CUT OUT

Thousands of British personnel serve in Afghanistan – some bring back more than memories...

TV producer Dan Simmons wants to film it all. He gets himself embedded in a regiment about to be deployed to the Afghan war. He shoots some film. Then he shoots himself. The Ministry of Defence puts Military Police captain Stef Maguire under pressure to file it all away, but the TV man's dying words lead her to ex-cop Tom Fletcher, now living the perfect life in the country. Fletcher doesn't know why the TV man shot himself, but some very dangerous people think otherwise – and when they begin to threaten his family it's time for him to act.

CUT OUT

CUT OUT

by

Patrick Lennon

Magna Large Print Books
Long Preston, North Yorkshire,
BD23 4ND, England.

British Library Cataloguing in Publication Data.

Lennon, Patrick
    Cut out.

    A catalogue record of this book is
    available from the British Library

    ISBN   978-0-7505-3381-2

First published in Great Britain in 2009 by
Hodder & Stoughton Ltd.

Published in Large Print 2011 by arrangement with
Hodder & Stoughton Ltd.

Magna Large Print is an imprint of Library Magna Books Ltd.

Printed and bound in Great Britain by
T.J. (International) Ltd., Cornwall, PL28 8RW

*This one's for the sixteen-year-old soldier
Alf Lennon.*

And I have asked to be
Where no storms come,
Where the green swell is in the havens
    dumb,
And out of the swing of the sea.

Hopkins

Monday Morning

Captain Stef Maguire was twenty-eight, tall and muscled-up, a good shot with a hand-gun. But she got in a real mess in Afghanistan, so the army lifted her out, gave her counselling, and sent her home. That first morning in her new post, she opened the office door to find blue sky, white clouds and a teenage soldier holding a small pig under his arm.

The pig's snout was sticky with blood.

She straightened her tunic, smoothing out her few hours' sleep on the office couch. The boy soldier had one eye on her buttons, panting, naming himself as Private Swilter.

She said, 'And who's the pig, Swilter?'

'It's the regimental pet, Captain.'

'Well, take it to a frigging vet. I'm the Royal Military Police. I don't treat sick animals.'

But the pig – a grey, smooth-haired thing – looked excited more than injured, licking the blood off its cheeks with its pink tongue. She did *not* like the look in its little eyes.

'I was walking the pig, Captain, and we found a body.'

'A body?'

'A dead man in uniform, by the perimeter wire. So I came straight here to the MP office. And I found you, Captain.'

She thought, *First day as well*, putting her boots on.

Waterton barracks – now she could see it in daylight rather than in the darkness of her arrival the night before – was no different from any other British Army base. Jogging beside the soldier still clutching the damn pig, she passed a jumble of buildings – some left from the world wars, others new office types – all slung down on an expanse of turf steaming in the sun.

She said, 'Why were you walking the pig?'

'It's my duty, Captain. 0600 hours, I walk the mascot. Her name's Trixie–'

'Just show me the body.'

They came to the edge of the buildings where a row of old store huts ran down to the edge of the base. The soldier led her between the huts, saying, 'Trixie ran off down here and didn't come back, so I followed–' the pig in his arms began squealing '–and I'm sorry Captain, but Trixie made a mess.'

They rounded the corner of the last hut, into a clearing that couldn't be seen from the barracks. They stopped running.

In front of them, the sun was steaming the dew off the perimeter chainlink fence. Sitting back against one of the concrete fence posts, there was a man in desert combat fatigues, the rank of private. His head was leaning to one side, his chest darkened with blood. A lot of blood, still wet. The thick grass was drifting with vapour.

'Who is he?'

'Don't know, Captain. You think he shot himself?'

She walked over to the man. In his lap there was an army-issue Browning pistol. His hands were loose by his sides and blood had formed a pool beside his thigh. She could see what Trixie had done: the wet grass had hoof prints, and the pig had been snouting at his blood. She lifted the gun off the man's lap, applied the safety and placed it behind her. Then she squatted down and looked at him.

A gunshot wound to the chest. His face was blue-white and his lips were grey – but she realised he was *breathing*. Still alive. She turned and gave a series of instructions to the boy behind her and saw him salute and start running back to the main area, carrying the squealing pig.

It was quiet. She looked around. Beside the man, a single 9 mm cartridge lay in the grass, glinting pale through the steam. She squatted down again and looked at it. There was something not right about it. She put her face close to his and said, 'I don't know if you can hear me, but the medics are coming. It'll be a few minutes, OK?' She inhaled, breathing an unexpected scent.

He opened his eyes, looked at her. His eyes were red and dilated, probably unseeing. He tried to say something, but failed. She said, 'Don't worry, you'll be OK.' But she believed he was close to death.

He tried to speak again, then closed his eyes.

She looked him up and down. This isolated place, the gun in his lap, a single spent cartridge. *You think he shot himself?* It did look like that. But there was something not right with the 9 mm cartridge – and, looking at the man, she saw there was something not right with *him*. She lifted one hand and felt for a pulse, found a weak trace, looked at the hand closely, put it back on the grass. She looked at his uniform, his boots.

What exactly was going on here?

She knew what was wrong with the cartridge. It was the wrong colour – a white alloy, not army-issue brass. That meant a foreign-made cartridge, maybe a civilian product.

A minute passed. In the field behind the trees, a water irrigation spray started hissing. Then she figured out what wasn't right with the man.

He was no teenage soldier. She guessed he was mid-forties – an unusual age for a private in the modern army. And more, most private soldiers have polished boots and callused hands. This guy was the other way round. He had scuffed boots and smooth, manicured hands. Something else too. She put her face close to his for a second. Yes, it was there again. The scent was unmistakable. How many private soldiers wear premium cologne while in uniform? She thought, *Is he even a soldier?*

'Help me.'

The man was speaking, his cracked lips open, his eyes fixed on her.

She said, 'Take it easy. You'll be OK.'

'They're here.' A whisper, his eyes fixed behind her.

She looked round. Between the huts, she could see Private Swilter – minus the pig – and two paramedics approaching at a run. She said, 'Yes, they're here. You want me to call someone?'

'The honey man.'

The paramedics slammed down beside them, began unpacking their kit.

She said, 'Who do you mean?'

'The honey man. He's got–'

His voice failed. She put her ear close to his lips. That cologne again. She felt a paramedic kneel beside her, saying, 'Let me see him, Captain.'

Then the wounded man whispered something else. It was faint, hard to catch – but it was a name, she was sure of that.

She let the paramedic attend to him.

She picked up the dodgy cartridge and the pistol and stepped away a few paces, wondering what to do with them. Then she used a plastic wrapper from the paramedics' kit and stowed them in that.

News was obviously spreading – more people were arriving from the main barracks now – men and women, various ranks, all in the desert camouflage uniform. Some of the junior ranks began crowding the scene, and she pushed them back, got them to form a cordon to keep the others away. An MP sergeant appeared, and she handed Private Swilter over to him.

She took out her notepad and scribbled on it.

The Honey Man. He's got–

But she wasn't sure of the name he'd whispered.

Looking up, she saw people standing aside to let through a Military Police officer, rank of major. She thought, *Great way to meet the new boss.*

They saluted each other and she explained what she'd seen. Meanwhile, the paramedics had the unknown man prone on the ground, were cutting open his camo jacket. She got a glimpse of his torso: coated in blood, spasming. No ID tags – something else not right about him.

Major Ward stood staring down at him. She'd heard about Ward, good things too –

and seeing him, she could see why – mid-thirties, green eyes assessing it all. Assessing her, too. He said, 'Good start for your first day. What happened? Was this self-inflicted?'

'Possibly, sir.' She showed him the pistol and cartridge in the plastic bag. 'The Browning looks like one of ours, but the bullet's foreign. A few things to be explained here.'

'Agreed.' Ward moved his eyes onto the wounded man. 'So who is he?'

'No tags on him. And he said something – at least I think he did.' She showed him her notepad – *The Honey Man*.

'What does that mean?'

'I don't know.'

From the main road, she heard the wail of a civilian ambulance, and the medics heard it too and looked relieved. Ward stood looking at the man. She saw his eyes narrow, creases deepening around them. Suddenly he said, 'Oh God. It's *him*.'

'Who?'

'Bloody hell.' Ward leaned down, lifted the man's face up, looked at it. One of the medics said, 'Please, sir. Space.' Ward stood back, picked up the piece of camo jacket cut away, lying on the grass. One end was dripping with blood, the other was part of the chest, with buttons and a flap pocket, no name on the label. She watched him feel inside the pocket, pull out a thin leather wallet, flip it open.

19

'It *is* him.'

Ward handed her the wallet. She looked at the name on the first credit card and recognised it from somewhere, but couldn't connect it to the man on the ground.

One of the medics looked round. 'He's going.'

Ward said, 'Now *this* is a problem.'

'He can't have. Not now.'

In the Ministry of Defence Main Building in Whitehall, three people sat in a small office on one of the upper floors, grouped around a desk smelling of polish.

The man speaking was Bill Downey: aged around fifty, a civilian suit, cool oblong glasses. Downey was in the government – low profile, but still the best image builder around. He adjusted his glasses and looked at the much younger man and woman opposite him, both in uniform.

'And not there, of all places.'

The two looked back at him. They were the army – Summers and Haines, always known by their surnames, the best of the MOD public relations team.

Together, the three people made up Team Defence – the MOD's media face.

Downey said, 'You're sure this really *is* him?'

Summers, the uniformed man, nodded. 'It's him. Dan Simmons, the TV document-

20

ary producer.'

'God almighty. What happened?'

Haines, the uniformed woman, said, 'He was embedded with the Cambs regiment, making a film–'

'I know, I know. I arranged it. He came to me personally with this plan to make a documentary about army life. I said, *But you're an academic, you make films about ancient religion.* He said, *I want to relaunch myself. I want to be cutting-edge.*' Downey shook his head. 'So how did it happen?'

Haines said, 'He was found at 06.30 this morning at a point inside the base perimeter at Waterton Barracks. He had a gunshot wound to the chest. He was taken to hospital in Cambridge, where he died twenty minutes ago, at 09.10 hours.'

Bill Downey took off his glasses and massaged his forehead. 'Waterton Barracks. God almighty – not again. I thought we'd moved on.'

They all knew what he meant.

Waterton Barracks had been the site of the deaths of three young soldiers in the late 1990s – all found with close-range gunshot wounds. The inquest verdicts all came in as suicide – and the MOD *moved on* – but rumours of bullying had circulated for years.

Downey said, 'That's why I let him in there, to show how clean we are now.' He replaced his glasses. 'Alright. Either he shot himself – which is terrible, yeah – or some- one shot him, which is a lot worse. So which is it going to be?'

Summers said, 'We don't want to second- guess. The RMP and the civilian police are on site right now.'

'Come on, help me. We've got Operation Poppy Crush rolling out next week. We've got the Minister going *personally* to Waterton for the send-off parade *today*. So, suicide or what?'

Haines, the woman, fixed Downey with school teacher's eyes. 'Well, the initial im- pression is that he shot himself with a Browning army-issue pistol.'

'In the chest?'

'People do it sometimes. The gun was still in his lap.'

'Where did he get a gun?'

Haines said, 'It's army issue, with the serial removed – the kind of thing that pops up in civilian hands. And the bullet was some kind of foreign copy, possibly Croatian.'

'A civilian got in there and gave him a stolen gun with Croatian bullets to shoot himself? I said, help me, not bury me.'

'There's no reason to think it happened like that. The issue now is what to tell the wider audience. Considering the Minister is going there today.'

Downey looked at the wall clock. 'We'll have a statement out by 11 a.m. I'll do that personally. Maybe a press conference.'

The school teacher's eyes smiled at him. 'But why? The news today is full of big financial issues. Dan Simmons is just a small-scale tragedy, people will understand that. Incidentally, our sources say that he was troubled by army life.'

'Sources at the barracks?'

'Think about it. An academic suddenly finds himself embedded on an army base. He may not have adjusted successfully.'

Downey was scribbling notes. 'Adjustments *are* difficult. And for Dan Simmons of all people – they called him the playboy professor, didn't they? He had that suntan, that wavy hair. By the way, he was on a sabbatical from his college, but it was an enforced break.' He looked up. 'Playboy hits the reality of army life, can't take it. People remember the hair, that helps.' He closed his pad. 'Let's get this straight, here in the room. He was a nice guy, couldn't take it, he found a gun and shot himself. But I want to emphasise, *there was no bullying.* We have to spell it out – no mistreatment. We have to really take the momentum out of this now, before the big parade at Waterton later today.'

Summers said, 'I think it'll slow down.'

'We have to make sure. Who's the Military Police at Waterton?'

'Major Ward.'

'What's he like?'

'He's good.' He exchanged a glance with Haines. 'Though he's got a reputation for being independent-minded.'

Downey shook his head. 'This is too important. You two – get up to Waterton. Spell it out to them. Suicide, but no bullying. Spell it out.'

Stef Maguire escorted the civilian Detective Inspector across the barracks. His name was Brzinski. Dove-grey suit, narrow tie, and two assistants with briefcases. Brzinski was telling Maguire how clever he was, saying, 'Most of our work now is technology-based, did you know that?'

'Yes.' She pointed the way around the newer buildings, to the scrappy area of the old huts and the perimeter wire. The detective dived forward, his shoes making no sound on the tarmac. She walked beside him, her boots clicking hard. She felt her notepad in her pocket – the dying man's comment about a Honey Man. In the spirit of cooperation, she knew she ought to share it with the civilian team. But the attitude of this cop Brzinski was pissing her off.

Brzinski said, 'Been with the regiment long?'

'The RMP aren't part of army regiments. We're separately constituted in what are called provost companies, we get posted

24

alongside the army.'

'So you've been posted here long?'

'First day today.' She saw Brzinski look her up and down.

'And you're shipping out to Afghanistan next week.'

'The regiment is, not us in the RMP. We're staying here on the post.'

'Yeah? I'd've thought they could use some muscle like you. You're staying behind for a rest?'

She clenched a hand and breathed out. 'The scene is over here.'

He said, 'You guys know your job, absolute respect. But the science we've got now, the power of the forensics, we're lead country in the world, did you know that? You know in five years all babies will have their DNA taken at birth? We're building something here that's like out of the future. But it's the scene that's the key. The crime scene. We rule that, it's our territory.'

He hesitated, not knowing which path between the huts to take. She showed him the far one, the row of scrappy hawthorns rising beyond the roof. He stalked his way down there, the assistants behind talking on their mobiles.

He said, 'Give us a scene, properly preserved, and we can tell you anything. Hair fragments, fibres, microscopic flecks of saliva. Give us a well-preserved scene, and we rule the world.'

They rounded the corner and stopped.

In front of them, the perimeter fence enclosed the stretch of damp grass where Dan Simmons had been found. The area was trampled by army boots and strewn with debris – bits of bandage, tubes, plastic wrappers. There were a few cigarette butts and a vending cup half full of tea. On top of that, an irrigation spray in the farmland beyond the perimeter had started up, and a light breeze was spattering water over everything.

The wonder cop was speechless.

Against the perimeter fence post, where Dan Simmons had sat and suffered his gunshot, the blood on the ground had been trodden into a filthy puddle. As they approached, she noticed a few of Trixie's hoof prints and even a couple of excited little pig turds.

The police detective nodded, looking around, as if something was being confirmed. He went and spoke briefly to his assistants. Stef Maguire caught the word *'Animals'*.

At first she thought he meant Trixie. Then she saw the assistants smirking and she thought about it again. And that was the end of the spirit of cooperation between Captain Stef Maguire and the civilian police.

She opened the door to one of the blocks of troop accommodation and let it swing shut behind her. A long corridor painted gloss grey with doors left and right. The smell of floor shine and male bodies, total silence. This was a new building, and glancing through each door it seemed that private soldiers were sharing only two or three to a room, the beds perfectly neat under the pin-ups and family pictures tacked to the walls. Halfway, she came to a door with a huge poster taped to it.

She recognised this one. It was the poster that the MOD had designed for Operation Poppy Crush – copies distributed to every British military installation. There was a rumour it was planned to be put up on street billboards – but the Ministry had cancelled the idea at the last moment. It showed a British armoured fighting vehicle under an orange sky, ploughing through a field of poppies – the tank tracks scything down the flower heads, the words Poppy Crush in racing letters at the base, and a slogan:

Poppy Crush – crushing the Afghan heroin trade.

Someone had stuck a paper sign on the poster, with a scribbled countdown:

5 Days To Go

The nameplate on the door had two names.

Private Rick Godson
Dan Simmons – Temporary

She waited half a minute for the civilian

master detective. Then she thought, Sod it, and opened the door.

The usual cramped but Spartan layout. Two beds against opposing walls. One was in perfect order, the blanket turned over the required hand's breadth, the pillow in line with that, no dust on the floor beneath. The other one was unmade, with a pile of laundry at the foot, no pictures on the wall. She leaned down and sniffed the pillow. Simmons' cologne. Beside it, a wooden panel on two steel lockers made a desk with a radio alarm clock. She pulled on a pair of latex gloves and clicked the radio on. Radio 4. The 11 a.m. news just starting.

Interest rates, a banking crisis, a plane crash in Brazil. Then:

'The broadcaster and academic Professor Dan Simmons has died following a shooting incident at Waterton Barracks in Cambridgeshire. The MOD say that Military Police recovered a handgun from the scene, and at this stage nobody else is being sought in connection. It's believed Professor Simmons was living the life of an ordinary soldier at the base while filming a documentary. MOD spokesman Bill Downey told us, "This is a terrible tragedy, and our thoughts are with Dan's family. Army life is harsh and it doesn't suit everyone. Sometimes, people react in ways that are unexpected and tragic." '

And straight on to sport.

That was it. She had to admire it. Twenty seconds, nothing stated explicitly, options left open in case anything came up. But Dan Simmons was left in the listener's mind as the guy who didn't fit in, who couldn't take it.

She turned the radio off.

Nobody else is being sought in connection – who exactly decided that?

Is this because it's Waterton, with all the old rumours?

Under the desk, she opened one of the steel lockers – everything left unlocked, the regimental tradition.

Electric razor, herbal shower gel, male face scrub, a bottle of that cologne. Also a toothbrush, socks, an expensive brand of jockey shorts. *Army life is harsh, and it doesn't suit everyone.*

But what had Simmons himself been talking about – the Honey Man? He's got *what*?

She looked in the other locker. It contained a high-quality Handycam and its accessories. She played the stored video: the screen showed scenes of army life. Sequences of vehicle maintenance and mealtimes, jerking backwards. She placed it back with its attachments. She crouched and rummaged through them with her latex-gloved hands. Cables, a charger, spare battery packs. Also cables for a laptop or notebook computer. That would make sense if he was editing footage, but there was no sign of the computer itself. Finally, at the back, a small cardboard box sealed in packing tape. She took it out, felt its weight. The tape had been broken open, leaving an oblong hole. She shook it: a heavy rolling and clunk inside. Batteries, she guessed. AA size. More spares for his camera or whatever.

She tapped it in her hand again.

And again.

Then she emptied the box out on the bed.

They were the size and shape of batteries, but the similarity ended there. They came in a foreign-looking silver alloy, cheap casing around the grey tips. 9 mm ammunition, eight rounds of it, the same type she'd found next to Simmons on the grass.

Dan Simmons had the rounds.

Dan Simmons, with his face scrub – and his own bullets?

Would his fingerprints be on these rounds? Did he keep the ammunition that killed him, in a little box, right here under his desk? Did he bring it in here with him? Did that mean he brought the gun in here too? Why? Because he wanted to play at soldiers?

Or because he knew the old rumours about Waterton Barracks – that weak people were singled out and killed here in the past?

As she waited outside the door, she looked at the Poppy Crush poster again. '5 days to go' – would that have wound Simmons up?

Were the boys pressurising him, counting him down to the day of going out there and facing it for real?

Did that make him snap? Take the gun he'd brought in for self-defence, turn it on himself?

And even if that was true – who was Honey Man?

And by the way – where's Dan's laptop?

She heard the main door open. She kept looking, though, at the poster of Poppy Crush – the bulging Afghan poppy heads being scythed down by the British armour. She ran her hands up over her own arms, felt the muscles there. The last time a dying man had spoken to her, barely two months ago, he'd been covered in those seeds. A dying man's words, his breath in her ear.

She heard Brzinski's voice in the corridor, but for a few seconds, she couldn't take her eyes off the poppy heads. Seeds spinning in the air like insects. Breath in her ear.

Is that why this matters to me?

Because the words of a dying man carry a weight you can only understand if his breath has–

'Captain Maguire, are you OK?'

She pulled herself away, faced the civilian wonder cop.

'Brzinski. Yeah. Come on, you'd better see what's in here. You'll need to take some prints.'

Summers took a break from his Blackberry to watch the fields moving past the car. Green wheat and pylons beside the motor-way.

Haines on the seat next to him, her faint smell of soap. She caught his eye and passed him the sheet of paper she was reading.

Proposal for the embed of Dan Simmons with Cambs regiment.
Purpose of embed: to make a documentary showing the role of the British armed services in the suppression of the Afghan heroin trade. Professor Simmons will accompany the regiment to Afghanistan for Operation Poppy Crush.

He said, 'I only hope they can manage with-out him. You think Downey is overreacting to this?'

'No, he's being a politician. The Minister has put his name to Poppy Crush personally. They can't afford this to blur the message.'

'You sound like one of them already,' he said, handing the sheet back.

'And he's right. There is no bullying in the army.'

Private Godson, Dan Simmons' roommate, was in an interview room in the RMP post, staring at the wall. Private Swilter, the pig-walking boy soldier who'd found the body, was in the next room, chewing his finger-nails. Stef Maguire was in a meeting in Major Ward's office. She wondered briefly where the pig was.

She took a look at the other members of Ward's team who were present. A male captain, about her age, who looked hung-over. A female captain, called back in from a shooting competition, wearing a tracksuit. The male sergeant she'd seen earlier in the morning, devoid of any presence at all.

Ward dished out the inevitable instructions: recording who was where on a barracks of five hundred people. Finding someone who'd heard or seen something.

'Dismiss. Not you, Maguire. Your day is just beginning.'

It sounded grim, but when the others had gone, and he sat looking at her, she liked him – he was solid, unblinking. Then he smiled.

'Come on, take it easy. It's a bad one for your first morning.'

'Sir.'

'In the ideal world, our introductions wouldn't have been so rushed. But I want to say I'm aware of your background. And I want you to know. I mean. Damn it, I'm hopeless at this.'

'Sir?'

He stood up, reaching for his webbing belt. 'I mean, you made a good start and I know you'll do well here.'

'I'm not damaged goods, sir. No matter what anyone says.'

He held her eyes, then smiled. 'Have you got something to prove, Maguire?'

'Could be, sir.'

'OK. I don't mind that. In fact, the problem I've got here is that some people–' he gestured at his departed staff '–have nothing to prove. So *you* are a welcome arrival.' They stood looking at each other. He had a big presence, she had to admit that. He said, 'By the way, how are you getting on with the civilian police?'

'I'm showing them all due courtesy, sir.'

'They're annoying, aren't they?'

'Extremely.'

He smiled. A wide, angular face, hair cropped above the ears. Eyes the colour of perimeter grass. 'Come on, what do you think? Dan Simmons shot himself or not?'

'I don't know. But I heard the MOD statement on the news. I can see the way they obviously want to present it.'

'Some people from Team Defence are actually coming up here this afternoon.' He grimaced. 'To make sure we follow the official MOD line.'

'Thoughtful of them.'

'It's the political reality. These media people are the new chain of command now. If we're going to deviate from the line, we'll need something substantial to base it on.'

'OK,' she said. 'Why did he bring in a gun? I can imagine him sneaking one out, as a souvenir. But sneaking one in? Why?'

'Maybe he came expecting trouble. This barracks has a reputation.'

'What about his computer? He must have had a laptop to store his Handycam footage, but it wasn't in his locker. The charger's still there.'

'*That* is a good point.'

'And his final words. *The Honey Man. He's got something.*'

'You think he meant his computer? Sounds like he was delirious.'

'I can't quite make sense of it, no.'

'See what I mean? If we're going to rock the boat, we need something stronger.' He opened the door. 'Come on, let's interview some of Dan Simmons' comrades. Try to see if he really was being bullied. And if they know where his laptop is.'

'Sir, Simmons gave me a name.'

Ward closed the door. 'A name?'

'I only just caught it. It wasn't distinct. It sounded like Tom Fletcher.'

'Tom Fletcher? Who's that?'

She said, 'I don't know. But a minute ago I did an Internet search on Honey Man Tom Fletcher.'

'And?'

'Tom Fletcher is the name of someone

who runs a smallholding about twenty miles west of here. He produces organic honey. It seems remarkable. Simmons said Honey Man plus his name–'

'Or you think he did.'

'Sir. And he's just down the road. And now I'm thinking, sir. Does he have the laptop? And why – what's on it?'

Ward turned and leaned against the door, thinking. 'The team defence people are arriving in an hour. If there is something going on, I want to know before them, and before the civilian coppers.'

She said, 'So why don't I take a look at this Tom Fletcher?'

'Agreed. Take a look, say hello, just lowkey. See if he knows what was going through Dan Simmons' mind. Then we'll speak again and consider if he's relevant. And in the meantime, I'll interview some soldiers.' He opened the door. 'I'm glad you're here.'

She watched him walking away across the tarmac square in front of the MP post. She reminded herself of rule number one in the captain's handbook. Do not start fancying senior ranks.

Monday Midday

In her own quarters, Captain Maguire changed into jeans, a shirt and a hiking jacket. She stood looking at herself in the mirror.

Have you got something to prove?

Yes. I can listen to the words of a dying man, and this time I can get it right.

Anything else?

Yeah. I'm still RMP.

She took a pool car and went out through security onto the main road. She passed a civilian police car, a TV news crew and a solitary peace protester.

It was the kind of early summer day when you don't want sunglasses – blue sky, high cloud cover, irrigation sprays in the fields pulsing rainbows. Even the dead animals along the tarmac looking fresh and clean.

She unfolded the directions she'd printed from the simple website of this person named Tom Fletcher. She left the big road, drove between huge fields of emerging wheat, the remains of a village – a pub turned into a house, some executive homes, a boarding kennel. Then the road turned off onto a single lane for a hundred metres, down into a slight valley that broadened onto a plain.

The fields here were planted with a crop that looked like bamboo – or a grass related to bamboo, the fronds reaching two metres in height, making a wall right across her field of vision, except for the thin road snaking through it.

A sign at the side of the track said, *Honey straight on*.

She drove slowly along the road, the grass leaning over her car on either side.

Honey Man, Tom Fletcher.

Whoever he is, he's really cut himself off from the world.

She rounded a curve in the road. Ahead was a large whitewashed cottage fenced off against the giant grass.

She approached, coming onto a driveway that led through a timber gate, into a gravel courtyard planted with shrubs. Two cars: a new German estate, and an old Land Rover with a trailer bar and a front winch.

She stopped and got out. Quiet, except a bird calling from the grass fields. The house was old, but cleanly restored. Blinds down on all the windows, the front door studded with bolts. She rang the bell. No answer.

She stepped back and looked up at the house – got the impression that one of the upstairs blinds had moved. Silence, though – except the sound of the grass.

She walked around the house, past a padlocked tool store. At the back there was a kids' play area – then a wide meadow planted up as an orchard – scores of saplings stretching down a turf slope. The grass surrounded the smallholding here at the back too, rising on either side of the orchard.

From beyond the trees, she heard a sound. A steady thudding, a space of five or six seconds between each impact. She walked towards it, into another field sloping downwards again, this one full of beehives – maybe fifty of them, she guessed. White boxes in long lines on the turf. She could hear bees, could see them spiralling out of the hives around her. She thought, *What a great life. Civilian peace and quiet, honey and apples.*

After the hives, the slope ran down to a stream that fed across a flat plain in the ground. The water made a small round lake before escaping on the other side. The shallow water was pocked with trees – the biggest a felled oak in the centre, its limbs half-submerged. In the middle of all that, a man was chopping the fallen trunk with an axe.

She watched him.

He looked mid-thirties. His head was shaved down to stubble, sunlight in the hollows under his shoulder bones. Wide shoulders too, under an old T-shirt. Serious strength in there. Standing thigh-deep in the water, wearing workman's trousers plastered in clay and silt. Swinging at the trunk with an axe, trying to separate a side branch. Thud, the axe sinking in, him wrenching it out, lifting it up, thud.

The Honey Man?

Thud.

Does he know something about Dan Simmons?

Thud.

Him, here in this quiet place with his beehives and apple trees.

The man wiped his face with his forearms, and glanced up.

They stood looking at each other for a few seconds. He had a beautiful, calm face, that, with his shaved hair and shadowy chin, made him look like some kind of monk. His eyes moved over her. She realised how tall he was – way over six foot, his reflection spreading across the lake.

She said, 'Are you Tom Fletcher?'

'Yes. Are you here for some honey?'

She said, 'No, I'm Stef Maguire. I'm a captain with the Military Police at Waterton Barracks.'

It was hard to read his face. He swung the axe up, catching the light, and down into the tree. Thud. He left it there and waded through the water to the edge of the lake, up the earth slope, leaving a trail of water. When he got close to her, she could smell clean sweat and wood sap. His trouser cuffs wet from the lake, rubber sandals on big tanned feet. He reached into a bucket for a water bottle and unscrewed it, looking back at her. He looked at the ID she was showing him.

Then his blue eyes met hers.

'Military police? What's up?'

'Have you seen the news today?'

'Not really.'

'Maybe you've heard of someone called Dan Simmons.'

'Dan the TV professor?'

'You know him?'

'I met him a few times, years ago.' His blue eyes didn't blink. 'Why, what's he done?'

'He was making a documentary at Waterton Barracks, and, er, sadly he shot himself last night. He's dead.'

Tom Fletcher stared at her. Then he shook his head, screwing the top back on his water and wiping his tanned hands on his shirt. 'That's terrible. He was a nice guy. But why are you here?'

'The reason I'm here is that just before he died, he said your name.'

Two bees droned past. 'My name?'

'Well, he said *the Honey Man, he's got–*. And then I believe he said your name. And obviously I'm asking why that would be.'

'I really don't know. The poor guy.'

'He might have been referring to his computer. Did he send you information of any kind?'

'Information? No, I haven't heard from him for years.' He stopped to think, staring at the water. 'That's really strange.'

'Do you have any idea what he might have meant?'

'No. I'm sorry. Would you like a jar of honey? It's the best I can do.'

He seemed genuine. She gave him her number at Waterton. 'If anything arrives from Dan Simmons, you must let me know.'

'Sure.'

As they walked back up the slope, she said, 'How did you know Dan?'

'About four years ago, we met a few times through mutual friends. I haven't heard from him since then.'

They came to the slope leading up through the beehives, the giant grass swaying beyond them.

He said, 'Like it? It's Indian elephant grass. We grow it here as a biofuel crop.'

She said, 'Doesn't it make you feel isolated? I mean, anyone could be observing you from inside there.'

He laughed. 'You're thinking like a soldier. I'm a beekeeper.'

Monday Afternoon

Private Godson, the soldier who'd shared Dan Simmons' twin-bed quarters, had exercised his right to have a comrade present at the interview with Major Ward. So his platoon sergeant was standing in the corner, utterly still, eyes on the door. The sound of their boots coming to attention was itself like a gunshot.

Sitting at the desk, the civilian policeman flinched. Ward wasn't surprised. They were stuck in a battered 1960s' prefab room reaching thirty degrees, with round-pin electric sockets, a picture of the Queen, and steel mesh on the window.

Private Godson was nineteen, shaven-headed, with bruises on his jaw and one green tooth. Earned sixteen grand a year, minus tax, minus the charge for soldiers' accommodation.

'Good boots you have, Godson.'

'Bought them, sir.'

Minus the money that a soldier spends on quality kit that the British Army doesn't provide. Ward knew from Godson's file that he'd climbed into the back of a burning Land Rover to pull out his platoon corporal in a training crash. People such as Private Godson made the British Army function.

Godson's eyes unblinking.

Ward said, 'Private, you're aware who I am, and this is Inspector–'

'Brzinski.'

'Brzinski of the civilian police. Tell me how you got on with Dan Simmons.'

'He was quiet, sir. When we had a joke, he didn't always appreciate.'

'A joke?'

Godson blinked. 'We called him Sleepy, sir, because he couldn't get out of bed in the morning.'

'You called him Sleepy to his face?'

'In a friendly way, sir. Everyone has a nick-name.'

'Would you say he was enjoying his time at the barracks?'

'No, sir. The sleep, the laughs we had. The food, even. It wasn't him, sir.'

'Was he being treated unreasonably?'

'He was treated the same as other com-rades, sir. He said that's why he was here. Treat him the same.'

'He found that challenging?'

'Yes, sir.'

'Was he being bullied?'

'I never once saw anything you could describe as bullying, sir. We'd say "Hello Sleepy" and that.'

'Describe last night, May 11th.'

'We were stood down from 1900 hours, sir. We went to the other ranks' mess. Saw a DVD, sir.'

'Where was Simmons?'

'He stayed in quarters, sir.'

'When did you last see him?'

'1900 hours, 19.05.'

'Did you invite him to go with you?'

'Yes, sir, he said no.'

'What were his words?'

'No.'

'Just that?'

'No, I'm busy, I've had enough. Sir, something like that.'

'I've had enough?'

'Something like that, sir.'

'What state was he in?'

'Not good, sir. His hands were shaking.'

'Why?'

'Exhaustion, I think, sir.'

'Not fear?'

'He was afraid of deploying out to the Stan with us, sir. He told me that, sir.'

'He wasn't afraid of bullying? Being the butt of your humour?'

'Totally not, sir.'

'Did he say where he was going last night?'

'No, sir.'

'Where do you think he went? Or what he did?'

'I don't know, sir. Sometimes he used to walk around the barracks for fresh air.'

'What time did you come back?'

'Around 1100 hours, 11.10, sir. His bed was empty.'

'You didn't report that?'

'No reason to report it, sir. We were all in a good state, sir, everyone was positive. We were just glad he wasn't around.'

Ward gave it a pause. Godson was unsweating, hollow eyes focused. His sergeant hadn't shifted a millimetre. The Brzinski guy was undoing his shirt collar.

Ward said, 'Where's his computer gone?'

'No idea about his computer, sir.'

'So he did have a computer?'

'A Sony VAIO, sir.'

'You noticed that, then?'

'Yes, sir. He was always on it in the evenings, connecting to his camcorder.'

'Godson, did someone nick that laptop? Just for a laugh, for a joke?'

'No knowledge of that, sir.'

'A joke is OK.'

'No knowledge, sir.'

Ward rocked on his feet for a second. 'Godson, did you ever see Simmons with a Browning pistol?'

'No, sir.'

'Did he refer to such a weapon?'

'No, sir.'

'Do you know where he could have obtained such a weapon?'

'No, sir.'

'Did you see Simmons with 9 mm rounds?'

'No, sir.'

'But he had a pistol and rounds at some point last night. The rounds were in his locker this morning.'

'I never saw inside his locker, sir.'

'Never, Godson? Just a peek?'

'Never, sir. And never expected him to look in mine. That's the regiment, sir.'

'Look at me, Godson.' Ward looked the kid in the eye for ten seconds. Scared eyes, but not hiding anything. Ward said, 'Alright, enough for now. Anything you want to ask?' Silence. 'I mean you, Inspector.'

Brzinski stirred. He was the only man sitting on a chair, but looked by far the most uncomfortable. He said, 'Private Godson–'

'Sir.'

'Did Simmons strike you as being in a state of mind to kill himself?'

'I wouldn't know how to tell, sir.' Godson's eyes remained fixed on the wall.

Ward took Brzinski back to his office to compare thoughts, and poured him a glass of water.

Ward said, 'What do you think?'

Brzinski gulped the water. 'Where's the CCTV?'

'There's no CCTV.'

'Why not? This is an army barracks.'

'You've just asked and answered your own question.'

'But you've got it on the gate.'

'On the gate, yes. But in here, these people don't even use locks. They're comrades. They die for each other. We don't need CCTV.'

'No cameras, the scene's a mess, no DNA, no cameras. What am I supposed to do?'

'You could ask some questions.'

'Well here's a question. Who came onto this base around the time Simmons died? You keep records?'

'Not of barracks personnel. Only outsiders.'

'Outsiders, great.'

'The last non-base person was a plumber from Cambridge.' Ward checked a notebook. 'In at 15.10 and out at 17.03. I phoned his wife. She says they were in the bingo by 1900.'

Brzinski frowned. 'But the noise of a gun, Major. On an army base? It would bring people running. Why did nobody notice? You've got to think of that.'

But he didn't say it in a way that meant he'd spotted a new angle. It sounded as if he was trying to shore up the suicide idea.

Ward said, 'I checked the manifest. 23.48, a helicopter landed on the pad near the golf course. Helicopters are noisy things, and that's close enough to where Dan Simmons was found to mask the noise of any gun-shot.'

The copper said, 'You see, that points to suicide. I mean, if someone wanted to kill him, why not shoot him twice and finish him off?'

Ward watched him, wondering what exactly was going through his mind. He said, 'Between you and me, Inspector, have you been given an official line to follow?'

'No way.' Brzinski swallowed. 'Look, I'm heading back to base now. We'll be getting the forensics back – what there is, anyway. And I'm going to work on that idea: he shot himself when the chopper came in.'

Ward saw him out. He thought, *If anyone's going to challenge the official line, it won't be this guy.*

With Brzinski gone, Ward went back to the interview room.

'Off the record, Godson. Describe Dan Simmons.'

'A useless wanker, sir.'

'Alright. Did he ever talk about honey?'

'Sir?'

'Did he ever use the phrase Honey Man?'

'Never heard that, sir.'

'Did he ever mention the name Tom Fletcher?'

'Never to me, sir.'

'You're sure?'

'Sure, sir.'
'Dismiss.'

Tom Fletcher gave the Military Police woman a jar of honey and shook her hand. She had strong, callused fingers – like his own – but there were lines around her eyes that were deeper than her age. When her car had gone, he turned and looked up at his house. An upstairs blind was slowly going up. Then his wife leaned her hip against the window frame, looking down at him. Her coppery hair was tangled with the clouds in the glass. She was smiling, though; he could see that. Nobody smiled like Cathleen.

He opened the front door into the porch. Kids' shoes and boots, coats on a peg. A big Thai woodcarving of a dragon. He opened the inner door, locked it behind him.

Fletcher's kitchen was a big space, half the ground floor of the original house. A stone floor, a woodburning stove for the winter, a central island for cooking, where Fletcher poured himself a glass of water.

Beside the tap, a note from Cathleen.

In bed for an hour.

He could hear the shower running upstairs, the open door Cathleen's invitation to him. Any other day, he would have joined her. But he turned on the radio and waited till the news started, then stayed listening to another banking crisis while his wife soaped her body upstairs and his apple saplings spread in the sun outside.

The second news item was Dan Simmons.

He heard the shower stop.

He heard the quote from the base commander. 'Army life is tough, it doesn't suit everyone.'

The Honey Man.

What was that all about?

He heard his wife on the stairs. He turned off the radio.

'Hey, axe man.' Cathleen came in. Wet hair, wearing one of his shirts over jeans, bare feet, all lit up by the sun. His heart moved the way it always did when he saw her, but she was frowning. 'I saw you giving honey to another woman, Tom. And the physique on her, too. I'm jealous.'

'She's a captain in the military police.'

'Military police? What did she want?'

Cathleen was flipping papers over at her workstation, getting ready for her afternoon session. She ran a small business in partnership with a friend who lived a few miles away, importing artwork from the Far East.

He said, 'Cathleen, you remember Dan Simmons?'

'Old Dan? Is he back on TV?'

'He's dead. He was filming at Waterton Barracks, and they say he shot himself.'

Cathleen's body movements slowed down, and she turned to stare at him. 'Shot him-

51

self? *Dan?*'

A few years before, Cathleen had worked for Dan Simmons on one of his documentary series – just a short stint as a researcher. Back then, Cathleen had commented on how fragile the man seemed to be.

He said, 'That MP lady was there when they found him. She thought that Dan might have sent me a message.'

'A message about what?'

'She said, *The Honey Man, he's got something.*'

'But what does that mean? Maybe he emailed you something, or posted it.'

'But why would he? I hardly knew him. I met him – what, two or three times?'

He went over to her and smoothed the damp hair from her face. She had the freckles he remembered from when they'd first met, as teenagers, plus the new lines forming around her eyes.

She said, 'Better check, Tom. Did he send something?'

Together they opened the post, checked Fletcher's email and went through his phone. There was post from friends and the Farmers' Union and the bank. But nothing from Dan Simmons.

He said, 'It's all a misunderstanding, then. Unless he sent me something and it hasn't arrived yet.'

'So what are you going to do?'

'I'm going to get on with clearing the lake.'
She lifted his shirt and rubbed his chest and told him she loved him and his axe.

Passing the beehives, Fletcher lifted the roofs, checked the honey. Bees bumped him, but he was practised – not needing a protective suit. Then he went down to the lake and retrieved his axe from the trunk. He began to swing, but paused.

Dan Simmons – with his hair, his cologne. Shooting himself dead? It didn't seem the Simmons's way.

Fletcher chopped a limb in half, and watched the split wood cartwheeling across the water. Then his eyes went up to the elephant grass.

Anyone could be observing you from inside there.

He felt the breeze rising.

Summers and Haines arrived in a Ministry car and came into Ward's office. They were both in uniform, but the man named Summers had his hair too long, and the woman, Haines, was wearing lipstick. They looked like politicians.

He gave them a summary of the Dan Simmons situation, and they sat nodding. Summers said, 'This has got to be really clean.'

'If you're concerned about him being bullied, the answer's probably no.'

'Excellent.'

'But I'm keeping an open mind.'

Haines smiled. 'That's why we're here. The message is, Not too open.'

Ward said, 'Personal visits, messages. There's a lot of focus from the Ministry.'

'You know what they've got riding on Poppy Crush. It's turned into a personal battle of wills between the Ministry and the anti-war movement. They've both chosen this as the time to draw their line in the sand. You see what I'm saying? Poppy Crush is bigger than just an operation. It's become a kind of symbol.'

Ward pointed at a newspaper on his coffee table. 'Some cynics say that a bit of flash and bang distracts people from the economy. Bloody civilian cynics, eh?'

Haines said, 'This is the world we live in. There's a lot riding on it, you know that. If this turns into a scandal while the regiment's out in the Stan, there'll be bollocks on the carpet.'

'Not yours, though.'

She smiled and held his look. She had the coldest smile he'd ever seen.

2 p.m. in Britain, 6.30 p.m. in Afghanistan. The sun was red on the lip of a valley where carrion crows were circling on the thermals, making shadows across the boulders leading down to the valley floor.

54

Halfway down, a cluster of houses stood around a stream: clay walls with slit windows, doors with iron spikes. There was smoke coiling against the red sky, the smell of *aush* cooking, dust settling in the air as the heat turned to night chill.

Away from the houses, on a boulder above the stream, a man was sitting in the shade of a ragged sycamore tree, cross-legged, his hands on his knees. His eyes were closed. He was European, white, in his thirties, with hair in grimy dreadlocks hanging around his face. Dressed in traveller's gear: hiking boots, jeans, a zipped jacket. A rucksack beside him.

The dust of the many roads he'd been travelling stuck to his clothes, in his hair. Breathed in the smell of the cooking, the tang of the water, the village cesspit.

He heard footsteps coming along the path, low voices discussing him – he'd picked up enough of the language to know they were worried. He got to his feet as they approached, his legs tired from the travelling.

Two men faced him: a village elder, sixties, big white moustache – and behind him a guard, an old Kalashnikov pointing at the traveller's belly.

The older man said, 'Assalam alaykum.'

'Walaykum.'

The elder spoke in Pashto, 'What do you want?'

Bare metal glinting on the gun. The night

breeze carried dust and bird cries. Along the valley floor, poppy heads were nodding.

The traveller smiled.

'I am looking for peace.'

Monday Night

Major Ward stood on the steps of the MP office, watching a TV news crew setting up across the roadway, on the corner of the parade ground. They weren't here because of Dan Simmons – he knew that. They were here for Poppy Crush.

From the direction of the parade ground, he could hear the sound of the regiment forming up. A hushed noise punctuated by occasional shouts – a sound that hadn't changed for three hundred years, he guessed. The men who'd paraded on the square here had gone out to Normandy, the Rhine, Korea, Suez, Cyprus and Northern Ireland. Then the women had joined and they'd gone out together to the Gulf, Iraq, Afghanistan.

The Stan, they called it.

He stepped down onto the road, stood with his hands behind his back, watching the camera crew. The sky overhead turning orange, streaked with cloud.

Now the regiment was going back to the Stan again for Poppy Crush. People had to believe in Poppy Crush. People had to buy into it, that was the phrase. Its poster campaign, its own promo video on the Internet, a dedicated PR team in Whitehall.

He knew that Summers and Haines were around somewhere, making sure their parade went well for the media.

'Major Ward.'

He turned. Captain Maguire, at attention, under the orange sky.

'Sir, I've been to visit Tom Fletcher.'

'Easy.' She stood at ease, big shoulders swung back, but shadows under her eyes, her pretty face with its wide mouth, hair looping over her ears under her cap. He had orders to look after Stef Maguire, after everything she'd been through. He had a feeling he was going to enjoy that task.

He said, 'Let's go and see the show. Tell me while we're walking. Dispense with *sir* for now.'

They made their way past the TV equipment. He could feel the presence of the massed ranks around the corner, almost like static in the air.

She said, 'Tom Fletcher really does make honey. It's a nice lifestyle.'

'Lucky chap. Did Dan Simmons send him something?'

'He says not. He insists he doesn't know what Simmons meant.'

'You think that's true?'

Maguire dropped her voice.

'I don't think he's lying. But he knew Simmons in the past. So Simmons might have tried to send him something before he died.'

'But send him what exactly?'

They rounded the corner onto the parade ground.

Haines and Summers were standing right in front of them, close together. Beyond them, the regiment was assembled in a block, their backs to Ward and Maguire, five hundred men and women facing forward. There was an explosive crack – their boots coming to attention – then silence.

Beyond the troops, Ward could see the Colonel on a platform, flanked by the Defence Minister himself, and a minor member of the royal family.

The Minister began speaking, his flat un-accented voice rolling around the square, the echoes filling the pauses he left for effect.

'You are the spearhead. You are the next phase in this war. You've shown you can fight the Taleban. But now our youth are being attacked by a new enemy.' Five hundred soldiers stood utterly still, the wind lifting the Union flag and the regimental ensign above the platform. 'That new enemy is heroin. Afghanistan is the world's largest exporter – not just of opium, but of finished heroin. That export is corrupting our people. Look in any market town, you will see the victims. This is our front line now, and you are the first wave. You will seek out opium crops and you will seek out the middlemen who ship this cargo of death to our streets. Poppy Crush means just that–' the Minister clenched a fist '–we crush the poppies in the fields, we crush their distribution. And we in government have every confidence in you.'

There was silence, the flags billowing over the sunset.

Then the royal took over, his hairpiece twitching in the breeze. After that, the Colonel spoke: a punchy minute's-worth. It finished with cheers for the royal – *hip hip*, then a mechanical shout echoing out over the barracks, into the farmland outside where irrigation sprays were sputtering.

Summers and Haines turned round, smiling, acknowledged the two MPs and walked away.

Ward said, 'I had a lecture in politics from those two this afternoon. And at present, we don't have anything to challenge them with except some guy who makes honey.'

'But something is going on.'

He watched her profile. He thought, *Poor kid. Everything she's been through, she must be hurting. She's tough, she's just right for the RMP, but she's latching on to this because she wants to show what she can do.*

A strand of her hair flickered in the breeze.

The last cheer sounded around the parade square.

Late afternoon, Fletcher ran a bath for his children. The bath was an old enamel tub from a scrapyard. He'd restored it, knocked a wall down to take it, plumbed it in himself. He loved that bath. He heard Cathleen's car on the stones outside, bringing the children back from their nursery school. He grinned at the sound of them: their yelps, clambering out, coming up the stairs.

They were twins, but not identical. At three years old, the differences were there. Evie was tall for her age, quiet, with big green eyes. Sally was a little shorter and rounder. He washed them gently, bronze light coming off the fields. The spirals of wet dark hair on their scalps looked like a fingerprint he was leaving.

Sally said, 'Daddy's quiet today.'

He kissed her forehead. 'I'm just thinking.'

They ate together in the big kitchen, the door open on the garden, a mesh screen in case the bees wanted to join them.

The girls ate in big mouthfuls, saying mmm after each one.

Later, when they were asleep, Fletcher went into the little upstairs room he used as a study. There was still some light in the sky over the field of elephant grass. He put the lamp on and looked at his email again.

He glanced up and saw Cathleen watching him from the door.

61

She said, 'Dan Simmons?'

The name sounded out of place in the warm room with its view of the mauve horizon.

'I keep thinking, has he sent me something? Did he really want me to know something?'

She walked over and put her arms around him. 'It's some kind of misunderstanding. You remember what Dan was like, he was so damn fussy about everything. It must have been a nightmare for him on that base.'

'Then why say my name to that Military Policewoman?'

She rubbed his chest, letting her nails dig in a fraction of a second. Then she took her hand away, and with the same nails tapped a photo on the study wall. 'Remember this?'

It was a photo of the house they'd taken before they bought and restored it – a wrecked shell with trees growing through the roof. Next to that, a series of her sketches showing their plan for how the smallholding would look when all the work was finished: the beehives in their fields, the apple trees in blossom, and then, at the base of the final slope, the little lake fully cleared and turned into a shallow bed for growing watercress. Around all that, the elephant grass crop encircling the house and land.

She said, 'See, it's starting to come true.'

'It's starting. It'll take another three years

to pay for itself.' He rested her up against the door frame and slowly unbuttoned her shirt. 'And then we're independent. Poor, but independent.'

She undid the last button, slipped her breasts into his hands. 'Don't let anything spoil this, Tom.'

'The kids are asleep.'

'I mean the plan. It's everything we've got. This is our whole life, right here.'

He kissed her. 'So let's forget about Dan Simmons.'

Cathleen closed the bedroom door. Then she opened the window and turned the slatted blind to show slices of red and mauve cloud and long trails of aircraft. She undressed facing the horizon, watching the vapour trails break up, feeling the cool air over her skin.

She turned round and saw Tom on the bed, watching her. The sunset light angled across him in v-shaped lines. She liked watching him. The last few years, in this house, his chest had shaped up like clay slabs, all the manual work coming through in his arms. Tan on his wrists against the cream sheets, and cuts left by splinters and thorns. She climbed onto the bed, and kneeled over him. Her hair flickered in the night breeze, her hands pushing him back on the bed. She squatted on his belly for a minute, her knees gripping his ribs, looking down at him while he ran his hands under her, moving as he opened her up. She tipped forward and bit him – a real bite, marking her territory. She felt him grip her hair, and she pushed her face in his shoulder while she bucked and twisted. When she came, she couldn't help crying, her face against his ear, his hands spinning out her hair.

She lay on him with the cool draught across them both, drying her tears on his cheek. Noise of a jet plane in the distance. In a while, she reached out and felt the bite she'd left on his shoulder.

He said, 'What was that for?'

'For giving your honey to a soldier girl.' But she liked the marks her teeth had made. She said, 'Ah, sweet. Like if you take stones out of a riverbed. See? Those little dents are gone by morning.'

She kissed it.

'You're a good wife, Cathleen.'

She smiled, holding her husband, listening to the grass outside in the breeze, while her heart slowed down.

The villagers gave the traveller a bowl of goat meat, hot *mourgh*, a room for the night: a three-metre-square storeroom, with an earth floor, a bucket, a paraffin lamp, a pile of engine parts in one corner. He sat against one wall and closed his eyes. He heard women's voices in the next house – just the voices, the women themselves never visible out here in the villages. That was something he missed, something he wanted to go home to. The sight of women.

He lit the lamp, put it beside him, closed his eyes, crossed his legs over his rucksack.

These were long roads he'd been travelling – but his journey would be over soon. He would have what he wanted: peace and love.

He heard the rat before he opened his eyes and saw it: a grey shape moving between the door and the ground, its head swaying, sniffing. Village rat, used to people. The paraffin light showed its eyes, its fur in wet furrows, the curve of its tail.

The traveller smiled. There was room on earth for all these creatures. The rat came closer, eyeing him.

He said, 'Don't be afraid, little friend.'

Its head turning.

He stunned it with his boot, splashed paraffin over it, set it alight and threw it by the tail out of the door. Its arc lit up the whole room for a second, little claws casting jagged shadows. It landed in the open drain, went under with a hiss.

The traveller turned the lamp down and waited for the morning.

Captain Stef Maguire sat on the bed of her

quarters, her back against the concrete wall. The window was open, bringing in a smell of the farmland outside the barracks.

She was naked, covered in a sweat she knew would chill her. She shook her head.

When she slept, it was usually dreamless. Sometimes, though, Afghanistan would come back to her.

Back to the Stan.

A long field of boulders, the skulls of goats close up, houses in the distance made of clay, dug into a hillside. The crackle of a diesel fire right next to her. The words of a dying man in her ear.

She went to the sink and washed her body down with her hands. Lean muscles on her arms, water in the stubble under her arms, sluicing off over her ribs, over the floor. She dried herself and lay back on the bed. On her desk, the pot of Tom Fletcher's honey glowed like a diode.

She thought, *How good to have peace, like that guy. Living with bees and apples. But what the hell did Dan Simmons mean?*

She closed her eyes and saw the animal skulls again, shadows of men too, walking towards her between the boulders.

She flexed her arms. She said out loud, 'I'm not damaged goods. I'm not imagining this. Something's happening.'

It echoed around the cheap little room.

Fletcher woke and listened. Cathleen was asleep with her arm over his chest, her fingers holding his collarbone. He lifted it away carefully and turned on his side. The bedside clock said just after two. He closed his eyes. He opened them. Whatever had woken him was still there.

He sat up. Cathleen's arm fell loose.

He stood up, naked in the moonlight, listening. Outside, he could hear the elephant grass making a sound like waves. It wasn't that.

The noise again. It wasn't one of the usual night sounds: a fox barking, or a truck on the main road, or a motorbike echoing down the long stretch. He listened, heard nothing more.

He looked down at Cathleen.

Cathleen was stretched out asleep on her front, her hair across the sheets. He put out a hand to feel it. It lifted in his fingers, her face turning. He touched her lips, felt them open. He ran a hand down her spine, into the small of her back, lower, between her thighs. Her head lifted and fell.

He heard the noise outside again.

He heard Cathleen sigh.

The noise again.

He stood at the bedroom door. The noise came from the front of the house. A chinking sound. Footsteps – going across the court-yard gravel. Faint, but audible. He looked

67

back at Cathleen winding herself in the sheets.

He crossed the corridor and stood at the top of the stairs. He could hear Evie turning over in her bed, nothing from Sally's room. Then an owl calling, and the sound of the grasses. He went down the stairs, into the hallway, cold stone under his feet. He unhooked his work trousers from the rack. He slid them on quickly and turned to the doorway. Moonlight lit his hands as he unlatched the inner door, opened it, stepped into the porch, clicked it behind him. The Thai dragon bared its teeth, eyes wide.

He listened again. He knew he hadn't been mistaken. Somebody had been out there. He unlocked the front door, held it partly open.

Through the gap, he saw grasses dipping under a big oval moon. He heard that noise, and then – unmistakably – the sound of a car moving away on the main road, going north. Then silence. He opened the door fully. Moonlight spilled in, and cool air smelling of the fields. The courtyard was empty. He looked around at the open gate, the stars above the elephant grass.

He glanced down at the doorstep.

Right in front of him, on the flagstone, there was a shape the width of the step. He crouched down to see.

It was a dead animal.

A large rabbit. It was lying on its side, its long ears lined with fur that was lifting in the breeze, its hind legs curled defensively.

Jesus.

Fletcher glared out at the road. He turned and flicked the porch light on, looked at the animal again.

Around its head, someone had tied a piece of rag, covering its eyes like a blindfold. Another rag had been tied around the muzzle. More than that, its belly had been slit open very recently – the emerging blood still steaming. Fletcher realised the animal was female, had been pregnant: a string of fetuses had been pulled out. They lay on the step in colourless shapes, scattered in blood and fluid across the stone.

He heard the click of the inner door opening.

'Tom?' Cathleen was already crouching beside him, wearing one of his shirts, pulling it around her knees. 'What's this?'

'Go back inside. I'll clear this up.' But the porch light was painting the corpse on their retinas.

'This is revolting. The babies.' She reached out a hand. 'With a blindfold.'

He stopped her hand. 'Go back inside.'

'Who did this?'

'Vandals, maybe. Or poachers.'

'What vandals? What poachers? Why?'

He asked himself the same question, locking the front door, going to the metal tool shed at the side of the house. His axe was glinting inside, in the dark. He took a spade.

He went out of the gate and looked along the tarmac track that led through the grass to the main road. It was empty and silent.

But someone had parked out there, left the dead rabbit on the doorstep, driven away. Why?

He walked out past the sign for *Honey*, dug a hole at the edge of the fields and buried the animal, let its fetuses slide off the spade in the moonlight, and covered it all with earth.

Then he swung the gate shut, padlocked it, left the porch light on, locked the porch and inner door.

Back upstairs, he lay beside Cathleen. The bed was rumpled and damp. It felt violated now.

She said, 'Who do you think did that?'

'I don't know. Maybe some idiot farmer playing a joke, he got the wrong house.' He closed his eyes, listening to a new breeze running over the grass. He could still see the rabbit's ears, the fur lifting. A gag around the mouth, a blindfold.

The message was clear. See nothing, say nothing.

Say nothing about what?

And if you do – what happens?

He couldn't escape the timing. It happened now, tonight, after Dan Simmons said Fletcher's name.

At least, according to that Military Policewoman, he said Fletcher's name.

He lay smoothing Cathleen's hair. An hour later, when the breeze died down, they were both still awake.

Tuesday Morning

When the traveller went outside, he saw sun bursting over the sides of the valley, massive slopes of rubble, magpies hopping across them. From the village, a group of men setting off to work in baggy clothes and flat hats, pulling carts behind them. And down below, on the valley floor, their workplace: the poppy fields stretching into the middle distance. Millions of red flowers.

The traveller watched the poppies, eating from a plate they'd left outside the room. Tea, an apple, berries dipped in sugar. Still cool enough for the drains not to stink too much.

The tribal man was watching him from across the street.

The traveller showed appreciation of the food.

The man came over and looked at him with the wide amber-green eyes these people had.

'What nationality are you?'

'Swedish. We're neutral, everyone loves us. I'm a journalist, I'm writing a book about today's Afghanistan.'

The man chewed and spat. 'They say the British are coming here to burn the fields.'

'They'll come here, they'll go away again.'

'Why do they want to burn the poppy? For the cost of their army, they could buy it all and throw it in the sea.'

'If I ever meet the British, I'll ask them. Listen, I need to hire a car and driver. Take me to Kabul.'

The man chewed. 'My brother-in-law has a cousin in Sweden.'

'Yeah?'

'In a big town near Stockholm. Tobo? Tubo?'

'Täby. Nice place.'

'The time to Kabul is seven or eight hours. A car and driver would be–' he spread his hands '–five hundred dollars.'

'I have the money with me.'

'You travel in Afghanistan with that money? You trust your fellow men.'

The traveller picked his teeth. 'That's right. And I'll pay another hundred if he gets me to Kabul before tonight.'

Fletcher stood in the early sun, looking across the yard. Warm light on his face, mug of coffee steaming in his hand. A perfect six a.m. moment. But the gate was still padlocked shut, and the pale doorstep still had a dark smear.

He was sure of three things.

One, Dan Simmons hadn't sent him any message.

Second, whoever left the dead rabbit obviously thought Fletcher knew something.

And finally, any other producer of organic honey in the entire country would be phoning the police by now.

Fletcher didn't do that. He finished his coffee. He unlocked his tool store and took out his axe, felt its blade with his thumb. Ran a bucket from the rain barrel and soaked a whetstone in it, then ran the stone over the axe head. Soft, slow strokes, water dripping between his fingers. Stone granules flecking the water. He wiped the blade with his sleeve and held it up to the light, still thinking.

Back in the kitchen, he fished Stef Maguire's phone number out of the bin. Then he picked up the phone.

In the RMP post, Stef Maguire had the kind of headache that comes from broken sleep. She massaged her temples, reading the document that had popped up in her inbox. Copies to her, Major Ward, Inspector Brzinski's team, the coroner's office, Summers and Haines on an MOD address.

The post-mortem report on Dan Simmons.

The man died with his contact lenses in place, an ulcer on his inner lip, a fungal infection of his toes, the imprint of a boot on his calf. Grass seeds and hawthorn blossom in his hair. No alcohol in his bloodstream. A gunshot wound to the right of his chest, consistent with self-infliction from a left-handed man. The skin of his left hand, under ultraviolet, showing residue from a gun mechanism in close proximity, fired recently. Its pattern spread across the thumb and wrist, characteristic of using a handgun.

Also a note from Brzinski the wonder cop: fingerprints. From the 9 mm rounds in Dan's locker: no usable traces. From the pistol itself: two full prints, plus one partial, one unusable. Both the full prints matched the victim's left hand.

Dan Simmons next of kin confirmed he was left-handed.

Team Defence would love that.

OK, let's say he did shoot himself. *Why?*

The desk phone rang.

When she ended the call, she went to Major Ward's office and found it locked, with a neatly printed note on the door. She followed its instructions and found Ward on the firing range. She spoke to the armourer on duty at the pass desk, let him log her in, hooked a pair of ear defenders around her neck, walked along the back gallery, past twos and threes of regiment troops standing at the firing stations. She noticed some of them nudge each other and indicate her, others nodding in greeting although she didn't know them.

Ward was at the last station. Standing, without ear protection, firing an SA80 on single shot. He had an assertive stance, back muscles sloping forward, taking the recoil, easing. The air reeked of gunshot.

He looked round at her. 'Seen the post-mortem on Dan Simmons?'

'Looks like he was falling to pieces physically. Something kept him going.'

'It's called the army.' They were making the transition away from using 'sir'. What retired generals would call *this regrettable familiarity between the ranks*. He said, 'His prints on the gun, but not the rounds. Notice the residue on his hand?'

'Yes, looks like he fired the shot.'

'Uh-huh. And did you check?' He rested the gun and turned to face her.

'Check what?'

'Don't tell me you didn't check. Even Brzinski phoned me to check. Damn, and I thought you were a star.' His eyes unblinking, though rounds were banging off right beside him.

'Check–'

'The armourer's log. You've just walked past the guy.'

She thought about it. 'Dan Simmons used a gun here? On the range?'

'Yesterday at 1500 hours. He was filming some men at firing practice. The armourer says they let him shoot off some rounds

76

from a Browning. Took the piss because he couldn't hit anything.'

'So then he'd have residue on his hands anyway. He may not have shot himself.'

'That's a bit of a jump. What's the step in between?'

'Check the residue on his hand against the spent cartridge. It's non-army issue. He fired a gun here, but did he fire the shot into his chest?'

'That's what I said to Brzinski. Problem is, there was so much residue on his skin, they'll never tell the difference. They call it forensically marginal.'

Ward turned and aimed, but didn't fire. He looked back at her. 'What's up, Stef?'

'Tom Fletcher has just phoned me. Someone left a dead rabbit on his doorstep last night, gagged and blindfolded.'

'You're joking. No, you're not, are you? But why phone *you*?'

'He says there's something about himself I should know. Something significant.'

'Sounds like something for the civilian police.'

'I think this involves us.'

He frowned. 'What do you propose to do?'

'We can be there and back in an hour.'

'We?'

'I think you ought to meet him yourself.'

Ward squinted along the range. Sunlight was flooding down through the roof panels, tinting the gun fumes. He said, 'Team Defence went away happy. It would be easy to keep them that way, but I don't like politicians telling me what to think. So I don't mind rocking the boat if I've got something to rock it with. But a gagged rabbit?'

She stood looking back at him.

Do not start fancying senior ranks. You're just getting straightened out, girl, don't blow it again.

He said, 'Come on then, hotshot.'

The MOD car moved slowly in southbound rush-hour traffic. Haines and Summers used the time to review the previous night's news programmes and the morning papers. The parade was featured well. At 8 a.m., the phone rang: Bill Downey. They put him on the speaker.

'How are things in that barracks?'

'Solid. You saw the news?'

'Well done. The guys looked fantastic. Some ethnic ones at the front, too. The minister looked good, really talking from the heart. And they kept the prince to a minimum – quite right, he looks bloody useless. Well done again. Pleased with yourselves?'

Haines said, 'There's some negative stuff, though. Interviews with the anti-war lot. By the way, there are peaceniks outside Waterton Barracks now. The broadsheets are saying this is a battle of wills now between the government and the protesters.'

'It'll pass,' Downey's voice said. 'When people see the guys on the ground, burning the poppies. We are going to get that, aren't we? Fields burning?'

'We'll make the first one a dawn raid – you get sunrise, flames.'

'Excellent. That broadsheet attitude will pass.' A long pause, reception crackling, road noise. 'The ghost at the feast, eh? What about Dan Simmons?'

Summers said, 'It feels like old news already, doesn't it? The inquest opened and adjourned yesterday. It could be six, nine months before it's back on. The civilian police are off the base now, they're seeking nobody else.'

'What about the RMP man, Major Ward?'

'We had a talk, and he's on board. He understands politics. No signs of bullying, that's really significant. Plus, the post-mortem is pretty clear, Simmons was holding the gun himself, so there you are. News coverage, Simmons gets mentioned foot of the page in broadsheets, more like an obituary than anything else. It's tagged onto the Minister's speech in the redtops. Lots of blogging and muttering, but there always is. So it's blowing over.'

Downey said, 'And maybe it's even *helped* us. Shows the pressure the guys face, a sense of risk. Could we use that?'

The car picked up speed. Summers said, 'Let's just let it die.'

Tuesday Afternoon

Fletcher told Cathleen he was going to clear the trees in the small lake. But he walked through the orchard, through the beehive field and up to the wall of elephant grass. He stopped, with the axe over his shoulder.

The grass was two metres high, with leaf blades sharp enough to cut skin. Someone *could* slash their way through the fields to watch the house, but going through all that stuff would take for ever. It was planted, though, in fifty-metre blocks, which were separated by channels just wide enough to walk along. He looked into the nearest channel. Dry earth, littered with the fallen grass blades.

He walked into it. The grass almost closed over him, the light jagged and flecked with dust. Could someone get out of a car at the main road, hide in here, watching the house?

Yes, easily.

Was someone here now?

Fletcher walked along the channel. Powdery earth after the dry winter. He crouched and examined the dusty soil.

It looked completely unmarked.

He checked the other channels around the

81

house. He found an old jerry can and a dead fox. Nothing else – no sign that anyone had been in there.

Fletcher walked out and got to work on the lake that would become a watercress bed.

By eight a.m., he'd cleared two of the smaller trees and dug their roots out of the sediment. He could start to see the way it would look: a wide, shallow lake with cress sprouting through the water.

The elephant grass shivered in the breeze.

He hadn't stopped thinking about the dead rabbit.

He heard the twins coming across the field, down the slope. Laughter over the sound of birds. He sank the axe in the one remaining tree trunk – the massive old oak – then waded out to meet them. They came swaying down the incline and jumped up at him, shrieking. He lifted one in each arm and whirled them around, laughing, put them down again.

Evie presented him with a twig she'd found.

Sally said, 'Daddy smells of trees.'

'Hurry, girlies.' At the top of the slope, Cathleen was waiting, hands on her hips. She was going to drop the twins at their day nursery, then work at home, calling retailers to sell her Eastern art. The twins staggered back up the slope and disappeared with her over the rise. He felt the little pang he always did when they left. In a while he heard her car start up. Then there was just the sound of the grass. He waded around the oak stump for five minutes, thinking where to start.

'Mr Fletcher.'

He turned. Two uniformed officers were standing at the top of the slope, bareheaded, outlined against the blue sky. They came down towards him, and he waded to the bank to meet them.

Stef Maguire plus a man in his thirties – major rank – tall and wide. He introduced himself, looking at the axe. 'Not going to chop us up, are you?'

Fletcher swung the axe into one of the stumps. 'I didn't expect a visit in strength.'

Ward looked around the site, nodding. 'Captain Maguire told me you had a nice lifestyle. She's right.' He looked at Fletcher. 'But I heard about the dead animal. There's something you want us to know?'

Fletcher said, 'It's about Dan Simmons. Back when I knew him, I wasn't a beekeeper. I was a private investigator.' Maguire raised her eyebrows. 'And before that, I was in the Cambridge police. Detective Inspector rank. Dan Simmons knew that, of course.'

The elephant grass swayed.

Maguire said, 'Well, that's significant. That makes me think that Simmons passed you information *because* he knew you were an investigator. Maybe he thought you were still a policeman. How about that?'

'The point is, he did *not* pass me any information. Maybe he planned to, or he thought he had, and it didn't get to me. But the fact is, I don't know what he was talking about. But somebody out there–' he gestured beyond the grass '–evidently thinks I know something. Do you know who it could be?'

Maguire said, 'Are you saying you feel at risk here?'

'This place is pretty isolated. I have three-year-old twin girls.' The grass rustled and bowed.

Ward walked over to the axe. 'Can I?' Fletcher nodded. Ward lifted it free. 'I have absolutely no idea who might have left an animal on your doorstep. But why not phone the police about this? They're your old friends.' He began to swing the axe.

'They're not my friends. I'm not on good terms with the police.'

Ward lowered the axe. 'And why is that?'

'We fell out.'

'Over what?'

'Quite a few things. Now I solve my own problems in life.'

'I see.' Ward lifted the axe again and swung it down into the trunk. It exposed a hollow of parasitic larvae squirming in the light. He kicked them away. 'Look, you can solve problems on your own or you can get some help. If Dan Simmons was in some kind of situation, I need to know what it was. If something arrives from Dan, you have to let us know. I mean that.' Ward slammed the axe into the trunk and left it there. 'Why the axe, anyway? Why not get a digger in here, clear it in an hour?'

'I like cutting wood.'

Ward straightened up. 'Must be very therapeutic.' He smiled, looking around. 'You know something, I'm jealous. I envy your life here. I'd like a place like this, later on.'

'After the army?'

'Yes, after this.' Ward's smile faded. 'Anything from Simmons, we have to know about it.'

In the courtyard, an old red Alfa stood next to Cathleen's car. When the two soldiers had driven off, Ward at the wheel, Fletcher swung the gate shut and padlocked it. He saw Cathleen watching through a downstairs window.

In the kitchen, she said to him, 'This place is turning into an army camp.'

'Maguire again, and a Major Ward.'

'Were they any help?'

'They want us to phone the police.' There was a long silence. Fletcher knew that Cathleen shared his view of the police – that they made things worse. She looked at him, twisting her hair up. 'Such a nice-looking man.'

'Thanks.'

'I meant the major.'

'You're trying to be brave.'

'Yes, I am, Tom. I am trying.'

Ward drove them back through the farmland. Irrigation sprays in the sunlight, a Hercules from Lakenheath crawling along the horizon. He said, 'So what do you think?'

'It's obvious. Dan Simmons thought of Fletcher because he was an ex-police officer, or an investigator. That in itself is significant – it means Simmons wanted something to be investigated. But I also believe Fletcher – I don't think he knows what Simmons was talking about.'

'Aw, you're a sucker for a man with an axe.'

'Yeah, every time,' she said. 'But seriously, Simmons thought of an investigator – in his dying moments. Why? What did he want to tell him?'

They drove in silence for a minute. Then Ward said, 'How are you doing, Stef? In yourself?'

'Permission to be patronised, sir.'

'Sorry.' He caught her eye. 'I think you're doing OK.' Thinking, *She is so damn pretty*.

The traveller sat in the back of a twenty-year-old Nissan jeep. The driver took the centre of the road, swerving past the goats and the mopeds on the hill roads. The valley sides gave way to the route across the plains. A steady ninety k.p.h., passing trucks loaded with barrels and planks. An Afghan army column at the side of the road. The traveller settled back and opened the window as the sun climbed.

He saw the driver watching him in the mirror, the eyes flicking away.

The traveller closed his eyes. He leaned on his rucksack, put his arm around it. Four hours passed with occasional stoppages, six hours, eight hours. Late afternoon, they hit Kabul.

Think of Kabul, think of a hellhole, maybe. The traveller knew it wasn't completely like that. He had the Nissan take him to a quarter near Cloud Town, a residential district that had been claimed by a mix of journalists, NGO staff, government agency people and their entourages. An Afghan police checkpoint at each entry gave an idea of security.

He said *Khodahafez*, goodbye, waited till the truck turned the corner, looked around.

The streets were shady, lined with palm and eucalyptus. There was a bakery, a grocery store, a barber shop, an English language bookshop, apartments to rent by the week, a row of hotels behind steel railings. The traveller went into the largest one: the Palace Hotel. Four storeys, air conditioning, family-run, two guards on the door. Staff who spoke English.

He shook hands with the desk clerk. The man brought him out a security box – the real thing, steel and a combination lock. The traveller slid the lock and took out credit cards, six thousand dollars cash, a satellite phone, his ID in a leather case.

Michael Jason. That's me. Not some Swedish hippy.

So Jason took a seat in the deserted lobby and ordered tea and a bread roll. He watched the tea steam in the sunlight, watched smart European women walking past on the pavement. He hadn't seen women walking like that for weeks. He wanted a shower, get cleaned up. He checked his phone. A few odds and sods, but also a message from yesterday.

Call me. There's a problem.

From his main contact, the man who called himself Guru.

He dialled. 'What's up, Guru?'

A pause. Sounds in the background he couldn't identify. Then, 'Who've you been talking to?'

'Nobody, Guru.'

'You're sure?'

'Yes. Why?'

'Listen. There's a reporter, a journalist

called Dan Simmons. He's been digging around. He found out about us.'

Jason felt adrenaline rush his scalp. 'OK. So shut him up.'

'Simmons is dead. On the barracks. The army are saying he shot himself.'

'Good.' Jason grinned. 'So what's the problem, Guru, man?'

'I think Simmons backed up his information, sent it to someone. Have you heard of Tom Fletcher?'

'Who is he?'

'Simmons called him Honey Man. Sent him his information.'

'So shut him up too, this Tom Fletcher.'

'More dead bodies, attracting attention? I sent him a sign last night, to keep quiet. But it looks like he's ignored it. Things are getting out of control.'

'What does that mean?'

Guru said, 'Fletcher's been talking to the Military Police. There's this female who's sniffing around, captain rank. She's brought in a male officer.'

'What rank?'

'Major.'

'Jesus. Now you've got to shoot Fletcher too.'

'Shoot him while he's talking to the Military Police? You don't think much, do you?'

Jason thought about it, the palm trees

89

spiking shade across the lobby. 'You know this is my last trip. Feels like it's unlucky.'

'Keep your head.'

'Look, just sort out Honey Man, Fletcher, whatever he calls himself. If not you, then send someone. There must be someone you can send.'

'I think – yes, there is. It can be done. Tonight, or tomorrow morning.'

'Just get it done, then.' He took a gulp of tea. 'I want to come in now, Guru. I want to come home.'

'Wait. If Fletcher's been talking – you understand what it means? Wait till the morning. Stay off the map.'

'Off the map? I'm in the Palace Hotel.'

'So relax. By the time you wake up, Honey Man won't be a problem.'

Jason ended the call, thinking about Guru. Up there, controlling everything. Stress in his voice.

Then Jason started thinking: *This could be a lot worse.* Of all places in Afghanistan to be stuck for the night, this was among the best. A toilet, not a bucket. A hot shower and a seat in the lobby, unwinding, watching Euro girls walking past. After his trip eating goat and sugared bread, talking to hairy villagers, he could do with this.

He paid for a room for the night. He knew he had to change his rucksack, so he went to the hotel shop – full of rugs and bubble pipes – and picked out a Samsonite roller suitcase and a padlock. He paid in cash, took the Samsonite key. He bought some chinos and a new shirt too – overpriced crap, but he needed something.

Taking it all up to his room, he noticed the lobby wasn't completely empty. There was a young woman sitting on her own, her back to him, braided hair, stirring coffee. He caught her profile as he walked past – she looked bored, wanting some company. At the stairs, he looked back, got a quick smile. Maybe this trip wasn't so unlucky after all.

Fletcher went on digging and chopping the trees in the pool until late afternoon. Then he went back to the house. He retrieved an old packing case from the attic, brought it down to the kitchen. Cathleen closed her laptop and came over as he opened it.

'I didn't realise you'd kept all this, Tom.'

'I thought we might need it at some point.'

She put her face against his shoulder for a second. He could feel her stress, and he put his arms around her and hugged her for a minute.

She said, 'I'm OK.' Then she reached for her car keys. 'Annabel's away for a week, she wants me to check on her house.' He nodded – Annabel, Cathleen's business partner, made frequent trips to the Far East, sourcing carvings for British stores. 'I'll do that, then

I'll pick up the kids from nursery.'

'OK. I'm going to get this working.'

As she left, he took out of the packing case some of the kit he'd used in the days before becoming a honey and watercress farmer.

A set of cameras, button size.

He went out onto the road, pushed a wooden spike into the ground under the bushes and taped a camera to it. For such a tiny piece of equipment, it gave a pretty clear infrared image in darkness, and could transmit it to the computers in the house. He put a plastic cup over it with an aperture for the lens. Protect it from rain and make it look like litter. Then he went around to the back of the house. He fitted another camera to one of the apple trees, hiding it under the leaves. It would give a good view of anyone approaching the house out of the channels in the elephant grass. Anyone carrying dead animals or other objects.

The sky was turning deep blue, clouds glinting aluminium. Night was a few hours away.

Tuesday Night

Jason had the best room in the place: top floor, a balcony over the gardens of the old palace. He stood there, looking out. Warm breeze, and the hotel lights spreading shadows of cypress trees. He turned to face the room. A big box TV, a shower stall like something from a slaughterhouse. Smell of wax and soap. Luxury.

He locked his valuable stuff inside the Samsonite and used the padlock to secure it to the air conditioner. Some bugger could take it, but they'd make a lot of noise, and he'd only be out of the room for a while. Then he took a quick shower and changed into the new clothes, clean pants and socks from his rucksack. He told himself he wanted to take a walk around, get some air before the long night in the room.

Yep.

In the lobby, the girl was still there, sitting cross-legged on a couch, twisting her hair braids in one hand, stirring a bowl of coffee in the other. She looked up. He smiled. They got talking.

He was thinking, *Has Guru organised it yet?*

At dusk, Fletcher went onto the main road. The skyline was purple-black, an ovoid moon low on the fields. The only traffic was a beet lorry rumbling past. Fletcher watched its lights disappear, then walked back to the house, a bat circling overhead.

He checked the camera in the bushes, then the padlock on the gate. He locked and bolted the front door and went around checking the windows.

In the kitchen, the TV was still on, the sound down low. A newsman's voice was saying, 'The battleground for Poppy Crush is in the remote valleys of Afghanistan.' Fletcher turned from the window to watch. Graphics lit up over the still of a poppy head. 'In 2001, Afghanistan exported fifty per cent of the world's illegal opium. Today – after seven years of democracy backed by NATO forces – it exports ninety per cent of the world's supply – and not in the form of crude opium, but of ready-made, refined heroin. Ironically, the southerly Helmand province – scene of the fiercest British fighting against the Taleban insurgency – produces the bulk of this. But let's not forget the other battleground – here at home.' The graphics turned to outlines of male shapes against a map of Britain. 'The importers are here, the big men who've grown rich on pure Afghan heroin. They sit in unknown locations, giving orders, showing no mercy.'

Footage of a street scene, police recovering a handgun from the site of a shooting, an undertaker's van pulling away behind them. 'Poppy Crush opens a new front against them. Not only in the south of Afghanistan, but throughout that country, including the regions around Kabul itself. It will cut the oxygen of supply from these big men of heroin, the British distributors.'

There was a rushed quote from the Defence Minister. Then on to the economy. No mention of Dan Simmons at all.

Fletcher turned it off. In the silence, he heard Sally and Evie singing in the bath.

He brought them milk and biscuits. They ate in their pyjamas, swinging their legs off Evie's bed. He read them a story about a whale making friends with a mouse. Evie fell asleep on his lap. He kissed them both and tucked them in, smoothing their hair on the pillows.

If anything happens to them. If anyone hurts them.

Outside, the clouds were darkening.

He went into his study, looked at the pictures of the twins on the walls, and Cathleen's sketches of the finished smallholding. He turned the PC on and brought up the two camera inputs, placed them both on the screen. The front of the house, with the gate and the road between the grass. At the back, the field of apple trees going into the dark.

He sat at the window, watching the court-yard. Around ten p.m., a cat jumped onto the gate, bristled its fur, jumped down again. He heard Cathleen checking on the twins, then going to bed herself. He stretched his arms, feeling the ache from all the axe work, listening to the sounds of the house cooling down. Back on the screen, a fox was standing in the orchard, leaking thermal blur from its jaws. He heard occasional vehicles on the main road, not stopping.

He was asking himself a question. What might Dan Simmons have wanted to tell him from the barracks of a British army regiment that was counting down to Operation Poppy Crush.

See nothing, say nothing.

On the screen, the fox eyes turned brittle green.

Captain Stef Maguire turned it over in her mind. If Tom Fletcher couldn't explain what Dan Simmons was talking about – who could? The question might have to wait for a few hours now.

She knew that outside of theatre oper-ations, a substantial amount of service life is spent on sport and socialising. Tonight was socialising.

She sprayed some gel into her hair and combed it through, tied it up into a neat ponytail. Tonight wasn't just another cocktail party or meet-your-comrades hour. She'd heard the Cambs regiment had some kind of ceremonial dinner before a new deployment, hadn't realised the damn thing was tonight. They called it a *feast* – so important that even the on-base RMP were invited. She looked at herself in the mirror. She hated regimental dinners.

When she reached the mess hall, she realised this was worse than anything she could have imagined. The whole regiment was mingling in the central space – making a noise like a machine in low gear, oiled by booze. Around the walls, there were trestle tables laid for the soldiers to dine, and at the far end a raised platform for the commanding ranks. In the centre of that, Trixie the pig was secured in a wooden crate, a tinsel crown catching the revolving disco lights, little eyes twinkling.

She caught sight of Ward on one side, surrounded by a knot of people: some MP team, some regiment. She made her way over. Just outside the group, she was cornered by a man who introduced himself as the regimental chaplain – his bald head gleaming, a fancy cocktail in his hand.

He said, 'Sex on the beach.'

'Sorry, Chaplain?'

'The name of the drink.'

'Isn't that extremely dated?' But she was listening to the conversation behind her –

97

Ward's group. They were talking about an operation, something from a couple of years ago.

The chaplain leaned close to her ear. 'Settling in OK? Any way I can help?'

'Why is that pig at the top table?'

The chaplain laughed. 'Goes back to Empire days. The colonel's pet was always head of the table. King of the feast.'

She remembered what Trixie had been feasting on the day before. She said, 'Did you ever meet Dan Simmons?'

'Poor, poor guy. But we have to move on.'

'So you met him?'

The chaplain nodded, put his mouth to her ear. 'He came to me for a chat. He was terrified. You could see it in his eyes.'

'Terrified of what?'

But a gong sounded over the noise, and the regiment fell quiet. A voice called, 'Be seated for the feast.'

Jason told the girl in the lobby that his name was Pete – the first name that came into his head. She said her name was Anna, and she worked for a Belgian NGO – coordinating charity action in the field, assessing its benefits. She said she didn't mind the fieldwork, the open spaces. But Kabul scared the knickers off her. That's what she said, straight out, laughing in good English. She had nice teeth, crinkles beside her eyes. Made her twenty-five, twenty-six, he guessed.

She said, 'So what are *you* doing here, Pete?'

'I'm travelling around, writing a book.'

'That's so interesting.'

She flicked her hair and shoulders back. Her blouse open three buttons, smooth and tanned inside. Hope she doesn't go shopping like that. They'll fucking kill her. She saw him looking.

He said, 'Anna, I hope you don't go shopping like that.'

She glanced down. 'Why?'

'They'll – there'll be a negative cultural reaction.'

'That's why I stay in the hotel.'

'Don't you get bored?'

She kicked her legs up, rested one foot against his, let her hair fall down over her face. 'I've got three bottles of gin in my suitcase.'

'Where's your suitcase?'

'In my room.'

He thought of his own room: the Samsonite padlocked to the air unit – the whole reason he was here. Can't just leave it there. He looked at Anna. Can't just leave *her* here.

In the lift, he stood close enough to smell her hair. She had her eyes closed, humming to herself. Daft, spaced-out charity girl. Sometimes, trips just work out. It all ends up sweet. Anna here is sweet.

In her room, Anna leaned over the suitcase, got two bottles out, gave him a full view of her boobs. Straightened up and smiled. He kissed her against the door and she put her thumb inside his belt at the back.

He said, 'We're going to my room.'

'OK, Pete. Wherever you like.'

After the dinner, when the toasts were all done and the national anthem sung, the regiment broke into loose groups clustered around the bar or the various side doors giving out onto the sports field. Stef Maguire found herself outside one of the doors, breathing in the night smell of the barracks. The sound of voices and laughter from the mess hall a steady drone.

'Well, well.'

Two men of her rank standing in front of her, the disco lights playing across them. Regiment men, not MPs. One smoking a cigar, the other swirling a brandy glass. The big, chopped hairstyles of public school cadets, not grown up. She said, 'Well?'

'Maguire,' the cigar man said. 'The hard girl. With a taste for the hard stuff.'

'Meaning?'

'We've heard about you.' They both grinned. 'Hopefully when we're out next week, we'll do a better job than you managed

100

to. Like, we might manage to burn it, not consume it.' They laughed. 'That is why you're here, isn't it? To recover from the experience?'

She snatched the cigar and threw it in the brandy. When the brandy man pushed at her, she flipped him over so that he landed on the glass with a dull breaking sound, sat up with blood running from his hand. The other one clenched his fist, pulled it back. Things about to get illegal.

She cupped her hand, got ready to slam it under his chin, break his daddy's expensive dentistry.

Ward appeared beside her, looked at the two male captains, and smiled.

Stef flexed her fingers.

Ward kept smiling, watching the boys walk away.

He said, 'You did well there. Classy.'

She said, 'I take it everyone here knows what happened to me.'

'Don't worry about it.' His boot crushed the broken glass into small pieces. 'I mean it, don't worry. You're OK, I'm OK. We'll stick together.'

Fletcher's watch said after midnight. Through the window: moon over the elephant grass. On the screens: the yard with the gate and the wall of grass. No animals. No movement. He checked the view of the orchard. Apple leaves twitching in a breeze he couldn't feel in the humid study. A moth drifting past. He watched it fade. He looked away. He looked back.

He felt the stubble on his cheeks rising.

The elephant grass showed as a grey wall. The nearest channel showed as a dark block. Inside it, completely still, the outline of a man, face and arms visible. Just standing there, looking up at the house. Then stepping back into the channel. Fletcher watched the screen for another minute. The man didn't reappear.

Fletcher went out into the corridor. He checked that Sally and Evie's doors were closed. He heard Cathleen move in bed, closed her door too. Downstairs, he watched the garden from the kitchen window. He thought of turning the floodlights on, decided against it. He let himself out of the kitchen door and locked it quietly behind him.

The moon threw some light – but he was standing in the shadow of the house. The air was warm and smelled of dust. He moved along the wall to the side, walked quickly across the turf, up to the grass itself. It was hard to hear anything from inside there – the stems were rustling in the breeze. He went along the edge to the channel near the camera, and stepped in.

The channel was almost completely dark,

the moonlight sending jagged shadows above his head as the stems dipped. Fletcher walked along the narrow space, blades scraping his face. He could just see a few metres ahead – nothing except the grass. Nobody visible. In two minutes, he knew he was approaching the other edge of the field, where it bordered on the main road. A sound made him stop. It was a different sound from the creaking around him. It was the clunk of a car door shutting – or maybe a boot lid. He could see the end of the field a few metres ahead, moonlight on the road. In the shadow of the last clump of grass, he stopped.

He could just see the front of a saloon car, the lights off, the plate unreadable. Moving his head slightly, he could see the front window, which was down, an elbow leaning on the sill. The car started up, but the lights stayed off. It reversed off the verge, then moved forward. As it passed, Fletcher got a one-second view of the inside. It stayed on his retina, tinted ash-colour by the moon-light.

The driver was a thin man in dark clothes. The passenger was huge, big arms bare in the moonlight. He was in the action of put-ting something inside his jacket, under his left arm. It didn't fit first time, because he took it out and placed it back in, adjusting it with the heel of his hand.

Then the car was past him, going back to the main road.

He stepped out into the road and heard it move away slowly, not accelerating, as if patrolling around the edge of the property.

Fletcher turned back into the channel. He began to run, the grass blades whipping at his face. He was sure he'd seen what the big man was trying to fit back under his arm. In the moonlight, it was bone-coloured. But he'd seen enough of them back in police days to know what it was. A Browning 9 mm pistol.

He saw that again in his mind, then saw from the previous night the rabbit's dead fetuses. And the twins asleep in their beds. He ran faster.

In his room, Jason opened the balcony and showed Anna the palace gardens, standing behind her. Moths clunking on the open doors. His hands on her waist, then his mouth on the back of her neck. She bent it forward for him. She tasted of fine sweat and some kind of fruit soap, just like a Belgian would taste, he thought suddenly.

She said, 'Pete, I don't make a habit of this.' He laughed and ran his hands inside her shirt. 'Really, I don't. It's just I'm lonely and this place scares me. And I'm feeling hot today, like I need it, you know how a woman feels that sometimes?'

He tipped her forward onto the old bed.

He pulled her blouse off – no bra, but half a dozen big freckles across her shoulder blades. He kissed them, undoing her jeans. She slid them down herself, kicked her feet out of them. He said, 'I'm glad I took a walk in the lobby.'

'Me too, darling.'

He slid her thong down and slapped her butt. She laughed and wriggled. Moths banging into the windows, looking in. He rolled her over, saw she had her hand between her legs, getting ready for him. He thought, *She's too good to be true.* The sound of gunfire from the other side of the palace – just a few shots, then quiet. He heard her say, 'Here, I can help you.' One hand on the back of his neck, the other tugging at him. Her eyes closed, tugging. She ripped a condom open with her teeth and put it on him one-handed, eased inside just before he came, still holding his neck.

She didn't ask for anything else. He really liked this Anna.

She stroked his hair slowly, her face turned away.

Jason woke, put out a hand. The sheet was warm but empty. He stayed still, thinking. He turned his head to see the room. It was still night outside, moths on the windows. The table lamp was on, with a towel dropped over it to dim the light. Below that, on the floor,

Anna was squatting naked beside his suitcase. Her hair was stringy, just-fucked, and she was massaging a boob in one hand. He stayed completely still. She'd somehow got the case open. How did she do that? Its lid was black against her white freckled skin. She was rummaging inside, the thieving bitch. Squeezing her boobs with one hand and turning over his clothes with the other. He didn't move. Maybe she thought it was all just laundry in there. But then she lifted her hand out, holding his ID. Before he could move, he saw her lift the gear too, the whole reason he was here. She took her hand off her boobs and smoothed the plastic. A big frown of disbelief.

Fuck.

She had her fucking nails in it now, was trying to open it. He stood up. The room was so small he was barely two metres away from her. She jumped. She said, 'Oh, hi Pete.' She dropped the packet. Shuffled over on her knees and reached for his cock, opened her mouth.

He hit her hard enough to put her down on the floor. She sobbed and curled up. He stepped over her and lifted the towel off the lamp, checked the packet she'd been scratching at. Big scrapes from her nails, but still intact. He dropped it back in the case, closed the case, masked the lamp again. He picked her up and sat her on the bed, pulled the chair over and sat in front of her. She smelled of shagging and she was twitching, screwing her eyes up.

He said, 'Who sent you?'

'Nobody. Pete, I'll forget about this. I'll just forget. Please.'

'Who sent you?'

'Nobody.'

'How did you open the case?'

'The hotel shop has spare keys for the luggage. The man lent me this one.'

'Lent you?'

'I – you know. I did something for him. Personal.'

Jason couldn't believe he'd fallen for this. 'You're not a charity worker.'

'I am. I swear to God. I just do this sometimes.'

'Yeah? Why?'

'I'm confused. I'm vulnerable.'

'You fucking are now.'

She twisted her hands together. 'I like you Pete. You're so good in bed. I didn't want to open the case, but I thought, well, I've got the key. No harm.'

'Did you see my ID?'

'What ID?'

He slapped her head against the wall. 'You did. And what else did you see?'

'Nothing. Just a plastic packet.'

'You know what was in there?'

It was cool in the room, and her nipples

were hard. She said, 'No, Pete. Please.' She stretched back on the bed, damp creases on her stomach.

He was thinking, *Could just leave her, who's she going to tell? But she saw my name, I know she did. She saw my name and she knows what's in the packet. One or the other, OK. But not both.*

Looking at her on the bed, her hands slipping behind her waist.

'Anna, get dressed. I'm taking you back to your room.'

She rolled sideways, reaching for her shirt.

In her room, Jason kept the lights off, locked the door. He made her drink a quarter of the last bottle of gin. She didn't complain much. He made her show her passport: it had the name Inna Feltoum.

'That your real name?'

'Yes, look.'

It was on her NGO card too, and a letter from the Belgian Consulate addressed to Mlle Inna Feltoum, 76 Rue Balzac, Ghent.

He checked her phone: family pics, a cat, texts in Flemish.

He said, 'OK, Inna, come here.' She came and stood by the window, streetlights flashing on her face. 'We can be friends now.'

'Oh thank you.' She put her arms around him and he held her face against his shoulder. She was crying as she said, 'I'll forget everything.'

'I know you will, Inna.'

'Already I'm forgetting.'

'I know you are. Listen, Inna. I'm going to promise you something. I'll always be there for you.'

She smiled, squeezed him. 'And me for you. Anything you want, you can call me, OK?'

He opened the big window, and street noise spilled in, the smell of smoke and cooking. Light from the hotel awning lit her face. 'You're really pretty, Inna.'

'Thank you.'

'What I mean is I'll always find you. If you ever speak about what happened tonight, I'll find out. I can come and locate you, even if you move house, move country. You know I can.'

Her lip started shaking, her nose running.

'Please. I don't know your real name. I didn't see anything.'

'Just remember what I've said. OK?'

'Then you go?'

'Yes, Inna. I go.'

She smiled, wiping her nose.

A car hooted down in the street, and a food seller began calling. Jason checked the window: no balcony, just a parapet and then the hotel awning, three floors down. He leaned back from Inna, slipped his hands up under her arms, took hold of her there.

She looked up at him, scared and pissed,

wondering what he wanted now.

He threw her out of the window.

The last thing he saw was her pissed-up face twisting over the ledge, then her feet going over too, sandals kicking. There was a moment's silence, then the sound of her hitting the awning and the plastic roof over the street café – a big smash followed by lots of breaking, echoing out over the street. He stayed away from the window. The food seller had shut up, and someone was shouting. Apart from that, the sounds of the district went on.

He left the gin bottle under the window. He went to the door, hesitated over the key. In the end he left it in the lock – just what a pissed-up charity girl would do: let herself in her room and leave the key on the outside.

There was more shouting and cars hooting, but in half a minute he was back in his room, door locked, lights off, lying on the bed. One good thing about Afghanistan: no CCTV, no DNA, no fingerprints. You get a Belgian falling out of a window, nobody gives a toss.

He screwed his face into the pillow, breathing Inna's sweat and hair smell.

Nice kid in some ways.

Except she saw what was in his suitcase. And his name on his ID, she must have.

He closed his eyes.

What a trip.

Fletcher slammed on the floodlights and ran up to the bedroom. Cathleen said, 'What's going on?'

'We've got to move out.'

Thirty minutes later, two cars moved at speed along the road through the elephant grass, lights off until they hit the main road. A new German estate with Cathleen and two sleepy children. Behind that, an old Land Rover with Fletcher thinking, *They're all I've got in the world. And someone, somewhere, has sent a man with a gun to come and find us here. Who are these people, and why?*

And what do they think I know?

Wednesday Morning

At five-thirty, Jason was waiting in the lobby of the Palace Hotel. The street awning was flapping loose, and the glass roof was shattered, letting in the smell of diesel and street cooking. Jason asked the porter in English what happened? The man shrugged.

'Girl falls from window.'

'Wow. She OK?'

'No.'

'She alive?'

'Hospital.'

Jason watched the street – that bad luck feeling blowing in. But then his transport arrived, and he couldn't help grinning. Not yesterday's old truck, but a new Land Cruiser, darkened windows. The driver was twenties, British, tanned, shaven-headed. The driver looked Jason over: the braids, the chinos, the Samsonite.

'The fucking state of you.'

'Just get me out of here.'

They left behind the bookshops and bakeries, went through the suburbs: houses built onto workshops and factories, chimneys smoking against the lightening sky. Then an arterial road through the outskirts of the city, past bombed-out blocks with packs of dogs scrapping in the road, food vendors selling from oil stoves, corners manned by Afghan police in sandbagged emplacements, the mountains to the west grey-blue against the sky. Before the foothills, the road widened, letting the Cruiser speed up and overtake civilian tankers, lines of horses, three British army Land Rovers moving up the incline.

Jason said, 'Squaddies.'

The driver laughed.

After a further thirty kilometres, the driver took a turning off the major road, between two lines of chainlink fence. There was no signpost, but he confidently followed the track.

The driver asked, 'Feel good to be back?'

'What do you think?'

The small road curved onto a wide plain, the mountains ahead and the city under its smoke to the west. There was another chain fence, secured by cables and topped with razor wire. The Cruiser slowed, passed through a gateway in the fence, proceeded another hundred metres and halted abruptly at a checkpoint: two British soldiers aiming assault rifles from a concrete shelter. The driver rolled his window down, spoke to them. One of the troops walked around to Jason's side. Jason put the window down and spoke to him too. The soldiers spoke into radio sets, then waved the car on.

Another hundred metres, another road-block, staffed by more British troops, who waved them through. They zigzagged around concrete blocks in the road, climbed an incline and came into a flat area of prefab huts and steel-sided buildings. They passed a vehicle compound screened by netting. Jason noted a Warrior in there, and two Land Rovers with their engines raised on winches. They drove along a line of prefabs, behind a camo screen, came to the last one, pulled up. A sign in English:

Camp Omega
Base of the British Army in
Northern Afghanistan

The driver turned to Jason, shook hands. 'Welcome home.'

Haines walked into the squash court in the basement of the MOD building, went up to the balcony that ran along the back. She heard Summers before she saw him, his typical grunt. She leaned on the railing and watched him from behind, struggling a bit against an air force ace. Summers blew a point, looked round and saw her, called for a break. The air force star laughed.

Summers came up and sat beside her on the balcony bench, wiping his neck with a

114

towel. She took a corner of it and wiped sweat out of his eyes.

'Thanks,' he said. 'Why the glum face?'

'Something's come in from the Belgian Consulate. The one in Kabul.'

'Huh?' He wiped his hair.

'A Belgian citizen fell out of a hotel window. She's an NGO worker or something. In hospital, when she was coming out of anaesthetic, she started talking about what happened to her. The nurse was a Belgian volunteer who passed it straight to their Consulate. They've contacted us for clarification, in a friendly way. It's a tricky one.'

'*What happened to her?* What does that mean?'

She passed him a printed email. He glanced at it, then read it more slowly. He said, 'People hallucinate under anaesthetic. Don't show this to Downey. He's happy, keep him that way.'

'What if the Belgians chase it up?'

He handed the sheet back, wiped his hands and stood up. 'People hallucinate.'

It was Cathleen, in the end, who decided where she and the twins were going to go. Her friend Annabel's house – she wouldn't be back from the Far East for a week.

They'd made sure they weren't being followed, let themselves in around two a.m., put the twins to sleep upstairs, the two of

115

them curled up on the spare bed under the blankets they'd brought from their house. At five a.m. they cried and drank milk, then went back to sleep, Sally's arms around Evie's neck. At five-thirty a.m., Fletcher parted the venetian blinds and took a look outside. The house was a tidy 1990s executive box on a ribbon road of other similar houses. In the front garden, Annabel had crushed slate and a stand of bamboo, and a buddha's head watching the sky.

He released the blind and turned back to the living room. The walls were lined with Thai dragons and dancers in relief, fangs bared to the light. There was a massive TV too, its dark screen bouncing back the jagged sunlight from the blinds. Cathleen rubbed her eyes.

'What now?'

'Stay here, keep the kids inside.'

'Keep them inside? They're three years old.'

'They can play in the back garden. Just don't take them to nursery. Those men might know where it is.'

'Jesus Christ.' She pulled her hairband off and held it in her lips, began twisting her hair up, angry lines around her eyes. 'Maybe we've overreacted. Maybe those men were ordinary burglars.'

'With a gun, leaving dead animals blindfolded? I don't know who those men were.

But they came here with a gun because they think Dan Simmons told me something important.'

'But old Dan didn't tell you anything.'

'They don't know that. And there's no point me telling them that, because they won't believe it.'

'Then let's go away somewhere safe.'

He looked out through the blind again at the empty street. He began to speak, then stopped.

'What, Tom?'

'I've always gone away somewhere safe, haven't I? I left the police, I gave up the private detective business.'

'Because they weren't right for you—'

'Or because I didn't want to fight them. I wanted somewhere safe. I thought our house was the safest place of all.'

'It is.'

'Not now, Cathleen. We've run out of safe places.'

He stopped.

Evie was standing in the doorway, her big green eyes moving from Fletcher to Cathleen.

Cathleen picked her up and stroked her long dark hair, rocking her. Fletcher went and held them both very close.

Captain Maguire did an hour in the barracks' gym, then she went to the officers' mess at 0800 and found it almost empty except for Major Ward. The stewards were serving a ceremonial hangover breakfast to the few who had turned up. Maguire stacked her plate and sat opposite the major. She bit into a piece of fried bread.

Ward said, 'You don't look the type.' She raised an eyebrow. 'To eat fried bread.'

'Want some?' She held a piece out on her fork and he took it, washed it down with tea.

He said, 'Good time last night?'

'Yes, nice to mix with the regiment.'

'Mix? The punch on this girl, wow.'

'Thanks. Look, I wanted to ask you something.'

'I'll swap information for more fried bread.'

She passed him half a slice. 'Last night, before the dinner, I heard you talking about an operation you ran a few years ago.'

'I don't remember you being present at that point.'

'I was monitoring.'

He smiled. 'It's a good story. Operation Alloy.' He paused. 'This is where you say, do tell me the story.'

'Do tell me—'

'Well, it was like this. Back in 2003, 2004, the civilian police began to pick up on new kinds of weapons in the hands of criminals. British and American military-issue handguns, also older Russian- and French-made stuff. People say, hold on, this can only be coming from a combat theatre. Cue a lot of concern that army personnel were smuggling weapons out of Iraq, out of the Stan. Stealing them or trading for them in the field and bringing them back into this country, selling them on. Nobody could figure out how they were getting away with it. Operation Alloy said OK, if we were going to do that, how would we do it? I set up a team, and we went ahead like that, testing all the ways it could be done. Hide weapons in your kitbag? Not very clever.'

'How, then?'

'Hide them in vehicles. That's more like it. Lots of places in a Warrior or a Land Rover you can tuck away small arms. So where would you hide them? We took vehicles to bits, lifted out the inside panels, looked in all the cavities, the secret little places. It's the best way – test it out, then look around, do random checks, look in someone else's cavities, to see who is actually doing that. Bingo. We found two groups of soldiers at it. They pleaded guilty at the courts martial, saved us a lot of bad coverage.'

'What was the sentence?'

'Ten years. Military prison, no parole. It was a good operation all round. It confirmed my reputation for cleaning up a mess.' He poured tea for the two of them, looking around the empty room. There was a pause while she decided how to say what she wanted to say.

She said, 'You've been supportive of me these past two days. I'm grateful for that. And I think I know why.'

'Mm, why?'

'Because I think there's something not right in this barracks. And I think that you think so too.'

He looked at her for five seconds. 'I've cleaned up two piles of shit so far. There was Op Alloy, but before that there was this barracks. The deaths that happened here. Remember yesterday, at Tom Fletcher's house, the grubs inside that tree trunk? That's what this barracks was like. People hiding from the light. They brought me in to eliminate that, they've kept me here because of that. I'm the man who cleaned up Waterton. If I thought for a moment–' He kept looking into her eyes. 'OK. Dan Simmons worries me.'

She said, 'I got talking to the chaplain last night.'

'The boys call him Sex on the Beach.'

'After the cocktail?'

'After his posting in Gibraltar.'

'He said Dan Simmons went to see him. He said Simmons was frightened of something.'

'Of what? Going into a combat zone?'

'Or maybe something else? A man is

terrified of something, he has something on a laptop that disappears. Information about what? Why is he so terrified?'

Ward tidied his plate and set it aside. Dusty sunlight was coming through the windows. He said, 'You did well last night. You'll do well in the future. Oh, and you'll need this.'

He took her hand, opened it flat. He took the salt cellar and tipped a little salt into her palm and closed her fingers on it. His hand stronger than hers, not always the case with a man.

She said, 'What's this?'

'It's a big pinch of salt, Stef. You need to take it when you speak to the chaplain about anything. But yes, find out what the hell he was talking about. Just don't hit him.'

Fletcher drove into Cambridge, his home town. You go back home, you should feel warm, welcomed, like you belong. He didn't quite feel that way. He parked his Land Rover off Mill Road and breathed the air.

He'd been a police Detective Inspector here, six years before. Back then he'd been thirty-two, with money in the bank, a sweet little Audi to drive around in. A warrant card in his pocket that made people talk to him.

He breathed in again.

Pubs and traffic, the oriental food places

121

on Mill Road, the Indian wholesalers. Trains from under the railway bridge, rattling along the stretch of marshalling yard they called Electric Mile. It all felt like the past.

Four years ago, he'd been a struggling private investigator. But now he made honey. He wanted to branch out into watercress. He wanted it to stay that way. He wanted to make love to Cathleen and bring up their kids.

He climbed the fire escape to the first floor of a building above a printing shop. He pushed the door open.

Smell of pork stew. Twelve tables and a three-metre bar.

'*Cześć*, Stan.'

The man behind the bar watched him with morose Polish eyes.

'Tom Fletcher. *Cześć*.' He made the words sound like a prayer for the dead. Fletcher placed a pot of honey on the counter and Stan looked at it.

Fletcher knew what he was thinking. Three years ago, Fletcher and Stan had been partners in this restaurant, building it into a solid little business. Then Fletcher had handed back his share, moved out of Cambridge, left everything behind, shutting himself away with Cathleen and the twins in the old house in the fields.

Stan had shouldered the business himself, kept in touch, never complained. But the way he was looking at the honey said, 'You did that for this?' as clearly as if he'd said the words.

'You got trouble, Tom?'

'What makes you think that?'

'You're back in Cambridge.' His eyes on the honey.

'Did you hear about Dan Simmons, the TV professor?'

'Shot himself at the barracks?' Stan took the jar of honey and held it up to the sunlight. It flashed and glowed amber, enough to put a glint in his eyes. 'Dan Simmons, off the TV. He came in here once.'

'*What?*'

'It was, maybe, three years ago, just after you–' he paused '–left. He was looking for you.'

'Why?'

Stan looked into the honey as if it held all the answers in the world. 'He didn't say.'

Fletcher thought about that. 'He believed I was still a private investigator.'

'Yes, I think he said that.' Stan put the honey down, and his eyes grew still and black again. 'So what are you doing in Cambridge, Tom?'

'I'm going to take a look in Dan Simmons' house.'

Stan's eyes went back to the honey. It seemed to fascinate him. 'Is your new life what you wanted, Tom?'

'It's perfect.'

'It's pure. I can see that.'

Walking down the street, Fletcher realised that Stan meant the honey.

Cathleen watched the twins playing in Annabel's new-agey dining room. They were laying dolls out under a huge stone carving of a buddha's face fixed to one wall. The big blind eyes seemed to be looking down on them.

Dolls, teddy bears, a doctor's set.

She realised she was holding herself, wrapping her arms around herself. She went into the living room, stood looking at the phone in the semidarkness. In the end, she picked it up and dialled Thailand. A hotel, a room phone ringing out, then the hotel bar. Sounds in the background – birdsong, a swimming pool, clink of glasses.

'Annabel? I'm in your house. I just have to–'

She listened to the voice on the phone calming her, reassuring her.

She tried not to cry, but she couldn't stop it.

'Annabel, I just have to talk to someone.'

Wednesday Afternoon

Pretoria Road was a street of 1920s villas built in the honey-coloured Cambridge stonework. Some wisteria, ivy, cherry trees in full blossom, For Sale signs. Fletcher walked almost to the end, where the street met a footbridge running over the river to Midsummer Common. Dan Simmons' address was there on the right, the sun casting sparks of shade through its cherry tree onto a knot garden and a glossy red front door.

Fletcher crossed the road, went through the little gate in the wall, stood looking at the door. It was a beautiful house – solid, well-kept. Perfect for a TV professor. The tree moved in the breeze. A few flecks of blossom spun down over Fletcher.

A young cleaner answered the door, smiled.

Fletcher said, 'I was a friend of Dan–'

'Then you'll want to meet the sisters.'

'The sisters?'

She took him through the house – like a 1920s butler, except for the way she glanced over her shoulder. A tiled floor, scent of mature female perfume, a console table stacked with letters and cards, flowers in vases. He heard women's voices from behind the next door.

'–like the time he fell in the lake, remember? Poor Dan. He cried and cried.'

'To think of him in there with those soldiers, going out to that awful place. I mean, not awful because of the locals.'

'I do know what you mean.'

The cleaner knocked on the door and opened it.

The two women were sitting in easy chairs in a small, well-furnished garden room, spangled light from a wisteria flowing across them. They were both knitting, the needles still clicking as they looked up at him.

He realised they were sisters. Pale, putting energy into their knitting – displacing their grief, he guessed. The needles darting in the light, scent of the wisteria.

The cleaner slipped away.

He said, 'Hello. I'm Tom Fletcher.'

One of the women stopped knitting, looked at him. Her face was lined, her make-up wasn't great – but her eyes were clear grey.

'You're *Tom*?' As if she knew of him. She laid aside her work. 'I'm Susan, and this is Melanie.'

'Hello, Tom,' from the other one.

'We are Dan's sisters. Elder sisters.'

They all shook hands, Fletcher saying,

'I'm so sorry about Dan. He came to my wedding.'

Susan smiled and nodded. 'You must have been a very good friend.'

'Susan, why do you say that?'

'You're one of his people.' The click of her sister's needles again.

'Sorry?'

'Oh, I'm not making much sense today. So much to think about. Dan left some letters here for people he knew. Your name is on one of them.'

'My name's on a letter?'

Susan got to her feet. She was clearly the leader: Melanie staying intent on her work. Susan said, 'Come with me, Tom.'

She took him back across the hallway, into what could only be called a drawing room. A bay window onto the street, with a security grille. Floorboards, Persian rug, bookcases. Watercolours and tapestries on the wall. A huge antique desk, with scanner and printer. She said, 'It's a lovely house, isn't it? It's gracious.'

'It is, yes.'

'And now we have to decide what happens to it. So much administration. It's so impersonal.'

Fletcher nodded slowly, not looking at her. He was looking at the antique desk. It was covered with a series of manila envelopes. Maybe fifteen or sixteen in all, laid out across the dark wood. Each envelope had an address label, neatly printed, exactly centred. He could read the labels on the nearest two: a solicitor's office, and someone living on the south coast.

Susan was saying, 'Dan was worried about the future, we all know that. He was going out to Afghanistan, for goodness' sake. He left these letters for us to find. They're putting his affairs in order, basically. In the event of his death. His will, the house. Letters to old friends. In a day or so, I think we'll feel like sending them all out. But in some way, I like seeing them here. They remind me how thoughtful Dan was.'

'Yes, I can understand. And there's a letter for me?'

She went to the desk, picked up an envelope and handed it to him.

He held it in both hands. The label read *Tom Fletcher*

And his current address. He turned it over. The flap was unsealed.

He thought, *So this is it. This is what Dan was sending me. He didn't mail it, he left it here in case anything happened to him. Of course.*

This is why people came to my house with guns.

This is why my family is in hiding.

OK, Dan. What is it?

He put his hand inside. He looked in there. The envelope was empty. He showed it to Susan – she looked mystified.

He picked up the nearest envelope from the desk and turned it over. It was sealed with red wax and the print of a signet ring. He turned over a few more. All filled and sealed.

He said, 'Susan, do you have any idea where my letter is?'

'I don't know. This is just how we found it. Maybe he was still thinking what to write. Maybe he didn't have everything he needed.'

The house was dry and still. Fletcher swallowed. He could hear the faint click of the knitting needles, and from somewhere, the drone of a bee.

He said gently, 'Can I ask where the computer is?'

'The computer?'

'There's a scanner and printer here. But no computer.'

'It's missing. The army people were very frank. It's just gone missing.'

'I bet he had a smart little laptop, didn't he?'

'Yes, a shiny one. He was so proud.' Tears formed in her eyes. 'Like a boy.'

Fletcher took her by the arm, and she leaned against him for a second. Then she leaned back, smiling bravely, sniffing.

He wanted to ask if he could rummage around the house, but he couldn't find the words. *Dan was a nice guy, Susan. I'm sorry he's dead. But he's screwing up my life with his missing letter.*

Instead he wished her the very best and saw himself to the door.

Outside, in the little knot garden, he slit the envelope and opened it out. Nothing – no tiny scrap, no markings on the smooth manila.

Like a boy.

Invisible ink?

He put it away. Susan was probably right, Dan had been thinking what to put in that envelope. Or waiting for facts, hard evidence to include. About what?

He looked up. The cleaner was watching him through the window. He pointed to the front door.

She opened it. 'Mm?'

'They're sweet, aren't they? Susan and Melanie.'

'Yeah.'

'Did you know Dan?'

'Only met him once.'

'You know what I'd really like now.'

'Yeah?'

'I'd like a few minutes upstairs.'

She smiled, flicking cherry petals off his collar.

'That'll be fifty quid, love.'

There was a bedroom with a sleigh bed and

a mirrored wardrobe: cologne scent, suits on wooden hangers, evenly spaced. A bathroom with cologne on a glass shelf. A guest room with empty cupboards. A room lined with shelves holding porcelain figurines. No letter. No reference to Fletcher. Coming downstairs, he heard the sisters' voices behind their closed door. He liked them, the way they kept going. He looked quickly into the dining room: a bowl of fruit going speckled, on a starched tablecloth.

The cleaner whispered, 'Anything else you want to see?'

The front door shut quietly, her eyes glinting as the gap closed.

He walked up onto the footbridge and stood for a minute, leaning on the parapet, watching the river, thinking about how *thoughtful* Dan was. Knowing he was going out to a war zone, putting his affairs in order at his antique desk.

The Honey Man. He's got – what?

Dan knowing his life was in danger. Wanting to leave information with someone he remembered as an investigator. Someone who could investigate – investigate what? Who?

The river was green and speckled with pollen.

But you never wrote the letter, Dan. You thought you had, or maybe you were meaning to before you left for Afghanistan. So now I don't

131

know what you were talking about. But other people do – people who leave mutilated animals at my door. People who come to my house at night with guns. What do they think I know?

And they'll be back tonight. How long before they find us? A day, two days?

Who are they?

He felt nauseous, defenceless.

There was the sound of moving water.

A young woman rowed under the bridge on a skiff, her face raised to his for a second. Her neck tendons were tight in the sun, her eyes on his as she leaned back into her stroke, her lids lowering, a little cry from her mouth. He felt the way men do, that something had passed between them. But the next stroke found her looking at the trees, going away into their shadow.

He rubbed his chin and smiled.

She didn't even know I was here.

He ripped up Dan's envelope.

He walked down off the footbridge, quickly back along the street to his car.

He felt better now, more secure. The nausea had gone.

He was thinking of the night again, but with a sudden eagerness and a twitching in his hands. So Dan Simmons never wrote the letter – so what? Fletcher had just realised the problem that exists if you're an anonymous gunman who leaves dead animals at people's houses after dark.

132

You never know who else is there.

Jason felt like a tosser, walking into troop accommodation with a Samsonite roller case. He got over that by hoisting it on his shoulder like a kitbag. His bedding area – called a hutch – was stifling hot. He put the case in his footlocker and just left it. If you can't trust the army, who *can* you trust?

He went to the latrine and ran the hot water. He looked at himself in the mirror. Unbelievable.

He took scissors and cut off the hair braids, flipping them into the bin like worms. He took his electric razor and shaved his head almost bare, leaving just a millimetre. He ran water over his skull, wiped it off, looked at himself again. Then he went back to his hutch, opened the high locker. His uniform was in there, on its wire hanger. He took it out and smelled it. British detergent: nothing in the world like that. In two minutes he was wearing it, the red cap angled correctly on his head, the three stripes on his arm, the red RMP insignia flash, his boots laced. They clicked as he walked out of the accommodation, along the crushed stone path. A Chinook was landing near the perimeter, spreading a tornado of dust. He entered another of the prefab buildings, saluted the female captain at her desk inside the door.

She said, 'Sergeant Jason. Better late than never.'

She told him where to wait. He stood in a small, unventilated room, a ceiling fan washing hot air over him. He waited, enjoying just being back in uniform.

The debriefing lasted two hours. There was a captain from the RMP – a spiky-haired kid who'd been Jason's superior officer for three months now. Also present, a major from the Afghan army, an Afghan civilian from their anti-narcotics agency, and a liaison officer from the Cambs regiment. Sergeant Jason gave an account of his tour disguised as a hippy traveller. He used a map on the wall to identify nine villages where opium refinement was taking place, a further six he believed possible. He related the exact location of the machinery in each one, identified the village leaders where known. The Afghan major and the Cambs officer made notes, marked their own maps, conferred in basic English. The Afghan anti-narcotics guy asked if there was any evidence of involvement by the Afghan army. There was a brief confrontation in Pashto. The Brits winked at each other. At the wrap-up, the Afghans made a speech about cooperation, then left.

The Cambs man said, 'That was top class, good set of targets,' and walked out. The door clanged shut.

Jason sat facing his RMP captain. Spiky haircut, thin officer's face, sharp lips in a smirk. Lighting a little cigar, then clapping his hands dramatically.

'Excellent work, Jason. You made a good hippy.'

'Thank you, sir.'

'You were the last one back in, though. Everyone else has debriefed and gone. We haven't even heard from you for two days.'

'Been in dodgy places, sir. You saw that. There's tons of the stuff out there, mountains of it.'

'Well, we've got over a hundred factories targeted now, five hundred km square of fields. The Afghans are bringing these bloody great flame-throwers. It'll look great. You've been part of a big picture, a useful part. Well done.' Said in the tone Jason knew – the expensive school, talking down to the scum who'd been thick enough to risk his arse wandering the roads of Afghanistan for ten days.

Sergeant Jason smiled, but inside – not on his face.

'Thank you, sir.'

He waited for dismissal.

'You stayed at the Palace Hotel last night.'

'It was best, sir. I was still in civilian clothes. By the time I arranged the pick-up–'

'And apparently there was an issue there last night. A Belgian charity girl had a nasty fall.'

'I heard about that from the porter, sir.'

The cigar smoke coiled in the light. 'Thing is, she started talking in hospital, said a British soldier threw her out of a window. There's an email bouncing around. It has your name on it.'

Jason knew his face showed no emotion at all. But he felt a diesel rattle in his heart. Thieving little cow. And lying, too. After she made him fall for her. It shows, you can't trust them.

'Sergeant?'

'Can't explain that, sir. I did chat to a girl in the lobby, just some charity girl. Sounds like a misunderstanding.'

'I'll make a note that you said that. The operation's getting a lot of focus at home. Let's hope this hotel thing all blows over, eh?' The well-educated eyes patronised him for a while. 'You're all done here, Jason. You've got leave coming up, correct?'

'Yes, sir. I'm off back home.'

'Stay where we can reach you.'

Outside, the sun scalding his neck, Jason cursed the world. As soon as Honey Man gets sorted out, this Belgian slag pops up again. In his hutch, he threw his possessions into a kitbag. His phone rang.

It was Guru, sounding tense.

'Honey Man's gone.'

Jason zipped up the bag and kicked it flat. 'Gone? Where?'

'I don't know. I sent two men last night. They say the house is empty. He's not around, the family's not around.'

'Well that fucking proves it. He knows about this. He knows we're on to him.'

'I'm concerned now.'

Jason opened his locker, looked at the black Samsonite. He felt the key in his pocket. 'What men did you send?'

'Two local guys. Short notice, it's the best I could organise. They'll be OK, it's just *finding* him. I've told them to watch the house, see if he comes back.'

'Yeah, you see if he comes back. And get your locals to sort him out this time. For good.'

Stef Maguire asked a few people, and they said try the golf course. It was in a field behind the barracks: a little nine-hole set-up, sprinklers feeding the dry grass, a couple of bunkers that looked like shell craters.

She saw him out on the seventh hole, crouching over a ball by himself. The chaplain saw her approaching, and straightened up. He was in golf clothes, natty shoes, a yellow cardigan.

'Morning, Captain.' Behind him, the horizon was perfectly flat under mountainous white clouds. 'What would you suggest? It's a five-yard putt, there's a little slope and it's dry.' He crouched again, leaning on his putter, squinting at the hole.

She said, 'Could you bounce it off the back cushion?'

'That's snooker. That's a different thing.'

'Oh *yeah*. Duh.'

He laughed. 'Had the hangover breakfast? I bet Ward was there. Good guy, Ward.'

'He was just telling me about Op Alloy.'

'Good op. He banged those devious squaddies away for ten years, *and* we kept it quiet. Problem comes when they're out.'

'What problem?'

'He's had death threats, you know. *When we're out, we'll find you*, that kind of thing. Nothing he can't handle, obviously.'

She watched the chaplain rehearsing his shot five, six times. She said, 'I wanted to pick up on our conversation last night. You said Dan Simmons came to see you and he was scared.'

'I think I said *terrified*.'

'What of?'

The chaplain adjusted his gloves. 'The man was soft. Anyone could see that. Him and his toiletries, his face scrub. The boys were pissing themselves laughing. And he was shipping out to a war zone.'

'Poppy Crush isn't a war. It's a policing operation.'

'Oh *yeah*. Duh.' The chaplain took his stroke. The ball nicked the hole, circled around, flipped out again. 'Bugger.' They walked over to it. 'Last time I was in an Afghan poppy village, Captain, we found a Russian paratrooper.'

'A *prisoner*?'

'No, a body. They'd walled him up in about 1985 and just left him. He was mummified, I mean completely dried out, with these bits of leather in his teeth. We couldn't work out what that was – then we realised. He'd eaten his own belt before he died.' The chaplain sank the ball in the hole, picked it out and stood flipping it in his hand. 'When we were driving out, a roadside device detonated and took off one of our guys' legs. Well, we took everything away with us. Russian mummy, crippled English soldier, plus English soldier's legs. And the children all at the windows, *Khodahafez*, *Khodahafez*, waving goodbye. That was a friendly village. Well, you know all about that. How friendly they are.'

They looked at each other. The sun was reflecting off the chaplain's skull. He was sweating more than usual for a healthy man playing a little nine-hole set-up.

'Chaplain, why was Dan Simmons terrified?'

'He was an atheist. They're always afraid.'

'I'm an atheist, I'm not always afraid. What was the story with Simmons?'

The chaplain ran his thumbnail over the golf ball. 'He came to see me one night last week. He was rambling, talking about his programme, the research he'd been doing.'

'What research?'

'Putting Poppy Crush in context. Tracing heroin supply routes, the distribution system, the background.'

'Why didn't *we* give him that background? We authorised the film.'

'Maybe he wanted his own material.'

Still rubbing the golf ball.

'What are you saying, Chaplain – something in his research made him afraid?'

'He said – he said he'd found someone at the top of the tree. A big man.'

'He was afraid of that person?'

'He said he was ready to go public.'

'With what?' she asked. 'Something about a big man in heroin?'

The chaplain threw the ball to the last tee. 'Look, the guy was all over the place. He was confused. I tried to help, and I made a mess of that, I accept it.' He hunched over the ball, fingers twining. She didn't know much about golf – but he looked a poor player. Or nervous. Or full of regret, maybe.

She asked, 'Do you have any idea where his computer is?'

'No.'

The ball bounced off the turf of the last green, vanished into one of the bunkers. The chaplain watched it morosely. A shadow moved across him from clouds being pushed by the mounting breeze.

He said, 'Are you having counselling?'

'For what?'

'Your feelings of paranoia. I hear it's an after-effect of–'

'I don't need counselling.' She swept her hair away from her face. 'Chaplain, is something going on in this barracks?'

'Yeah. Duh.' He rammed his iron back into the bag, chose another. 'We're fighting a bloody war.'

She watched him trying to clear the ball from the bunker, the sand whipping away in the breeze. Then she walked away across the course. The metal flags creaking in each hole. Two things in her mind.

First, big men in heroin. Dan Simmons backed up his research about them somewhere. If not with Tom Fletcher – where?

Second thing, something Dan Simmons said to her before he died.

They're coming for me.

Thinking back, at the time she thought he'd meant the paramedics coming to help him.

But could he have even seen them?

They're coming for me.

In the afternoon, the air turned dusty yellow. Gusts of wind came across the fields beyond the modern houses, whipping the bamboo in Annabel's new-age front yard.

Sometimes the air carried sprays of dust picked up from the fens to the north – forerunners of the dust storms that the locals up there called Fen Blows.

Fletcher let the slats of the blind retract, darkening the room and its bas-relief dragons again. He crossed in front of the giant TV – his dark outline moving quickly – and went up the stairs.

The twins were playing in the front bedroom, making a train run around a wooden track. Evie looked up, pushed her black hair out of her eyes and grinned. Sally just focused on the train, her freckled hands moving it slowly, her tongue fixed between her lips. Then she looked up too.

She said, 'Where's Daddy going?'

He kneeled down. 'I'm going back to our house.'

Sally gave him the train to take.

He handed it back to Cathleen, inside the front door, before he kissed her.

She said, 'Will those men be there?'

'They think I'm hiding. They'll wish I was.'

Major Ward poured the chaplain and himself an inch of whisky. They sat in the two frayed easy chairs in his office, talking about Poppy Crush. Dan Simmons' name came up, and the chaplain put his fingertips together. Ward smiled.

'Stef Maguire's been to see you?'

'There's a word to describe her, I'm not sure which one. Fixated?'

'She's looking for something to prove. To show she can still do this. She's picked on Dan Simmons.' But he thought, *And she's right to. Good choice.*

The chaplain took a sip. 'What exactly happened to her? There are rumours, but it can't be true.'

Ward put his glass down. 'She was with a local interpreter, travelling between villages. She was driving, the Land Rover crashed. No enemy contact, it went off the road. You know those roads along the valley sides, I mean it's almost inevitable that someone's going to crash at some point. The interpreter was injured, died shortly afterwards. Maguire – well, what's the rumour?'

'Something about opium. She went native, got a taste for the stuff.'

'That's crazy. Think she'd still be here now?'

'What did happen?'

'You seem very concerned about her.'

The chaplain winced. 'I snapped at her. I said she was paranoid. That's bad.'

Ward said, 'What happened is simple. The Land Rover was wrecked, the radio was gone. The interpreter was dying, he had internal injuries. He asked her to do something before he died – I think get hold of his family, get a phone, let them speak to him.

Maguire herself had a spinal injury which caused severe pain. Some local tribal guys came out of their village and took her in, left her with their women. The women saw she was in pain, sedated her with some kind of opiate product.'

The chaplain touched his fingers together again. 'That could happen to anyone. Why the problem?'

'There was an incident, after twenty-four hours. Two of our men got into the house, tried to take her out. She didn't want to go. Thing is, the chemical they were sedating her with, it was some kind of old-fashioned opiate brew. You know the brain has a set of dedicated sensory receptors, like the ports on a computer? One for sight, one for sound, and so on. The weird thing is, we've got five senses and six receptors. The sixth one is biologically set up to handle opiates. That's the only thing it can do, take in opiates.'

The chaplain said, 'Why the hell is that?'

'It suggests that at some point in human evolution, our development was interlinked with the use of opiate, as much as with sound and vision and taste and so on. What I'm getting at, sorry, and going back to Maguire, is that if you expose someone to an opiate-based experience, it has a profound effect. In her case, she was hallucinating, she refused to leave with our men.

144

They had to drag her out. And the interpreter never got to speak to his family before he died. It was a mess.'

'Hence the aftereffects?'

'She's been to army psychologists, they're talking about effects such as paranoia and delusions, even hallucinations. Frankly, she's been posted here to recover. The idea is, while the regiment's away, it'll be deathly quiet and she can get back into shape mentally.'

The chaplain nodded. 'Paranoia. Always looking for conspiracies.'

'Thing is, though, she's a star, her whole file was top grade before this. We've got to help her get through it. And she comes with an objective point of view on this place, too.'

'On the golf course, she asked me, *Is something going on in this barracks?* Is that being objective? Or is that paranoia?'

'No, I don't think she's paranoid. She's on to something.'

The chaplain swirled his drink. 'I notice she's very beautiful.'

Clouds were filling the window.

Back in the RMP post, Stef Maguire took a knife and slit open the tape sealing the box of Dan Simmons' personal effects. She took out his branded jockey shorts, Handycam and cologne, herbal shower gel, face scrub.

She lined them up, parade ground style.

Dan did research, found things that terrified him.

They're coming for me.

Did he shoot himself in fear of Afghanistan – or in fear of what he'd found out? Or did someone get on to this base and shoot him? Before he could share his information.

So where is it?

She laughed at herself. *What – you're looking for secret messages? In his pants? In his herbal frigging toiletries? Come on, he must have backed it up somewhere online, somewhere we'll never find it.*

She dumped everything back in the box and went to the door. No wonder the boys took the piss out of Dan. Called him Sleepy, laughed at his–

She turned.

She looked at the box, sitting on the desk in the sun.

There's something in there that people keep mentioning. Something that people keep saying is typical of Dan Simmons. The reason he didn't fit in.

Not the pants.

Not the shower gel.

Face scrub.

The guys keep saying *face scrub*. Even the chaplain knew about it. Dan's face scrub was famous – an identifying mark. Also the stick to beat him with.

She went back to the box. The scrub was

at the bottom, twined up in the Handycam cables. She took it out and looked at it.

A plastic tube with a big, scientific cap.

Lancôme Pour Homme
Bio-molecular granules energize the profound levels of male skin.

Imagine your life is in danger. You need a hiding place quickly, but you're surrounded by people who mock you, despise you. You want the last laugh.

She held the tube to her ear and shook it.

She twisted off the scientific-looking cap. There was a nozzle clogged with scrub, giving off a raspberry aroma. She tried to peer into it. The bio-molecular granules looked frigging toxic.

She took out her pocket knife and cut the tube's throat. Red goo splattered out – a little cosmetic massacre. She gutted the thing and scraped out its contents on the table.

Lots of bio-molecular granules. If she ever got a boyfriend, she could use this to energize his skin. But underneath the mound of gunk, she picked up a small tube the length of her knuckle. Blue plastic, a removable cap showing a rectangular mouth that would welcome the tongue of any computer you introduced it to.

A cheap little computer memory stick – five quid in any high street. The most basic way to back up your information. She took it to the latrine, rinsed it under the tap and dried it carefully.

Dan wanted to leave a record of what he'd found. Even if someone stole his laptop. Even if he died.

God almighty, Simmons.
What exactly is on this stick?

Wednesday Night

Fletcher parked the Land Rover in a copse beside the road leading to his fields. Beyond the trees, past an empty field, he could see the edge of the elephant grass, twitching in the breeze. He waited while the sun began to set above it, watching a handful of ravens descend on the barren field and begin pecking for food.

He was asking himself what kind of numbers those men would return in – just the two of them, or more? Were they watching the house now? Probably. They'd probably hear or see him if he drove back in. Had they already entered the house, searched it?

More ravens dropped out of the woods and settled on the field, the sky above them turning mauve. Who sent those men?

He was back here to find out.

He walked between the trees, the scent of the May bluebells still in the air, dried stems crunching under his boots. When he came out beyond the copse, the field between him and the elephant grass was full of ravens – hundreds of them, strutting over the khaki earth. As the dusk intensified, they rose into the air, wheeling overhead in helix formations.

Fletcher sprinted under them, reaching the elephant grass in half a minute. He found one of the pathways and stepped inside.

There was still light in there, and he moved along, brushing past the sharp leaves. He came to an intersection in the channels and paused, listened. The breeze had dropped, and the stalks were making a low rustle, the ravens in the other field still calling. Nothing else. He looked around the corner, saw the long channel he had followed the night before standing grey but empty, too dry for footprints. One way, the road where the car had parked. The other way, the house itself. In a few minutes, the light would be gone. He jogged along the path, heading for the road. When he got there, he found it was empty, just the centre lines pale as bones in the final dusk. He turned and went back towards the house.

He could just see it at the end of this channel, the floodlights on automatically after dark. He moved slowly towards the block of light. He stopped and waited before the end of the channel, listening. Then he put his head out and looked around.

The orchard was there, untouched. The beehives stood white in the next field. The house itself, even the kids' toys in the garden, looked unchanged. Then, along the wall of grass, down towards the beehives, something that shouldn't be there. Just for a second, a red point moving at head height in the shadow.

Someone watching the house, having a smoke as he waited. Someone who would probably be coming back this way soon. Fletcher looked around, squeezed himself back between the stems, let one of them slant in front of him. He waited.

Sergeant Jason's kitbag was zipped and labelled, ready to go. The kitbag wasn't the problem. The kitbag wasn't going to do the work.

Jason hoisted a box onto his bed. It was a filing box, the type the army call a Lacon box. Like a packing crate, made of thin metal with a lid secured by roller catches. He released them and lifted off the lid. The Lacon box held a number of files, maps, wallets of photographs. Summaries of the debriefing information. He'd built this up conscientiously as a record of the trips he'd carried out, for future use and reference of the RMP. Officers love this stuff. It shows you're thinking of the future.

He was. He closed the door to his hutch. He put on a pair of surgical gloves.

He sat at his metre-wide desk and opened the Samsonite. Under unwashed clothes, the plastic packet that Inna had dug her thieving nails into. A kilo of pure, refined

151

Afghan heroin. Six thousand dollars in a mountain village, straight from a little factory where the powder was dried by fans running off moped engines.

Six thousand dollars at source in the mountains, sells for a hundred thousand dollars at sea level, in British towns. Normally that margin was soaked up by the men in trucks, lorries, ferries who haul the gear overland through the Stan countries, into Turkey and Europe. Cut out that supply chain, you're onto something.

And the first rule – don't open the packet.

You open it, try to divide it up – even if you don't touch it, it gets everywhere. Sniffer dogs will pick it up, and there are electronic sensor units that detect micrograms of drug on skin, clothing or on shoes. There were random dog checks at all British military airports now, RAF police with sensor wands.

Like they don't trust us.

Voices from the corridor – but Jason was the last of his team, and the people outside were new, chasing their own projects. They didn't disturb him.

He lit a cigarette, which felt weird with the gloves on. He took out of the Lacon box a sheet of thin white plastic. It was greasy and gave an opaque shadow. It was polythene, impregnated with PEC-PAK, a new chemical used in dry-cleaning.

152

He plugged in a soldering iron and went slowly around the sheet, fusing it together, sealing the kilo inside. The gluey smell of the chemical stung his eyes. It left a burn line in the wooden surface, in there with all the other dents and stains. Nasty stuff. PEC-PAK in high concentration masked the scent of heroin from dogs or electronic sensors, provided it was kept below 45 degrees Celsius. Above that, it broke down and the opiate smell could eventually find its way through to those little doggy noses. Forty-five degrees was OK. When the welding was done, he took out two chiller bags, picnic box type. Frozen solid in the fridge in the NCO's mess. He taped them around the package. That would keep it for ten hours, until the plane was well away. After that, an aircraft baggage hold at altitude is like a fridge. After that, England – where it might be 15 degrees tomorrow.

He removed the contents of the Lacon box. It was lined in heavy foam padding. He pulled one side of the lining away. The reverse of it was hollow. He fitted the package inside, smeared some adhesive on the surface around the foam and pushed it back into place. Then he rearranged the contents and put the top lid back, snapped the catches down. He stood looking at his Lacon box.

He was worried, more than he'd ever been

before. Not about the PEC-PAK system – he knew that worked. Worried about the Belgian NGO slag in the hotel. He'd been too soft on her, too forgiving. Too trusting – that was a lesson for him. And that Tom Fletcher person, that Honey Man, getting ready to foul things up back home.

His last trip, too.

When he got back to England, he was going to go PVR – request Premature Voluntary Release. With this kilo, added to what else he'd got through, there was plenty put aside. He could get out, start his new life. He felt the heat of the soldering iron, the chemical fumes.

His new life, his last flight. Going out at dawn.

Maguire went into Major Ward's office. She closed the door behind her and leaned back against it. He sat back in his chair and looked her over. She didn't mind that. She liked his hands, resting on his keyboard.

They didn't say anything for a few moments. Then he said, 'The chaplain stopped by. He's worried about you. He thinks the aftereffects of your experience are producing paranoia and a belief in conspiracies.'

'Is that what you think?'

'No, Stef.'

'Thanks. He's worried about you, too.

Death threats arising from Op Alloy, those men you put in prison.'

Ward smiled. 'I'll be fine.' Stopped smiling. 'What's up, Stef?'

'I've found what was on Dan Simmons' laptop.'

'Holy cow. Where was it?'

'Guess.'

'The *chaplain* had it?'

'No, it was in Dan's tube of face scrub.'

'A laptop in a tube of face scrub? How does that work?'

She held out the memory stick: tinted plastic showing skeletal circuits inside.

He whistled. 'You're good, aren't you? Is this a substantial development?'

'You'll see.'

'Substantial enough to upset Team Defence?'

'You'll see.'

He gestured for her to sit next to him. She plugged it into his desk computer and they watched the files come up. Just four.

Music
Pictures
Waterton Video
Documentary Research

He said, 'Try music first? Set the mood.'

There was Mozart, Coldplay, Billie Holiday. She opened them. Just music, nothing hidden in there.

Ward said, 'Hm. Let's see the pictures.'

155

They came up in a series of galleries. A smart house with a cherry tree and a red door. Monochrome studies of porcelain figurines. He sighed and he clicked on the next gallery. She touched his hand. 'Ready for this?'

The pictures flashed up.

He said, 'Whoa. I would not have expected that.' He flipped through them. 'Dan Simmons. You *were* a dark horse.'

Fletcher waited in the elephant grass for ten minutes, then twenty more. He knew the moon would be rising behind the house, but the floodlight glare made it hard to see. A moth whirled past, then many others – drawn by the floodlights. His ears began to hum with listening. When that faded, he heard a snap.

One of the stems being pushed aside.

Then a long, rushing sound. A man pissing into the dry earth. Some fumbling, a cough and a noisy spit. Then a shape appeared in the faint light at the end of the channel. A man in jeans and denim jacket, short hair, white trainers. Small and thin. Looking at his watch, kicking the ground. Beyond him, moths were spiralling over the apple trees. The man turned and looked into the channel, seemed to look straight at Fletcher.

Fletcher stepped out from the grass.

The man jumped, spun round, took a step

back. Then he reached inside his jacket and came out with a knife. Fletcher stepped to one side, saw the knife hand come up past him, and landed a big blow to the man's stomach. The guy doubled up, gasping, and dropped the knife. Fletcher grabbed his collar, but it ripped off in his hand and the man staggered back and ran off between the apple trees, heading away from the house lights. He was thin and fast, and got as far as the first beehive before Fletcher caught him by the back of the jacket. The material held.

He pulled him along the ground for a few metres, feet trailing, arms scrabbling. One hand clutched Fletcher's leg, and Fletcher hit him on the shoulder blade with the axe handle. A yelp of pain, no more resistance. Fletcher dragged him up to the next beehive, slamming the man down on his knees in front of it, ramming his face against the wooden casing.

'I'm just the driver.'

'Shut up.'

Fletcher listened. An owl calling, but no shouts or footfall, nobody coming to help.

Fletcher made him empty his pockets. Some cash, cigarettes and lighter, a cheap phone with nothing on it – no identity or pictures.

'Who are you?'

'Not saying.'

Fletcher could see he was the scrawny

junior of the operation. He didn't want to hurt him. Then he pictured the other man, the gun.

He pictured the twins in their beds. He swallowed.

He pushed the man's face against the hive. 'You know what's in here?'

'Fucking bees.'

They were making a low hum, feeling the disturbance.

'How many?'

'Lots, I don't know.'

'How many?'

'Let me go, man.'

Fletcher pulled his face back and slammed it into the wood again. 'Twelve hundred bees in a hive. If I lift the lid off, put your face in there, what'll happen?'

'Don't do it.'

'What'll happen?'

'They'll sting me.'

'Twelve hundred times.' The man stayed still, on his knees, panting. 'So who are you?'

Silence.

Fletcher tapped the hive. The humming took on a rasping tone.

'I'll put your face right inside there.'

'They'll sting you too.'

'Bees don't sting their keeper. Don't you know that?'

'You're crazy.'

A buzz as a worker drifted out, clunking

against the man's face, then another. Fletcher thought, *Is this right?*

Yes.

The man convulsed as it stung him on the cheek. Another one got him on the neck, then the hand he put up to protect himself.

'OK, stop it,' he shouted. 'OK.'

Fletcher pulled him back. The man was grunting, twisting his head. 'I'm Simon Wilks.'

'Where's the other one? The big guy?'

'He just told me to wait here, watch the house, phone him when you come back. That's all. I'm not doing anything else.'

'And what's he going to do when he knows I'm back?'

'I don't know, maybe come and talk to you.' The man's face was swelling up massively.

'You know what, Simon? I think you've got a bee sting allergy.'

'Oh fuck.'

'You feeling dizzy, nauseous? You need to be in hospital.'

'Please take me.'

'So what's the other guy going to do?' No answer. Fletcher picked him up again and brought him close to the hive, and this time raised the lid a fraction with his free hand. He saw bees flicking out, crashing into Simon Wilks' face. Wilks screamed and convulsed.

'He's going to shoot you. He's got a gun, he's under orders.'

'Orders from who?'

'I don't know. Please.'

Fletcher dropped the lid and threw Wilks back into the pool of light from the house. He lay curled up, his face bloated, one eye bigger than the other. 'So who is he?'

'I don't know.' Wilks was beginning to shake.

'The thing with bee stings, Simon, if you have an allergic reaction, you've got to see a doctor. Otherwise you get convulsions. You could have heart failure.'

'Take me to a doctor.'

'Who's your friend?'

'I don't know his name. I feel sick. I can't feel my hands.'

'Who is he?'

'We call him Little Tonks. He just said to me, watch the house, phone him when you come back, then he'll come down here.'

'Phone him on what number?'

Wilks gave a number– 'But it's just a number. It's a throwaway phone like mine is.'

Fletcher logged the number in his mind. 'How do you know Little Tonks?'

'He sells gear. I move it around for him.'

'What stuff?' Silence. 'You want to be stung again? What stuff?'

'What do you think? Heroin.'

'A heroin dealer wants to kill me? Why?'

'It's orders.'

'From who?'

'I don't know, man. You can sting me again, I don't know.' Wilks began to fold over.

'Tell me where I find Tonks. Then I'll put you in my car, I promise you that. You're in a bad way.'

'He sells out of a car. An old Lexus. In the afternoons, you might find him near Mepal. There's a lay-by he parks in.' He gave precise directions. 'Don't tell him about me.'

'Don't worry, Simon.' Fletcher helped him stand, the man's legs buckling under him. 'Why do you call him *Little* Tonks?'

'He's six-foot-six, twenty stone. Get me to a doctor. I can't see.'

'Don't worry. I'll look after you.'

Forty miles away, in the early hours, Fletcher opened the back gate of the Land Rover.

Simon Wilks tumbled out, rolled over and sat up, his face bloated. 'That was hours, man. Where are we?'

'Can't you tell?'

Simon tried to look around. There was a cold breeze full of salt. 'Near the sea?'

'Correct.' Fletcher slammed the tailgate.

'Where's the hospital?'

Fletcher crouched down.

'Simon, we're on a mud flat that goes out into the sea. In a couple of hours, the tide comes in.' He opened the driver's door. 'You can get out of here, but you'll have to work

161

at it. Now I've got to go. My wheels are sinking.'

'You can't leave me here.'

Driving off, he saw Simon's outline in the mirror, lurching after him, raising his bound hands, then spinning around and falling.

Simon had a good chance of finding his way out. Two hours was a long time, and the tide was slow. The exercise would do him good.

The Land Rover's wheels hissed on compacted mud.

Fletcher was asking himself why a heroin salesman and his simple-minded driver would come to his home to shoot him.

It's orders – whose orders?

He thought back to the TV news, the item about the big men of heroin, the blank outlines at the top of the tree. Did one of those people believe that Fletcher knew something about them?

He came off the mud flat, the headlights picking out the track through the dunes that led back to the coast road.

Heroin means Afghanistan. And that means Poppy Crush right now.

Dan, you idiot. What were you going to put in that envelope?

Stef Maguire sat on the edge of her bed, looking at Dan Simmons' files one more time. Partly because it fascinated her. Partly

162

because she didn't want to sleep.

She closed the screen, put her head on the pillow, didn't close her eyes. What did it prove?

There was the sound of a helicopter outside, its navigation light flashing across the window. She listened to the engine winding down, wondering if that was the same sound that Dan Simmons had used to conceal the noise of his gunshot. Dan Simmons, or whoever fired that shot.

She swung her legs over the bed again and clicked the laptop on.

Music
Pictures
Waterton Video
Documentary Research

The music didn't matter.

The pictures were a surprise, but surely not relevant. She opened them again. It seemed that Dan Simmons had been in the habit of asking women to pose for him. There were half a dozen of them. There was a skinny girl who looked barely out of her teens, sprawled on a Persian rug in a small academic-looking office, a view of Cambridge rooftops out of focus through the window, her ribcage and navel in harsh detail. That might explain Dan's enforced sabbatical from his college.

The others were a succession of women caught undressing, showering, lounging in gardens or beside swimming pools. Dan evidently preferred a frontal view, the women lying on their backs or with their legs drawn up, their labia jutting in the sunlight. One woman – a favourite? Or more photogenic than the others? – came up a few times: beside a pool, sipping from a tall glass, smiling, looking over her sunglasses as the camera focused on her spread thighs.

Dan, the playboy professor.

She clicked *Waterton Video*. The photos had amused Ward, the video had annoyed him. She could see why. It started off as tedious: the series of meals and exercises that she'd seen on the Handycam. There was an interview with Private Godson, the room mate.

Simmons: How would you describe army culture?

Godson: We get on OK.

Simmons: I mean, the life.

Godson: We get on with it.

Scenes on the firing range, scenes of an officers' drinks party. A clip of the chaplain. Sunset over the barracks. Then Dan Simmons filming himself in his room, face close to the camera, reality-TV-confession-style.

'What strikes me most about these people is the way nobody wants to talk about anything. I mean, they'll tell you about the new boots they've bought or the ligament they tore on the assault course.' On the film, voices outside, Dan flinching and waiting for them to pass. 'But ask people what they *think*–' Dan tapped his head slowly '–ask them what's really going on in here, and they'll still tell you about their boots. It's what I call *new boot syndrome* and it's immensely frustrating.'

Right, Dan. Like people who face roadside devices made of artillery shells and propane gas are going to spill their hearts out to someone with *your* accent.

She took a long swig from a bottle of cold water, eyeing the screen.

The file for Documentary Research.

Dan had arranged it as a tree, from ground level to top.

At the base, he had notes on *Users/Losers*. An interview with two street prostitutes who'd slipped into the life through heroin addiction. Just the kind of girls the government was holding up as victims of Afghan production, the British citizens that Poppy Crush was designed to protect. Then blurred video film of kids in hatchbacks, pulled over at the side of a road in British countryside, tying belts around their arms. The glint of syringe needles in the sun. Faces turning to the camera. End of footage.

The next step up in Dan's hierarchy was *Distributors*.

A series of notes about *Junior suppliers*. A photo of a blue car – a 1990 Lexus – evidently taken on a mobile phone. In the driver's seat, a hefty man with small eyes, in a bandana.

Dan's note: *Typical trade situation. Usually present, Mepal, mid afternoon. Very knowledgeable. Giving him time. Lead to the man at the top.*

The next level, at the top of the tree, was *Importers*.

Dan's note: *The man at the top is Guru.*

Guru?

This was accompanied by a photo of a red and gold canopy over what looked like an oriental storefront: sculpted dragons on the roof with bulging eyes, baring their teeth.

Dan's note: *Just a front. Laundering. Owned by a British citizen of Korean origin.*

Stef took another swig of water.

So the big man is called Guru, a British Korean?

She looked away from the dragons and scrolled down.

There was one more photo. A blurred image of an old building, like a big country house, semi-derelict, with a pair of timber gates made in an unusual diamond pattern.

Dan's note: *Guru's safe place.*

But who is Guru? Who's at the top of this tree?

She looked at the image for a few minutes.

A derelict house in fields. Needing to be repaired, restored.

She printed out a copy, folded it away.

There was nothing else about this building in Dan's files.

Beside the tree structure that Dan had drawn, there was a final section of his research.

Origin.

He had assembled a lot of notes on key poppy cultivation areas in Asia: Pakistan, Thailand, Burma, Afghanistan. He had notes on export routes across the Eurasian landmass, into Western Europe, over the sea into Britain. A long list of container ports, motorway stops, coastal towns, ferry routes. Exactly the routes that Poppy Crush was intended to cut off at the Afghan source.

She closed the screen and lay back, watching the green diode in the dark.

Guru. Sounds kind of Asian, Eastern.

Afghan?

Is *that* why Dan Simmons got himself embedded here?

Not to film scenes of service life – that was just a pretext. He wanted to go to Afghanistan. To get his big cutting-edge scoop about heroin.

So what was he afraid of?

Ask people what they think – Dan tapping his head – ask them what's really going on in here, and they'll still tell you about their boots.

A man in a bandana, a blue Lexus, usually there mid afternoon.

Ask people what they think – tap the head –

what's really going on in here, and they'll tell you—

She rolled on her front, dozed for a few minutes. She dreamed about the crash again, of course. The Land Rover on its roof in the poppies. A dying man's voice. The room they put her in, the taste of the poppy brew, straight from the fields. She woke. Pulled her legs up against her stomach and rocked herself.

Ask people what they think – tap the head – what's really going on in here—

She saw a red and gold dragon climb down off the ceiling and snap at her, its jaws trailing fuel oil.

She opened her eyes. She was drenched in sweat, but a cool breeze through the window was drying it off her skin.

The dragons were gone.

But Dan Simmons was still there. Tapping his head. *What's really going on in here.*

That wasn't right.

If Dan meant 'what's really going on in their minds' he would have tapped his head after saying *in here. But ask people what they think – tap – what's really going on in here.*

Here didn't mean *in their minds*, did it, Dan?

It meant in here, in the barracks. What's really going on in Waterton?

Or is that why you joined the regiment, Dan? Because you thought there was a link

168

between the heroin routes and the army?

In the locker, her uniform jangled on its hanger.

What is that link? Who is Guru?

A big man in a blue Lexus, Mepal, usually there mid afternoons.

Mepal was fifteen miles from Waterton.

She saw red and gold dragons coming at her out of the walls, whispering. She flicked the water bottle over them, and they vanished.

Paranoia. Feelings of conspiracy. Just the aftereffects of an opiate experience.

No. She dropped the bottle, put her head in her hands, screwed her palms into her eye sockets. Felt the tendons along her arms stiffening and twisting, dripping water.

'Not aftereffects. Real suspicion. I'll show you that.'

Fletcher cut the engine and let the Land Rover roll down the approach to Annabel's ribbon road.

He stopped it and watched the house for ten minutes. There was nobody outside that he could see, no cars he didn't recognise from the morning. The bamboo in the front garden swaying over the porch light. He got out. The Land Rover was splattered with mud and salt.

Upstairs, he lay down beside Cathleen. She was naked under the sheet, and the bed smelled of her neat body. The window was open and the metallic blind was chiming in the draught. He felt her wrap around him and rub her face against his chest.

'You smell of the sea.'

'Someone was watching our house. I took him to the Lincolnshire coast.'

She kneeled up and looked at him while he told her about it. The blind was jangling, throwing blades of moonlight across her that looked suddenly like Simon Wilks' knife. He reached out and swept them away, cradled her breasts in his hands. The kind of weight at the centre of his world. Skin cool and damp.

She said, 'This has to stop, Tom. I want us to go away.'

'I can't go away. This–' it suddenly made sense to him '–this is all the fights I should have had before. This is the big fight of my life.'

'What about us, me and the girls? What about our life?'

'One more day. I promise I'll sort it out.'

'No.'

'One more day.'

Cathleen made a sound in her throat, the sound she made when she was finally agreeing to something. She said it was the Irish in her, a Gaelic word that meant 'I don't like it but I'll do it'.

Or he thought maybe it was the way he

held her neck in one hand and with the other steadied her flank while he slid across her and between her thighs, her head turning so quickly that her hair crackled with static.

Thursday Morning

Bill Downey of Team Defence had a 7.30 breakfast with the Minister. Melon, Parma ham, orange juice, black coffee. The Minister was excited, trying not to show it.

'We're all set now, Bill. What do they call it – the final countdown?'

'Wasn't that a song?'

They laughed. 'Seriously, Bill, I want to thank you for the presentation of this. It's our war now. We've all put our names on it. What's the matter – something bugging you?'

'The anti-war people. They've made such a point of opposing this.'

'What – they care about heroin producers?'

'No, it's because they say that it's staged, it's a diversion from issues at home. They've even put a religious angle on it. They're starting to camp outside Waterton Barracks now.'

'It's our war, Bill. They can't stop us now.'

Bill Downey walked back along Whitehall, warm sun on his face. Inside the MOD, Summers gave him some bad news.

He listened, his smile turning to a scowl.

'Why didn't you brief me earlier?'

'We thought it was a minor thing. But it's spreading. This Belgian girl has a fractured pelvis, she may not walk again. And she claims the man who threw her out of the window was a British soldier. There are hints of further allegations still to come.'

'What allegations?'

'God knows. This story's been spread around a lot of blogs, now the mainstream are picking it up.'

'Have we had calls on this?'

'We had one at 08.10 hours from a Belgian TV channel. It's on their breakfast news.'

Bill Downey whipped his glasses off in frustration. 'Hold on. Why are we even discussing this? It's an internal disciplinary matter. It doesn't affect Poppy Crush.'

'This is the thing. You know the first stage of Poppy Crush, the reconnaissance phase, involved intelligence gathering. We had a number of people – predominantly RMP, plus Afghan police – scouting the villages, posing as travellers.'

'So?'

'This soldier is one of those people.'

Bill Downey took a few seconds to absorb that. He thought of the Minister slicing his melon, excited.

He said, 'What have we got on him?'

'Beg pardon?'

'If he's thrown a Belgian girl out of a

173

window – big if, but let's think about it. We need to be out there in front of him, managing perceptions. Otherwise it rubs off on the Operation. On us. What do we know about him? You must have–'

Summers took out an A4 sheet and passed it across. Bill Downey read it without touching it.

He said, 'No real education, but instinctive linguist. Went on the officers' selection course, failed it. One of those types. And what's this about his childhood? Get me some more on that, even if it's rumours. If we get a call from British media, we'll have that up our sleeves.' He still didn't touch the paper. 'Where *is* he, anyway?'

'He's on leave. He's on a flight back to Britain today, the TriStar into Brize Norton. We're inclined to leave him on it, show we're not knee-jerking. And we don't want Afghans involved, becoming a diplomatic thing. Get him back on home ground, we're controlling him.'

'Good point. Leave him on the plane, pick him up at Brize. No comment on unfounded rumours. Belgian breakfast TV – sorry, but we don't scrabble around for Belgians.'

'Brief the Minister?'

'No, leave it with me. And get me another page on Sergeant Jason.'

Getting into the British Military Airport,

174

Jason knew this was something else he hated about the army. They let you on an officers' selection course, then they fail you because you said all the wrong things at the drinks party. They do the PR films, the Internet campaigns, they tell you to risk your life for a traffic warden's pay, then they put you on trial if you shoot the wrong guy. And when they transport you around the world, they put you in a time capsule and take you back forty years.

The airport itself was an old civilian site, and nothing had changed from the 1970s except the razor wire. Pushing his kitbag and Lacon box on a luggage trolley, Jason came straight into the main departure hall. Asbestos ceiling tiles, rows of bucket chairs, check-in desks from Russian Aeroflot days. To cap that, through the distant glass windows, the RAF transport itself. Standing in a heat haze, streaked with oil. A TriStar airliner, a relic of the 1960s.

Seeing it all, he was glad this was his last trip.

He was going to miss the people, though. Sprawled on the seats, milling around, queuing at the check-in desks – his people. Hundreds of service personnel. Mostly young, tanned. Talking, laughing, sleeping. Kitbags and weapons wrapped in cloth bags, Lacon boxes like his. He looked for his queue, joined it, leaning on his trolley, feeling like a 1970s tourist, back from Benidorm to Gatwick on the TriStar. But the check-in clerks were in uniform, and this was Afghanistan to RAF Brize Norton in Oxfordshire, across four thousand miles and twenty countries, not all of them friendly.

A clerk walked down the line with next-of-kin forms – something the air force were fussy about on long-haul transports. People wrote leaning on each other's backs, or straight on the floor. Jason laid his form on the lid of his box and filled it in. Religion: Methodist. Next of kin: he wrote her name carefully and smoothed it down.

The queue shortened. He joined in the talk, the laughter. Everyone sweating – but the temperature nowhere near the 45 degrees that would worry him. He hoisted his kitbag onto the conveyor, watched the clerk tag it and send it away. Then he hoisted his box up there, didn't even glance at it, looking up at the cables hanging from the ceiling.

He heard the clerk say 'What's this?'

Jason focused on the ceiling. Cables, cobwebs, dust.

'What's going on?'

He swallowed. In the end, he had to look down. He felt sweat collecting between his shoulder blades – not just the closed-in heat, more than that. The clerk said, 'The power's down. Wait a minute, eh? Won't be long.'

And he waited, looking at his filing box with its kilo of heroin wrapped in dry-cleaning fluid, just sitting there on the conveyor. He felt sweat on his face, thinking this final trip was jinxed.

He looked behind him. A pretty female private soldier, one of the regiments rotating out to let the Cambs regiment in. Tan, freckles, a bruise on her cheek. She said, 'Typical,' and glanced at the box.

He smiled, 'Yeah, isn't it?'

Then the clerk said, 'Alright,' and printed a label, slapped it on the box and sent it off. All along the line, other labels being slapped on, conveyors rattling again. He winked at the girl and walked off. Just in time to hear an RAF porter with a megaphone walk across the floor saying, 'Flight to Brize delayed, Brize is delayed. Proceed to the waiting area.'

A massed groan went up. Through the window, the TriStar stood in the shimmer coming off the concrete, the three engines mounted around the tail making a shadow like the ace of clubs. He couldn't see any baggage trucks going out to it. Maybe they were going to change the plane.

In the latrine, the water was full of rust and an RAF man was being sick in the basin. Jason wondered how bad this trip could get. He found out a minute later, when his phone rang. Guru's number on the screen.

'Yeah?'

'The local men I sent to see the Honey Man.'

'Yeah?' He went out and saw the TriStar passengers being channelled into an external building. 'What happened?'

'One of them's disappeared. And I still don't know where Tom Fletcher is right now.'

Jason kicked the wall. Clever Guru, screwed it up. 'So you've got one local guy left. Pull him off, he sounds like a fucking idiot. When I get in, I'll come straight over and do it myself.'

'Do it yourself?'

'He thinks he can hide from me, he's all wrong.'

He rejoined the scrum. Through the doors, the waiting area looked dark and stifling. He saw the girl soldier going in, surrounded by her gang of mates.

He thought, *I get through this flight, I'm going straight to find Honey Man. He won't even know about it. Not till it's all over.*

'I do trust you, Tom.' Cathleen was pale, with shadows under her eyes, stirring a cup of coffee in Annabel's kitchen. 'But we're like prisoners in here.' The twins were playing on a decked area in the back garden. A wind was starting up, spattering dust on the windows – whipping out the girls' long black hair and making them squeal with laughter. Above them, white clouds were speeding across the sky.

'I'll find those men and I'll stop this. I promise you.'

'How?'

'The big man with the gun. His driver told me where to find him.'

'He was probably lying, Tom.'

'I don't think so.'

Fletcher went over to the girls and kissed them. Their hair was warm, and they laughed, running around him in circles. Cathleen was biting her nails.

In the driveway, the bamboo was heaving over the slate dunes, and the cars were coated in sediment that had blown off the fields in the night. Fletcher squirted the dust off the Land Rover's windscreen and drove away, heading east, then north. Through the clean semicircles in the screen, the horizon became flatter, the fields more intensively farmed, the few remaining hedgerows growing flat in the wind.

He was heading for where Simon Wilks had said his big friend Tonks could be found. Out in the fens.

Thursday Midday

From back in his police days, Fletcher knew the fenland. In the distant past, it had been an inland sea where people lived on marsh islands, married their relatives, brewed opiate tea from poppies to numb the malaria that afflicted them. Then the fens had been drained and turned into farmland, but the region still kept its defiant, inward-looking identity – and in its towns and villages, the old poppy tea had been exchanged for refined opiates imported from Afghanistan.

The road took him past the sign for Waterton Barracks itself, then curved so that Ely Cathedral stood against the sunlight streaming from brown-grey clouds. To the east, an American AWACS plane rose slowly from Lakenheath airbase, its radar glinting before it disappeared into the haze.

Fletcher pulled off the main road, into a side road occupied by a snack bar built from an old railway wagon, a chimney letting greasy smoke whip away across the fields. He pulled in ahead of it, behind stunted bushes that hid him from the road. From here the land sloped down a little, gave a narrow view of the lay-by that bee-stricken

Simon Wilks had claimed was the site of Little Tonks' activities.

What kind of people would send a Fenland drug dealer to shoot you? Fletcher thought about it, watching the empty lay-by, lined with scrappy bushes. Drug people, logically. Someone using local people at short notice, improvising. But dangerous people, believing Fletcher knew who they were and what they were doing.

He thought, *I don't – but I will soon.*

Midday came, then half past. The smell of greasy cooking from the snack bar, but Fletcher wasn't hungry for food. High clouds, specks of blue sky, the air full of dust. The lay-by down there empty except for a delivery truck, the driver pissing into the bushes; then a builder's truck dumping rubbish. Twice, a powered-up hatchback came past slowly, as if looking for something, then sped away.

Little Tonks' customers, expecting him?

The wind was really picking up now, flicking gouts of soil out of the fields. This kind of weather – the spring winds after a dry winter – had a way of producing Fen Blows, the dust storms that could run for miles across the open fields. He saw a whole ridge of dust being picked up behind the lay-by, then dropping like a curtain.

He squirted the dust off the windscreen. Through the clean glass, he saw a blue car pull into the lay-by. Fletcher reached for his binoculars.

It was a Lexus. It looked like trouble, too: a 1990s model, windows tinted, number plate deliberately corroded. Fletcher watched. In ten minutes, that same hatchback came past again, swerved into the lay-by, pulled up next to the Lexus. So close it was hard to see what was happening through the dust and tinting on the blue car's windows.

Then someone tapped on Fletcher's window. A middle-aged woman, greasy apron, hair flicking in the wind. He put his window halfway down, kept his eye on the two vehicles. The woman leaned an arm on his roof, bare skin showing old tattoos, age freckles, knife cuts.

She said, 'Yeah, that's what they're doing.'

'What are they doing?'

'He's selling them little plastic packets of something. You are the police?' She looked doubtfully at the Land Rover.

'No. Are the police coming?'

'They drive past sometimes. You a journalist?'

'Sort of.'

'Another one, then.'

'Why, who else has been here?'

'The nice one off the TV. The one who shot himself.'

'Dan Simmons?' Fletcher asked. 'He was here?'

'Very nice man. He took a little film of the needle field.'

'What's that, then?'

'See the next field, where the ground goes down? That's where the kids inject. Dozens of them, every day, going on for years. All full of needles down there. I gave him an interview, all what I've seen.' She ran her finger along the door. 'He paid me sixty quid.'

'Nice guy.' Fletcher gave her thirty quid from his pocket, which disappeared in her thin hand. 'You'd better get back inside.'

'Yeah, there's a Blow coming up. You ever seen a Blow?'

'I've heard about it.'

'A Blow's a bad thing.'

When he looked again, she was gone.

Dan Simmons here, filming. That was definite, then. Dan knew something about these people, tried to pass it to Fletcher.

Fletcher started the engine.

The hatchback moved off slowly. He watched it pause near the field – the needle field – for five minutes, then move away along the road. A minute later another car moved in – a green Peugeot, stick-on spoiler on the back window. Same procedure, parking close to the Lexus, then away.

Fletcher moved the Land Rover out and down the road, the few hundred metres to the lay-by. The wind was moaning, dust drifting in veils. He pulled up behind the

Lexus, close enough to see the outline of a man on the driver's side – a big guy, shoulders bulging out of the seat. Staring in the mirror, he thought. Fletcher took out his mobile and dialled the number that Wilks had given him. There was a second's pause. Then he saw the big paw reach out, rummage, lift a phone to his ear.

Fletcher said, 'Little Tonks?'

No answer. Then, 'Wilks? What the fuck–'

They didn't finish the conversation. Fletcher slammed the front winch of the Land Rover into the back of the Lexus, breaking the lights off and popping the boot open, pushing the car towards the bushes. The driver took a second to react, then got the engine on, a big plume of smoke as it started up, and tried to pull away. Fletcher slammed the power down, a big surge that forced the Lexus sideways, the wheels spinning, clipping the edge of the embankment and pushing the two side wheels right over, the car finally stopping at an angle, releasing exhaust and tyre smoke that went slanting away in the breeze.

Fletcher jumped out.

The dust stung his face. Soil was being whipped up in low waves across the fields, spattering on the side of the other car as he ran around to the exposed door. It was facing slightly upward, hard to see through the window, and he yanked it open, looked inside. A few plastic bags, fag packets, drinks cans, three phones, pages of a body-building magazine. Beyond that, the driver's seat was empty and the other door was hanging part open. Little Tonks had squirmed out like a rat.

Fletcher ran around the car and pushed through the bushes, treading on old junk and tyres, until he came out into the field. The view ahead was blurry with dust, but a shape was moving. Tonks. Fletcher ran after him. The shape out there looked like a short man, getting closer it looked like a normal-sized but very wide man, outlined against the dust.

Fletcher shouted, 'Little Tonks. Come here.'

The man stood up. He'd been crouching in some kind of wrestling pose, but now Fletcher could see he was huge, towering over Fletcher's own six foot three. A round, smooth face topped with a bandana, cut-off vest showing muscle-man arms shaved smooth, bulging legs in black jeans, every-thing with a coating of brown dust.

They stood there looking at each other, the wind rising and falling, changing dir-ection, spattering soil. Little Tonks was looking around, seeing who else was com-ing. No doubt deciding that the police don't ram you off the road, then turn up single-handed. He laughed suddenly, showing big incisors, small eyes glinting.

Fletcher said, 'Simon Wilks says hello.'

'Who?'

'Simon. He got stung by bees.'

'Oh, you're the *Honey* Man.' Tonks laughed again, jiggling his round head. 'The beehive man.'

Fletcher could feel the dust between his teeth, getting in his eyes. 'Who gave the order?'

Tonks wiped dust from his eyes. He glanced behind him, to where the Blow was getting bigger and darker across the fields. He adopted some kind of martial arts pose, his huge pale hands against the wall of dust. Then he leaped forward. One of the hands flashed out and chopped Fletcher in the neck – sending a jolt of pain into his skull. Fletcher punched the huge chest, twice, then again, but another hand was tightening on his neck, feeling for something, a nerve location. He punched the big face and got in return a blow on the side of the head that made his whole vision turn sideways. Then Tonks threw him down on the ground, kicked him in the stomach in a way that the oriental masters maybe hadn't designed. Fletcher bunched up, the world collapsing inside his spleen. He retched, trying to breathe, but the movement redoubled the pain in his stomach. He saw the big boots walk away, then turn and come back – a running kick. He rolled sideways, felt the kick scrape along his spine, lashed out a hand and grabbed the foot. Tonks crashed down on his knees, the dust cloud behind him kaleidoscoping brown and mauve. A whirl of dust blew over them both. Tonks leaned over Fletcher and raised a fist. Fletcher elbowed him in the mouth, saw a spray of blood that the wind blew clear. Tonks raising his fist, Fletcher getting an arm around his massive neck. Tonks began grunting and chanting to himself, some martial arts word, over and over, getting ready to punch.

An impact. Tonks went limp, and crumpled sideways.

Fletcher looked up. Someone was outlined against the glare, standing looking down at him. He rolled over onto his knees and got his breath back. Then he got up slowly. Just standing up sent a new spasm through his stomach, but at least he could see straight. It was obviously Captain Stef Maguire. She was wearing a civilian hiking jacket, dust matting in her hair. A telescopic baton in one hand. She crouched down and looked at Little Tonks, then turned to Fletcher as he got to his feet. A new blast of wind came across the field, hot and powdery.

She said, 'Let's get in your car. The dust's coming.'

'What are you doing here?'

'We need to get in your car.' At the edge of the field, something was happening: a high wall of dust turning over on itself like a wave, throwing out bits of debris. 'See that? You know where it's coming from, what it's picked up?'

She began jogging in the direction of the lay-by. He looked back at the wave. It was advancing fast – a ragged splash of muck rolling towards him. From where?

From the needle field.

Little Tonks was regaining consciousness, eyes rolling up in his head, grunting.

Fletcher said, 'Who gave the order, Tonks?'

Tonks coughed and spat.

'Who was it?'

Tonks said, 'Sung. Kim Sung.'

'Who?'

'Kim Sung. He's got a business in Newmarket.'

Glancing up, Fletcher could see the Blow was already halfway across the field, huge layers of dust rolling and tumbling to earth, but also hundreds of bright things catching the light. He turned and ran after Stef Maguire, seeing her outline already at the lay-by hedge. His stomach hurt with every pace. He ran the last few metres to the hedge, tripped as he clambered through the branches, looked round again, picking himself up. Something was flying through the air towards him, out of the advancing wave.

He saw it clearly as it went past and into the bushes – a hypodermic needle, orange plastic and a steel spike.

The Blow was sweeping up all the heroin needles.

He saw others tumbling out of the air, orange darts flashing against the brown mass of the Blow wave. He charged through the bushes, past the Lexus, quickly around to the Land Rover. He saw Stef was already inside, holding the passenger door open. He slid in, and she let it slam shut.

The wave began breaking over them, a wall of dust and clods, shreds of grass crashing down across the lay-by, and in the middle of all that, hundreds of orange needles spinning away into the road itself. A series of impacts as debris hit the Land Rover, a rasping sound as the dust seethed down on the roof, then repeated taps as needles rained down too, bouncing off the glass. One was filled with blood that spattered a tiny handprint, others went ricocheting off the bonnet. That went on for half a minute; then the rasping subsided to a low hiss as finer dust followed the main wave out across the road and away into the next field.

Fletcher could see the headlights of cars stopped on the road, bright points in a mist of dust, and overhead the sun just visible as a disc. The cabin reeked of earth. Stef closed her eyes. Her hair and face were streaked with dust. She was breathing deeply.

He said, 'Thanks.'

She didn't answer. Through her window, the dust was becoming finer, sunlight breaking through. Fletcher wondered what kind of state Little Tonks was in. Concussed, powdered and needled. He got a bottle of water from the glove box and handed it across. She cupped some in her hand and rinsed her eyes.

There was a smash from the road, cars colliding at low speed in the last of the dust. The sun was coming back, lighting a rainbow through the blood on the windscreen. She said, 'Welcome to the Fens, eh?'

He felt the pain in his stomach and spine, the knuckles on his right hand. He said, 'I still want that man.'

She started up, steered the Land Rover around the bushes, thumping down into the field, wipers making a clean arc that showed drifting brown mist, the high disc of sun.

She said, 'Who is he?'

He told her about the men at his house, Little Tonks, the need to find out who was controlling them. 'He just gave me the name Kim Sung. Something about a business in Newmarket.'

'He didn't use the name Guru?'

'No, who's Guru?'

'Dan Simmons was researching heroin,' the Land Rover lurched down into a depression and up the other side in a plume of dust, 'and he identified someone at the top, an importer. Guru sounds like a nickname, a codename.'

'Is that why you're here? This is linked to Dan Simmons' death?'

'Hold on.'

The Land Rover wallowed out into the field, tyres ploughing up the loose soil. In a few seconds, they reached the point of the brief confrontation with Tonks. The ground was covered in a shallow drift of dust, the tops of the furrows already breaking through, the ground littered with needles. A lot of dust and needles, but not deep enough to hide a steroid-bulked carcass like Little Tonks. The man had gone.

Stef said, 'Kim Sung. Guru. It's got a kind of Asian, Eastern feel. Let me show you something.' She pulled out a printed photo of a building – some kind of big store frontage – with red and gold Asian dragons. 'Does that look familiar?'

'No.'

'Dan Simmons said it was a front, for money laundering. It could be Kim Sung's business.'

He took out his phone and looked up Sung in Newmarket. He showed her the screen: an oriental food wholesaler. 'Think that's him, the Guru person? A heroin importer?'

'Lots of shipments in and out,' she said. 'A

191

good cover.'

'You think he killed Dan Simmons? On an army base?'

She turned the Land Rover around and ploughed back towards the lay-by. She crashed through the bushes. The Lexus was there, brown with dust, but no sign of Little Tonks. She kept going along the lay-by, out onto the main road, along to another stand of bushes about a quarter of a mile away. There was a plain saloon also covered in dust. She pulled up near it and said, 'Let me show you something else.'

She showed him a photo of a wrecked building behind a pair of creosoted timber gates that were made in a series of diamond shapes. A printed caption read, *Guru's safe place*.

He looked up – she was watching him for a reaction. He said, 'What's this?'

'Not sure. Dan Simmons took a photo of it. I remember you said that you'd rebuilt your house. Did it ever look like this?'

'No, it was totally different.'

She put the picture away. She fixed him with her dark eyes, dust streaked down her face. 'I don't know you, Tom, but you're a nice guy. I think you should take a holiday or something.'

'My wife says the same thing. What are you going to do now?'

'We've got a name now. Guru, Kim Sung.

But it's a civilian name. That's tricky. I'll have to discuss it with Major Ward.'

He said, 'Are you out to make a name for yourself?'

She smiled, showing those deep lines around her eyes. 'Maybe get my name back. Be careful, Tom.'

He watched her saloon drive away along the wreckage-strewn road, disappearing into the haze.

Fletcher thought about it all, using pliers to pick the orange needles still wedged in the Land Rover panels, dropping them into a paper sack. He dropped the pliers in too, folded the sack up. He stopped in a field and splashed petrol on it, watched the flames light the dust in the air.

Thinking about Stef Maguire, about Dan Simmons preparing a letter he never finished, wanting to bring in an investigator. To look into heroin people, someone named Guru. Maybe Kim Sung, food wholesaler, of Newmarket. A man who thought Fletcher knew all about him.

Maybe.

Fletcher drove the car down to the edge of a flooded clay pit, drove it in up to the wheels and washed it down with a bucket, brushed the sludge off, washed it down again.

Back in police days, they would have

193

called this *feeding the dog.* You want to know something, somebody pops up and very kindly tells you. Fletcher wanted to know who was controlling Little Tonks. Tonks kindly told him it was Kim Sung.

Thing with feeding the dog, sometimes you get fed tripe, offal, rancid meat. Sometimes you pick up a nice juicy bone.

Only one way to find out.

He washed the earth off his face and hands, brushed what he could off his clothes. Then he got back in the Land Rover and headed out of the fens. The road was lined with vehicles stopped by the Blow, people rinsing their eyes. Others, like him, driving slowly away from it all. In ten minutes, the sun broke through, and the dust behind him became a mist in the mirror.

Thursday Afternoon

Fletcher came back into open farmland lit by clear midday sun, water sprays pumping in the fields. He turned off, making for Newmarket. Still the taste of dust in his mouth, grit between his teeth. The road eventually led into a valley with fields of newly-watered lettuce glittering in the light. At the end of this, at the head of a trading estate, he found the Sung oriental food business. He pulled up in the largely empty car park.

It was a single-storey depot with an ornate red and gold canopy over the entrance – prancing dragons and dolphins – like the gateway to an earthly paradise.

Exactly the photo that Stef Maguire had shown him.

He walked in. Straight away, he felt there was something wrong about the place. It was clean, well ordered, fragrant. But on a Thursday afternoon, it was almost deserted.

It was the kind of store where you need to register as a trader before you can shop – and he showed his business card to a friendly Korean woman who peered at his dusty overalls, then signed him up as *T Fletcher honey producer.*

'Is Mr Sung here today?'

Suddenly less friendly. A shake of the head.

'When will he be here?'

'Can't say.'

'Can you phone and ask?'

'You go shopping now.'

He took a flat trolley and shopped around. It was warm, the sun coming through roof panels, raising a spicy scent. The aisles were stacked with noodles, rice products, jars of pickled fish, things freeze-dried in plastic sacks. Fletcher was almost the only customer: just a handful of other traders sniffing the bags and holding jars up to the light. He passed an aisle of freezer chests, saw sacks of frosty bones under the glass, then a recipe demonstration area where two female chefs in white aprons were stripping slabs of meat with cleavers. The only other staff on the floor were some young Korean men loading rice sacks onto the shelves. He looked back, saw them watching him.

The more he saw, the more he felt the place was a sham. He thought, *Yes, I've been fed a juicy bone. The place is a front.*

He thought Kim Sung was Guru, the man trying to kill him.

He came past an entrance with a sign in pictogram script and English: *Staff Only*. Clear plastic doors, no locks. He pushed through, into an unlit corridor, doorways left and right. He walked quickly along, trying to look as if he knew where he was going. Most of the doors were closed, the open ones showed offices with workstations and food samples, but no workers. Right at the end, there was a fire door with a glass panel.

It showed a sunny car park at the back of the building. Right in front of him, a man was heaving a set of golf clubs into the front of a Porsche, jiggling the bag around to make it fit. He looked up, into Fletcher's eyes.

He was Korean, aged around thirty, slicked hair, metal sunglasses, braces on his teeth. Cool golfing clothes, corny driving gloves and two-tone shoes.

Fletcher stepped out. The man took off his sunglasses.

Fletcher felt a hand on his arm. He suddenly found the recipe demonstrator women on either side of him. They were short women, but in their thirties, hefty and seasoned, looking like they'd done this before, each with a butcher's knife held loosely in their fingers. One of them stretched out her knife and pressed its tip against Fletcher's crotch. She looked up and smiled – one tooth chipped like a guillotine blade. The other woman looked to the golfer for instructions.

The golfer said nothing, just moved his chin to send everyone back inside.

The space was about ten metres square, concrete floor and walls, light from a single high window. A stale, refuse smell. A big double door that led to the loading bay, Fletcher guessed – the sound of a vehicle being driven away, trollies being trundled into the building. In here, a few plastic crates and a big machine that was some kind of rubbish compactor: a metal chute stained with food debris.

The recipe women were facing Fletcher, knives at half-arms. Between them, the golfer stood looking at Fletcher's driving licence, his big mouth glinting with metal, twirling his sunglasses in one hand. He tossed the licence back and put his sunglasses on, looked over them at the dust on Fletcher's clothes. Then he went to one of the plastic crates in the corner and opened it. He reached in and took out a shrink-wrapped chicken. He slit the plastic with his finger and let the shroud fall away. The bird was headless and plucked smooth. He threw the bird into the compactor, clang, and slammed a button. The machine groaned, metal plates grinding into life. That went on for half a minute, the man watching Fletcher, smiling. Then something popped out of the chute onto the concrete floor. The man picked it up and threw it to

198

Fletcher. He caught it, then threw it away, wiping his hands. It was the chicken, compacted into a cube, just one little claw standing proud of the flesh.

The man squinted at Fletcher. He said, 'This room is where we interview shoplifters.' He had a strong voice, with no accent. 'We have a pilferage rate of zero point five per cent. What do you think of that?'

'Sounds low. Are you Kim Sung?'

'It is low. The national average is six point one per cent. I am Kim Sung. Are you a shoplifter, Mr Fletcher?'

'No. I'm the Honey Man. And you're Guru.'

Kim Sung ran his tongue across his braces. 'What?'

'Someone sent a man to kill me in my home. I think it might be you.'

'I've never heard of you. I'm a food wholesaler. Who told you this nonsense?'

'A man called Little Tonks.'

Kim Sung leaned his head back. The movement of a man who has just understood something.

It was quiet in the concrete room, except for a low buzzing from the crusher. The compacted chicken lay between them, leaking fluid.

Kim Sung said, 'In Korea, there is a type of dog bred for human consumption.'

'Is that right?'

'That type of dog is degenerate and cannot be trusted. Just like some people. Mr Tonks has misled you. I know nothing about you. So you can go now. But don't ever come back to my food store.'

The recipe women showed Fletcher back to the Land Rover. The one with the chipped tooth said something in Korean. The other one whistled and rattled her tongue.

Fletcher said, 'Is Kim Sung a good boss?'

But they were already walking back to the store.

Fletcher drove away. The shining dragons and dolphins on the canopy faded in his rear mirror.

A façade, a front for money laundering, heroin distribution? Maybe. Dan Simmons did have a photo of the storefront – Stef Maguire had just shown Fletcher that.

But Fletcher had walked in there, seen the crusher, and walked out again unharmed.

He looked in the mirror again.

Nobody was following.

Fletcher believed that Kim Sung had never heard of him, didn't want him dead. He believed that Little Tonks had used one final stunt. Tonks had fooled him back there in the field.

And Fletcher believed that Kim Sung's pilferage rate was as low as zero point five per cent.

Major Ward noticed Stef wasn't in her office, wasn't answering her phone, and started to be concerned. She was effectively absent without leave. The words after-effects, paranoia, flashed through his mind, though he knew she was pretty stable all the same. When he knocked on the door of her quarters, she opened it in uniform – but her hair was wet, her eyes red and irritated. On the floor, he could see a tracksuit covered with brown dust, and a pair of trainers the same colour.

He said, 'What's happened?'

'There's something called a Fen Blow.'

He listened to her telling him. It started calmly, then it came out in a rush. Tom Fletcher, a field full of needles, a drug dealer, a Korean food wholesaler. Dan Simmons tapping his head. What's really going on–

He said, 'Listen–'

'Something is going on–'

'I said listen. God's sake, Stef. I said I wanted to get to the bottom of the Simmons case. OK. But when did we discuss observing civilian criminals in fields? When?'

The outer door slammed open and a soldier crashed past, whistling. He waited till the man had gone. 'Stef, we've got to tread carefully here. We're under a lot of focus, we've got to behave calmly. OK?'

'OK. But I've got a theory–'

'Look, let's discuss this tonight. I've got a

flat in the village. It's pretty grotty, but it's a change of scene. And nobody's going to be walking past.'

They walked out of her block, sun after the dark of her room, making them both blink. He thought, *Damn it, feels like we're lovers*. Thinking of the way her wet hair looked, not knowing how this whole thing was going to end.

Fletcher went back into the haze, back to the lay-by. The Lexus had gone. He pulled over by the clay pit where he'd washed down the Land Rover. A few anglers were sitting there now, like deluded men fishing for the reflected clouds.

The critical thing now was to find Tonks again.

Fletcher unfolded his road map and spread it on the dashboard. Where would Tonks be? The man clearly felt at home out in the fens, in his lay-by, in the middle of nowhere. Why use the lay-by? It was easy to enter and leave quickly. Plus the nearby field for quick injection work if the punters needed that. But where was his home?

Fletcher looked across the map. Tonks wouldn't sell from his own street, but he wouldn't travel long distances either. How far would a minor drug distributor travel from where he felt safe? Thirty minutes' drive? Fletcher drew a rough circle around the lay-by with his finger. It contained three small Fenland towns. One of those three? If so, what would Tonks do in such places? Fletcher thought of that martial arts pose he'd struck in the field, the hammy karate blow, the steroid bulk of the guy. The body-building magazine abandoned in the Lexus.

Where would a chemically bulked-up martial arts freak go to lick his wounds?

Small Fenland towns look much the same. They have cheerful Slovaks working the fields, modern estates, a high street, a Methodist church, a war memorial. Then a railway crossing, and, beyond that, a small business park with a car repair place, a discount carpet store, and usually, a gym.

The gym in the first town he went to was fire-damaged and boarded up. In the second town, the gym was holding a body-and-soul fitness day in partnership with the Methodists.

When he got to the third town, it was late afternoon. The wind had dropped, but the air still smelled of the dust that coated vehicles and windowsills. He had to halt at a rail crossing, beside the war memorial with its bronze plaque glinting in the sun. He read the plaque. *Afghanistan 1878* over a list of names that sounded like the kids he'd known at school. When the barrier went up, he crossed and pulled over in a road surfaced with loose cinders. There was a lumber yard based in an old Nissen hut, piles of cut wood, a wail of machinery from inside, *We make anything* in wooden letters over the door. Then the obligatory carpet store, then a vacant space showing a reddening horizon. After that – it looked good.

A two-storey concrete building with a spotlight picking out the signage *Pro Gym Martial Arts*. He locked the Land Rover and walked over.

Double entrance doors, the ground floor windows covered with mirror film. Shouts and grunts from deep inside. Fletcher walked around the building. At the back, there was a car park with two hatchbacks, a mattress and an old bed. And a blue Lexus, covered in dust. One orange needle still stuck under the wipers.

Behind that, a rickety fire escape to the top floor, sealed off at waist height with barbed wire. Fletcher climbed over the wire, went up the metal steps. Through a half-open window, those sounds of kicking and gasping. Then, at the top of the steps, a fire door caked with dust and bird shit. He tried the handle – secured only with a basic latch from inside. He took his bank card and slid it up against the frame, two, three times till it released. He opened the door slowly, looked in.

A corridor with a stairwell at one end.

Before that, a door slightly open, shedding electric light onto a scuffed floor. He listened. Echoes of the martial arts one level below. From the lit doorway, silence – but someone was in there, a shadow moving then settling. He stepped over to it, listened again. Breathing? Was that Tonks, sleeping off his experience?

He pushed the door open.

The room had a table, a floor lamp, two chairs, a single bed. Sitting on the bed, a woman in her twenties, dark hair down over her shoulders, denim shirt unbuttoned, breast feeding a tiny child.

He took a step back.

The woman looked at him – eyes wide but unembarrassed. She put a finger to her lips. The room was hot and smelled of female skin. She put her hand back under the baby, lifted it off her nipple. She put it to her shoulder and patted its back. She had a tattoo across her breasts, freshly done: a wet flower. The baby burped and she smiled, half closed her eyes.

She whispered, 'Are you the Honey Man?'

'Yes. Who are you?'

She smiled and stroked the infant. 'Tonks' little girl.' He wasn't sure if she meant herself or the baby. 'I thought you might be looking for him.'

He closed the door. 'Where is Tonks?'

'Downstairs. One of the boys had to bring

him back.'

'What boys?'

'The gym boys. Them working out down there.' She glanced down at her breasts, up at him. 'He's got concussion in his head, he's got dust in his lungs. You know what you did to him?'

'You know what he's trying to do to me?'

'He's a good daddy.' Patting the baby's back. 'You should see him playing with this little one. He's gentle, him. Like a baby himself.' She smiled. 'You got kids?'

'Yes.'

'You love 'em, boy?'

'Yes, I do.'

'Good.' She placed the child carefully in the centre of the bed, stroked the little face. Then she sat again, leaned forward and slipped her shirt off. Her breasts were swollen and creamy in the glow from the floor lamp, with conical nipples that she wiped gently with a tissue. The tattoo flower had branches and folds. He noticed tracks along her arms, red dots following the veins.

He said, 'I'm going now.'

She smiled. 'Don't go yet.' She reached for a metal tin on the table, took out a syringe, a spoon, a plastic wrap, a little box of gear.

He said, 'You've got a baby here.'

She scowled, glancing at the child, then smoothed the little face with the hand that held the spoon. 'It's the way we are, boy.'

'You're breastfeeding.'

She smiled, sweeping her hair back, her breasts swaying. Spoon in one hand, syringe in the other, nipples wet. 'Just look at us. And my mother before me. We go all the way back.'

He was torn between going down to find Tonks and stopping this woman from doing whatever she was about to. She laid her gear out on the table with long fingers that cast shadows on the wall.

'This is crazy.'

She mixed water and another liquid in the spoon – lemon juice, he remembered from his police days in Cambridge, to break up the active molecule. She dropped in a small pinch of white powder. 'I seen on the news about that Poppy Crush.'

'They say they'll cut off your supply.'

'Can't stop what's natural. That's perversion.' She warmed the spoon with a cigarette lighter, the flame showing sweat across her breasts, glinting on her tattoo. She leaned forward, legs apart, feeling the air over the spoon, a line of spit hanging from her mouth.

He was listening for sounds outside – none that he could hear, just the martial arts noises from the ground floor. He said, 'So what's it like?'

She looked at him quickly with slitted eyes, then took out a loose cigarette filter, slipped it on the end of the syringe needle with one hand in a practised movement.

'You want to try?' She placed the needle with its filter in the spoon, raised her thumb to draw up the liquid into the syringe. 'Try it with me, boy. You'll see the world is different.'

'No thanks.'

'Sure?' Her pupils were poppy-coloured, focused on the syringe. 'Help me, then. Tie my arm.'

'No way.'

She scowled and put down the syringe. It made a big shadow on the wall. The same sounds came from below, also a car in the car park, a plane overhead. In the corridor now – other sounds? He reached for the door handle, began to turn it.

He saw the light swerve, then something hit him from behind, smashing across his shoulders. There was a flash and the light went out, breaking noises. He was stunned for a moment, thought, *She's hit me with the baby. An exploding glass baby.* Then he heard the baby wailing, realised she'd hit him with the floor lamp. The door slammed open, smacking him on the shoulder, and shapes filled the space – at least three men crowding in, outlined against the stairwell light.

He took a swing at the first one, hit a cheekbone, which cracked. Out of the dim light, the other two men got him by the arms, punched him in the stomach, slammed his head against the doorframe. He felt vomit in his mouth, gasping for air. The baby still screaming in the dark, glass sliding and crunching on the floor. They got him out into the corridor, dragged him to the stairwell, threw him down. He rolled twice – first time with his shoulder on the concrete step, then with his arms bunched over his head, his legs crashing over in a somersault that left him sprawling on the cool concrete landing, looking up at the men outlined against the corridor light at the top of the stairs.

So they were Tonks' boys. And that was Tonks' little girl.

No more baby screams from up there, no more exercise noises from down here. He pulled himself upright. Pain in his shoulder, blood now with the vomit in his mouth. The door in front of him opened. Little Tonks kneeled down in front of him, clunk, just inside the doorway, shoulders wider than the frame.

'Get in here, Honey Man.'

The gym room smelled of sweat. It had wooden flooring, arc lamps hanging from a ceiling girder, throwing yellow light over Little Tonks. The man was sitting on a press bench, in a boxer's tracksuit, the hood around his face. Small red eyes, small mouth with cracked lips, baggy sleeves hiding those anabolic fists. He was rocking himself, looking at Fletcher sitting on the opposite bench.

A man-to-man talk was the idea.

There was a tread from outside. One of the gym boys, listening. Tonks scowled at the door.

Fletcher fingered his own abdomen, his ribs.

He said, 'So, er, who told you to kill me, Tonks?'

'It was Kim Sung.'

'Kim Sung has never heard of me. He's heard of you, though. Why is that?'

Tonks said, 'Know what this is?' One hand came loose from the sleeve, shaking out two pieces of dark wood linked by twine cords. Tonks let them sway, casting shadows on the floor. 'Know the name?'

'It's a–' he tried to remember '–a *Chi Chuan?*'

'That's right, boy. Chi Chuan. Developed by monks three centuries ago.' Tonks wrapped it around his wrist. He flicked his hood back, showing the big face with a bruise where Stef Maguire had belted him, small reddened eyes flicking about. 'You enter my home. You spy on my woman giving milk.' He laughed, eyes shining. 'One strike with this weapon, I could sever your main artery.'

Fletcher said, 'Someone very senior gave

you this job to do and you screwed it up and now you're worried. Who was it?'

Tonks said, 'I could blind you in one or both eyes.'

'Who was it?'

'I could break your wrists and ankles.'

'Tonks, who told you to do this? Someone called Guru?'

'No. It was Kim Sung.'

'Why do you keep saying that?'

'Sung. It was Kim Sung.'

'Are the boys listening outside? Is that the problem? Just drop your voice.'

Little Tonks bit his lip, wiped his nose with a massive paw. Eyes filled with mucus – like a baby himself, the girl upstairs said. Tonks whispered, 'Look, you're a daddy, right? Like me?'

'Yes.'

'So you know how it is. Sometimes you just have to do things. And sometimes you just have to say nothing. So I'm saying nothing.'

Fletcher looked into the bulked-up face. He thought for a few seconds. He was tired, hungry, dust in his eyes. He wanted to go home. He got to his feet.

Tonks stood up too, a head taller, the Chi Chuan dangling loose from his right hand. The overhead lamp swung its light over both of them.

Fletcher said, 'OK. You're a good man.' And he put his hand out.

Tonks grunted, flipped the Chi Chuan around his thumb, put his own hand out too.

Fletcher grabbed the weapon, pulled it right off Tonks' thumb, whirled it around and cracked Tonks on the temple. There was a spray of blood, Tonks slamming his big paws up, martial arts style, then making basic fists – all the ancient wisdom giving way to playground habit. Tonks flailed out – Fletcher dodging and flipping the thong around the man's neck, twisting it. Tonks gurgled and hissed, hands scrabbling at the cords, getting a finger under there, trying to pull it loose.

Fletcher brought his foot up, scraped it down Tonks' knee, crushed the upper arch of his foot. He stepped back. He could smell the air blasting out of the man's gaping mouth – onions, chemicals, dislodged dust. He slammed the man in the other leg, then followed him down with the Chi Chuan still around the bulked-up neck, lowering him onto the floor. Tonks gurgled and scrabbled. Fletcher twisted tighter, then slackened the pressure. Tonks got the idea, stayed still, his face sideways on the floor. Waiting.

Fletcher said, 'The Chi Chuan wasn't invented by ancient monks, Tonks. Only people like you believe that. It was made up by a film studio in the sixties.' He put his mouth close to the man's big left ear. He whispered, 'Your world is ending, Tonks. All you've got left are the boys sitting outside. They still think you're the boss. We can let them keep on thinking that.'

Tonks wheezed. 'Go back to your farm.'

'Tonks, tell me. If you give me the wrong name, I'll come back here. Give me the right name, you never see me again. You can tell your boys outside how you threw me around the gym, how I pissed myself. Just give me the name.'

'No. I can't. You don't know–'

Fletcher tightened the cords around the massive neck, saw them disappear into the hairless folds. It looked like packaged meat. Tonks gave out a low gasp, began sobbing.

Fletcher had doubts about what he was doing – Tonks was a small-town idiot who'd blindly, stupidly followed instructions. And the man was a father too, to the tiny child in the glass-strewn room upstairs. Fletcher hesitated, looking at his own hands, the same ones that washed his children in the bath. But Tonks made the decision for him.

Tonks wheezed out a name.

Not Kim Sung.

'Gary Neale.'

Fletcher kept the cords where they were.

Gary Neale?

He remembered the name from police days. Back then, Gary Neale was a vicious county-level thug based in Essex. There was a story about someone who tried to inform on him, something about a rope and a Range Rover. The man was a threat to society. *'Gary Neale?* You're bullshitting.'

'No, it's Gary. Don't tell him, man, please. I pick stuff up from Gary Neale's people. They told me to do this to you. It came down from Gary. It comes from Gary, you do it.'

'Why did you say Kim Sung?'

'Sung's a new supplier, building up distribution. He's eating Gary's territory. Gary wants him out. I thought, cause him some problems. That's good for Gary.'

'Gary means Guru, right? It's his nickname?'

'Gary uses names. I don't know them all.'

Fletcher thought, *Gary/Guru.*

Gary told Tonks to kill me. Gary is Guru.

He said, 'Where do I find Gary?'

'Nobody finds Gary. He's somewhere on the coast.'

'Where?'

'Nobody knows. You think I visit him? You think he asks me round? You think–' Tonks began to choke, gagging for breath. 'You think he'll forget about you?'

Fletcher loosened the cords, let Tonks flop to the floor. The big head hit the boards with the sound of a career ending.

In the street outside, he turned the Land

Rover around on the cinder road outside the old lumber yard. He took a last look at the Pro Gym, outlined by its spotlight against the dark sky. Faces were watching from the doorway, steroid arms flexing, the battle for succession beginning.

Fletcher forgot them. But not Gary Neale.

Thinking back. Five, six years before: Gary Neale had been the closest thing the eastern counties had to a gangland boss: a charismatic, devious figure with fingers in prostitution, cheap farm labour, above all Class A drug distribution. And that story about the men who informed on him. They were found at the side of a farm road in rural Essex, back in 2002 or 3. They'd been dragged up and down behind a vehicle until they died, then the bodies cut off with the rope still attached and the next live victim hooked up. Someone had taken a photo. The road was littered with shoes, clothing, teeth, shit and blood. Next day, Gary Neale put new tyres on his Range Rover.

Fletcher headed back to his house, between the water sprays churning against the last light.

He was experiencing doubt. It felt corrosive, eating at him.

People like Tonks and his friends were one thing. They were gym rats, inbred, corrupted, easily dominated. But Gary Neale – he was something else.

Fletcher stopped at a railway crossing, watched the red lights blinking, a cargo train rolling slowly across, the vibration shaking the ground.

He put the window down, listening to the train rolling away. The barrier rose, but he didn't move. Beyond it, he saw a space drifting with diesel fumes. The vapour cleared, and he saw a dark field, its crops flickering in the red lights.

Fletcher was thirty-seven, six foot three, had a police bravery medal until he threw it in the river when he left Cambridge. And all his life – he realised now, looking at the field – he'd been backing away from the big battles he should be fighting. Gary Neale was going to be the biggest battle of all, and this one needed to be fought.

A car behind Fletcher hooted, flashed its lights.

He drove over the crossing, into the dark.

On the other horizon, a dusty egg-shaped moon was rising.

Big clouds over the sea, the shape of knife blades. Smell of salt water, sound of waves against the hull of a large boat.

Gary Neale flipped his cigarette out into the dark and leaned on the railing, thinking.

Gary Neale was forty-seven, tall, big and heavy. Eight years in prison. Killed three people personally – a few more if you count the ones behind the Range Rover.

He inhaled the smell of the sea.

The ones behind the Range Rover.

And the one back when he was eleven. The one who was fourteen or fifteen. Behind the Odeon, in the rain.

He straightened up.

These days, Gary Neale lived on a boat. He had a house in Essex, obviously – a big Spanish-type mansion with an electric fence. But he spent most of his time on his boat. For one thing, he could move it between the five different moorings he kept at the marinas along the east coast of England. And a boat felt more private than a house. More secure.

He liked the smell of the sea too, and the sound of gulls.

Just lately, everything was making him think of the Odeon, the soft rain that day. Like it was yesterday. When he had nothing except a razor blade. And she was fourteen or fifteen.

The boat shifted a little.

He was standing on the forward deck, looking down through the open glass roof into the forward cabin. There was a girl down there, sprawled on the divan. Naked, hands behind her head, looking through the side window, chewing gum. He didn't mind them chewing, but he insisted they wait. To be dismissed, to be told they were finished with, could go and wipe themselves down.

He was still thinking of the alley behind the Odeon in 1972. The mess on the wall.

He adjusted his suit. One of the suits he liked to wear on his boat. Italian blue, with a stripe, a polo shirt under that. He turned away, leaned on the deck rail looking out over the sea.

He said. 'Tonks did *what*?'

The man next to him was tall and wide, in white trousers and a black T-shirt. 'Our two local guys down there. One of them's gone missing. The other one, Tonks, we stood him down, like you said. But this Fletcher guy, Honey Man, turned up at the gym. One of the other boys was listening outside. Fletcher said *Who's Guru?* or something like that. Tonks gave him your name.'

'I cannot believe it. Where is he now?'

'Fletcher? We don't know—'

'I mean Tonks.'

'Upstairs at the gym. He lives there.'

'Tell the boys to keep him in there.'

'What about Fletcher, Gary?'

Gary Neale thought about it, running a hand over his cropped scalp. 'Tonight, send some of those gym boys. They don't know where Honey Man is, but they know where his house is, right? Tell them to take a can of petrol. See if they can't screw that up too. He'll get the idea. Tomorrow, leave early, go and give Tonks a lesson, make sure the others

218

see and hear it.' He watched the clouds. 'And I'll ask around about this Fletcher guy some more. I thought he was organic. A pushover.'

'He is.'

'Yeah? There was a guy like that in Whitemoor when I was in there. He was doing three years for fraud or something. He was a vegan, imagine that in a fucking prison. His wife sent him organic biscuits. He used to meditate and all of that. Two black guys tried to take him at the sinks, him cleaning his teeth.'

'And?'

'He knew they were thinking about it. He had his toothbrush handle all sharpened up. He used it on their eyes. Sometimes that kind of person, they surprise you. Treat them with suspicion.'

Gary went back to the roof, looked down at the girl again. She was in half darkness, kicking one foot in the air to a beat only she could hear, her breasts shaking to the rhythm. He called down, 'You can go.' She rolled over, sat up and swivelled off the bed.

They watched her go, bruises on her back showing in the creamy light.

Gary Neale said, 'I know someone who can sort this out. Just wait.'

Jason waited through the afternoon in the prefabs beside the runway. It was OK in there – air con, hot dogs and coffee, a TV showing satellite. And hundreds of chairs.

Jason stayed by himself, watching the other passengers waiting for the delayed TriStar. The bulk of them from a single regiment, a dozen from the air force. The rest, like him, odds and sods detached from their units. He lounged in a chair, lowered his headgear over his eyes.

He tried to guess where his Lacon box was right now. In a hangar, in the shade. Enough in that box to get him out of here, into the life he'd always wanted.

Laughter made him open his eyes. Against the far wall, a group of half a dozen had made a mini emplacement out of their packs, sitting watching something. Laughter every now and then, whistles, jeers. In there with them, he could see the pretty girl soldier, the one behind him in the queue.

He got a coffee and walked over to the emplaced group. They were watching a video on a laptop. Eight men, just the one female, all private soldier rank. Friends together, winding down. Stubbled hair on the men, little ponytail on the girl. Deep tans, regimental tattoos. Burns and bruises on the arms. He circled around the back, looked at the laptop.

Professional quality. A woman being mounted by a dog, by a small horse. Then a beheading – looked like Bosnia from years ago, the old clips still in circulation, still favourites. The head coming away cleanly, the body shaking, leaking on the snow.

The group stamped and whistled.

Two dogs fighting in a whorehouse, the girls in the background in bras and pants, cheering them on. Looked like Belize or Sierra Leone. He guessed what the prize was for the winner.

Jason caught the eye of one of the men – the youngest, he thought, line of acne along the jaw. He shook his head in mock disapproval, the kid grinned and raised a can of Coke.

He went and watched Sky. The emplaced group got to the end of their DVD and broke up. The girl soldier brushed past him. She said, 'I need a smoke after that.'

They opened a fire door and stood looking out. Mid morning, warm but not boiling. Jagged hills in the distance. RAF people working on the TriStar, using ladders and hammers. They laughed at that, smoking. They saw a baggage truck approaching the TriStar, and she said, 'That's a good sign.' A big smile, catching his eye.

In the afternoon, they got clearance to board the plane. They shouldered their kit and trooped out across the runway, up the creaky steps like a gang of the weirdest tourists on earth. Inside, the forty-year-old panels groaned as three hundred personnel piled into them. He got a window seat near an exit, so at least he could stretch his legs OK. The girl soldier dropped into the seat next to him, undid her hair and shook it loose. He didn't want to breathe it, but he did. He wiped his mouth.

She touched him on the arm, said, 'What's the first thing you're going to do when you're back?'

He said, 'Now you're asking.' But he was thinking, *I'm going to kill that Honey Man.*

Thursday Night

After dark, Stef Maguire changed out of her uniform and let Major Ward drive her to his flat.

He said, 'I warn you, I make conversation before discussing theories.'

'Well, OK.'

'And here we are.'

It was in a modern block on a development near Waterton village. Neat lawns, flower baskets, neighbours unloading groceries from cars. A communal hallway, then three flights of stairs to the top floor where Ward unlocked his front door.

'This is me.'

It was tidy, Stef Maguire noticed – looking around the little sitting-dining room – but it smelled hot and closed-up. A framed Victorian portrait of a cavalryman on the wall. Dust on the shelves and the top of the TV, but on the dining table a huge vase of flowers.

'Something I learned from my ex-wife. Big bunch of flowers, people don't notice the dust.'

'Well, that works.'

'Good.' He opened a window, letting in

warm night breeze and the sound of traffic.

'Seriously, what do you think?'

'It's, er, cosy.'

He turned to her and grinned. 'I lost out in my divorce, in a big way. This is what I've got left, but at least it's mine.' A lorry passed on the road, and the window vibrated slightly. 'Want to see the kitchen?'

'I'm tempted.'

It was a tiny galley, dominated by a fridge. Ward opened it and produced a bottle of white wine slick with cold.

Stef asked, 'Where's your ex-wife now?'

'Somewhere spending my pay.' His bitterness surprised her, but then he laughed, pouring wine. 'But you know how the army pays. We earn about as much as sales reps, but without the company car.'

'Here's to the army.'

They clinked. 'I wouldn't have my life any other way.'

They were both wearing jogging suits, trainers – anonymous, civilian gear that helped them relax. He cooked two thin steaks, green beans, new potatoes. She sat on the counter and watched his hands at work, smiling. They talked about life before the army: she'd been a graphic designer, he'd gone straight in from college. Eating, they opened a second bottle, watched the lights of the traffic beyond the trees, the moon casting shadows through the flowers.

Life after the army too – five years in, she wanted to stay in for the usual eighteen years. She had no idea after that.

'Maybe horses.'

'Horses?'

'I've always wanted a stables.' She laughed. 'That regiment kid, Swilter, he walks the little pig. You know he's sixteen? When I was sixteen, I was still collecting pictures of horses.' She looked at a picture on the wall: the Victorian horse-soldier. 'You a riding man?'

He smiled. 'Strangely, my ex-wife didn't want to keep that picture. It's my great-grandad, colonel of horses in the old Rhodesia.'

'You're an army family? I didn't know.' His eyes stayed on the painting. 'Is that why the men threatened you from prison?' He didn't answer. 'Sorry, I–'

'It's OK. I put them away for ten years. I'm everything they hate. Officer class, the old families.' He smiled. 'A stables, yeah? Good plan.'

'And you?'

He told her he wanted to buy a small hotel in France, read the paper at the bar every morning. He looked up at the moon. 'Not much chance of that. It'll work out alright, though. Everything always does.' He brought a bowl of strawberries and they ate them on the couch, their feet up. He said, 'You're good to talk to.'

'You're not bad yourself.'

He smiled. 'Come on, then, Captain. Tell me your theory.'

She took a long breath, inhaling strawberries and Ward's soap and water smell. 'The person that Dan Simmons called Guru. Tom Fletcher thinks it could be someone named Kim Sung, who's a food wholesaler. The civilian police can look into him. My interest is, where's this Guru getting it from? Heroin comes from Afghanistan, according to the government. What else comes from Afghanistan?'

'What?'

'Soldiers. We've got eight thousand people out there. If one per cent of them were inclined to do this—'

'Do what?'

'Import heroin. OK, half a per cent. That's forty people.'

'Our people importing heroin from the Stan? That's crazy.' He threw a strawberry back into the bowl. 'Come on.'

'We lose fifteen hundred people a year to random drug tests. The media call it the lost battalion.'

'The lost battalion are our people taking drugs, not importing drugs. Big difference.'

She said, 'Think of it. Think of the temptation out there, our people are surrounded by the stuff. You know the potential for squaddy crime, you ran Operation Alloy.'

'But smuggling guns isn't smuggling heroin.'

'Correct, heroin pays more. A handgun weighs half a kilo. It's worth what, three hundred quid round the back of a pub? Half a kilo of heroin must be worth more than three hundred quid.'

She watched him thinking, refilling their glasses.

'Import it and do what with it, Stef? Sell it round the back of a pub?'

'That's the point. Distribution. Imagine British troops getting together with these big drugs men, the kind of people Dan Simmons was researching. Imagine what they could do together. The biggest courier service available. Straight from the fields—'

'Straight through military airports with sniffer dogs and sensors. You'd have to know your way through all of that. And you'd need bollocks of steel. No, in fact, you'd need to be completely stupid.' He took a swig of wine.

'Half a per cent is forty people, remember. Are half a per cent of our people that stupid? Are there forty idiots in the British army? I think quite possibly. And that's my theory.'

He shook his head and was quiet for a long time. Then he said, 'Jesus. At first, I thought that challenging the Team Defence line meant saying Dan Simmons really *was* being bullied. That seemed pretty radical. Now you've come up with this. If you're right, this would totally humiliate the army on the eve of a major operation. And if you're wrong, it would leave us both with plenty of free time for stables and hotels, because we'd be unemployed. The reaction this will get, they'll say we're crazy–'

'But this is not paranoia.' She slammed her glass down. 'I'm mixed up, I'm not mentally ill. There's a fucking big difference.'

'Yeah, I know.' He seemed to come to a decision. 'OK. We'll take the lid off this thing. It'll mean breaking some bad news very carefully.' He looked at his watch. 'We won't get any sense out of people now. So we might as well get some sleep.'

They were silent for half a minute. Then she said, 'I have trouble sleeping. I get flashbacks. I see dragons coming out of the walls. And I just want to sleep.'

He led her into the bedroom and she stretched out on the bed. She saw him sit on the end of the bed, straight-backed, his head turned away. She kicked her trainers off. She stretched out a leg and rested her foot on his shoulder.

He said, 'I'll sleep in the other room, Stef. Or in the office.'

'I wanted to ask, do you get many visitors?'

He laughed. 'You're the only one who's been here.'

She hooked her toe around his neck. 'Something's going on here.'

'The way you talk, you're scaring me.'

'I mean us,' she said.

'Yes, I mean us.' He rubbed his eyes. She rubbed his shoulder with her foot. 'I'm supposed to be taking care of you.'

'Do it like this.'

She kneeled up and unzipped his jacket. Unzipped her own and rubbed her chest across his back. He turned round and lowered her down on the bed. His face in shadow, car headlights passing behind him, his hands feeling across her.

It was like being fifteen again, she thought, ruffling his hair. The way he cupped her boobs and rubbed them, nuzzled them. Like some kind of big, overgrown boy. But then he rolled her over and stripped her down like a gun – calmly, silently, without scratches or explanations. Running a hand over her, testing her out. She rolled again and did the same to him. She knew then it wasn't like being a kid again. She was twenty-eight and she needed certain things and she was in the modern army, it was here and now, two people who shouldn't be getting it on just doing it anyway, because she'd been through a lot and he understood all that and she really, really liked him.

Ward watched her sleeping, her breasts sharp in the moonlight, her arm muscles hard and damp. He thought *What have we just done? This is going to make everything so difficult.*

He thought about waking her, talking to her. He sighed and rubbed his chin. He pulled the sheet over her, walked through to the main room. He picked up his wineglass and sipped, looking at her laptop on the table.

Was she really on to something? He opened the laptop and flipped through the files again.

Music.

The Waterton footage.

Heroin. An oriental storefront. A derelict building. A pair of slatted timber gates. *Guru's safe place.*

Photos. The sprawled women. One on a rug, one on a bed. One climbing out of a pool.

He shut it down, went to the window. Looking at the moon without really seeing it. An idea was coming to him, something that explained what the hell Dan Simmons was talking about.

No, it was crazy.

But was it crazier than Stef's idea?

He sat down and thought about it.

Stef. God, we have to be so careful now.

This is in motion and we can't stop it.

He got back into bed and slid his hand between her cool thighs. She woke and spread her legs. He stroked her, felt how wet she was. He stopped.

She said, 'What?'

He said, 'I've had a new idea about the Dan Simmons thing. I think you may be part right, but I need to check some facts and speak to a few people. This has colossal repercussions. So listen, will you do something for me?'

'Such as?'

'Tomorrow, work a normal day. No chasing after drug barons. Then we'll catch up later in the day.'

'Here?'

'Play your cards right, yes.'

'Arrogant sod.'

'Will you do that for me?'

'Is that an order?'

'Yes. Let me take it on from here. Let me keep you safe.'

They kissed for a minute. Then she turned her head to one side, raised her knees, took his hand in her own grip, using his fingers like her own.

The TriStar levelled out and cruised like an old whore. The lights stayed dimmed, the windows blacked out. Jason could smell the girl beside him – women soldiers always a different smell from the men. She brushed his arm, said, 'I'll tell you what I'm going to do.'

'Go on, then.'

'I'm going to Southend and swim in the sea. Just jump in and roll around.'

She turned her face to him. He thought, *She's lovely, not like that Belgian thief. She's one of us.*

She said, 'What are you thinking about?'

He settled back. It was nice to tell someone you could trust.

'There's a little place in Spain called San Tierna. It's a good class of people, holidays, families. On the waterfront there's a little restaurant, with a bar, does boats for hire too. There's a villa up the road that's got a pool and a gate that slides across, electric. And a lovely garden, lovely soft grass.'

She nodded, getting the picture. She said, 'I can just see you running a bar. But I can't see you as a gardener.'

'The garden's for my aunt.'

She wriggled closer to him. 'Your *aunt*?'

'She looked after me, when I was a kid. She's the best, you know what I mean? The best.'

The girl stroked his cheek. Then she put her head on his shoulder and slept. He closed his eyes. He pictured his Lacon box down in the hold, pictured the property in Spain. It was all coming together, nothing could stop it or screw it up. He smelled the girl's hair. He smiled. He saw himself touching down at Brize, running straight along the tarmac, straight into Honey Man like a locked-on missile.

Fletcher let himself into Annabel's house. There was a single light on, but the ground floor was deserted. He stopped at the top of the stairs. Cathleen was sitting on the floor, asleep, her back against the door of the room where the twins were sleeping. He stood watching her. The light showed the copper colour in her hair. He sat beside her and she opened her eyes.

'Tom, thank God you're OK.' He put his arms around her and breathed in her hair. She said, 'Did you find out who's doing this?'

'Yes.'

He heard one of the twins whimper in her sleep.

Cathleen whispered, 'And?'

'There's a top-level psychopath called Gary Neale. I remember stories about him from police days. The men he sent were just locals, but he'll send someone else now, someone better.'

'*Why?* What's the reason?'

'He wants to keep something quiet. He's connected with drugs.'

'Where does he live?'

233

'People like him stay hidden. You can't look them up on the Internet.'

'So who will he send next? And when?' Her voice grew louder, and one of the girls turned over in bed again. She waited a few seconds, then she said, 'Come and see.'

She opened the door. The room smelled of the children sleeping. In the dim light, he could see their faces – eyes closed, mouths open, their long black hair spread out on the pillows. Evie had her cuddly rabbit next to her. Sally had her hands curled under her chin. He leaned down and pulled the sheet higher over her.

Outside, he closed their door. Cathleen whispered, 'We have to leave, Tom. You, me, the girls. We have to get out and stay together. Go to the police tomorrow.'

He bowed his head and thought for a while. He saw the dark space under the barrier of the train crossing, drifting with fumes.

He said, 'No. I have to find him.'

'You just said he'll send someone else. What if he finds us?'

They listened to the twins breathing. She said, 'You remember when we were fifteen, you said you'd look after me?'

'I said I'd always look after you.'

'So phone the police. Then let's all go away.'

He thought for a minute, with his head bowed. 'OK. I'll get some things from the house.'

234

Approaching the house, he could see it across the fields, the floodlights on, showing white against the sky. As the Land Rover bounced over the road through the elephant grass, though, he could see something was wrong.

Pale smoke was rising behind it.

Sliding to a halt at the gate, he smelled wood smoke as he jumped out, grabbed the fire extinguisher from under the dashboard and ran around the side of the house.

At the back, the low apple trees were casting jagged shadows – lit up by a fire beyond them, in the beehive area. Not just one fire, he realised, but dozens of them, stretching right across the field, sparks twisting up.

The beehives were on fire.

The wooden boxes were giving out tongues of flame, blue and orange lighting up the grass, thick grey smoke rolling out towards him. Under the smoke, he could smell petrol. He saw the top of the nearest hive crisp up and slide off, releasing a cloud of bees, some on fire, writhing with sparks.

He thumped the extinguisher into action and put the fire out – a burst of the foam did it quickly. But beyond that, maybe two dozen of the other hives were blazing, the bees flashing past him, an enraged buzzing that was as loud as the crackle of the flames. He saw one collapse, the whole contents on fire – bees, the honey core, the cell structure exploding. He ran from one hive to the next, using the extinguisher until the foam ran out, and he was left with a few that were burning like torches. He ran back to the house and unwound the hose, managed to wet the nearby hives down to stop them catching too. There wasn't much he could do after that, except run the water over the remains of the last burning hives until the fire was out and the field was covered in smoke.

He walked through the hives, his feet crunching the bodies of dead bees, then sliding on the collapsed slabs of honeycomb that had fallen free. He picked up the extinguisher and hurled it out into the elephant grass where they'd come from – staying in the dark, afraid to enter the floodlit area near the house.

He shouted, 'Come out here.'

No answer, just the crack of cooling embers.

He took out his phone and dialled Cathleen.

'Tom?'

'Change of plan.'

He listened to her swearing at him down the line. Then he heard her catch her breath and weep. In the background, one of the twins began crying too.

Smoke drifted up to the swelling moon.

Friday Morning

In the yard of the Pro Gym, Tonks' woman waited with his little girl in the passenger seat of his Lexus. The back seat was piled with their things – blankets, clothes, the baby's toys. Tonks himself was still inside, though. The gym boys wouldn't let him out.

So she waited. The baby woke up and she fed it. The sun was heating the car, making her skin clammy.

A man in white trousers and a black jacket came walking across the yard. He had cropped hair, sunglasses, was tall and wide. He glanced at her without stopping, then went past the car, into the gym.

He was in there just the length of time it took to feed the baby. When he came out, he stopped in front of the car, watching her patting the baby's back. The baby whimpered.

She began crying.

The man lowered his glasses to see better. He hitched his trousers up, scratched his balls. He spat. Then he walked away, out into the main street. From back there, she heard a car pull up, a door slam, the car pull away fast.

Little Tonks had told her it happened like this. He'd said, 'When they come for you, they do your legs first. Then your hands. Then your eardrums.'

Little Tonks just like a baby himself, no better or worse.

She sat in the car, rocking herself and Tonks' little girl, crying. There was nowhere else for her to go.

Haines got up at five, jogged three miles through sunlit streets, drank a litre of water, was at her desk by seven-thirty. When Bill Downey put his head round the door, she passed him another three pages on Sergeant Michael Jason. It was a mix of notes from social workers when Jason had joined the army, aged seventeen, and a report by an army psychologist ten years later.

Downey read it, standing in the doorway. Then he said, 'You think this is true? He had some kind of relationship with his own aunt?'

'Well, there was a scandal on the officers' selection course. He had a few drinks and started talking about her. He subsequently left the programme.'

Downey grinned. 'Good. If we've got a problem with him, and I'm not saying we have, we'll come out with this. His aunt is still around, is she?'

'He still names her as next of kin.'

Downey nodded. 'That'll help. The perception will be, we took him in, trained him, gave him a lifeline out of all that. We entrusted him with important work, even on Poppy Crush. But he's dysfunctional. He snapped, did this thing to the girl in the hotel. Regrettable, but he pays the price, we all move on.' He paused. 'Why the face?'

She said, 'He's a serving British soldier. These are just allegations.'

'I said, *if* there's a problem. But the Belgian girl won't go away, and there's this reference to further disclosures. What the hell is that going to be? We've got this anti-war thing brewing up at Waterton, we have to look clean.'

'But we don't want to be accused of betraying our own troops, throwing them to the dogs.'

He scowled, thinking it through. 'So what do you suggest?'

'He's due to land at Brize today. I want him picked up, securely but discreetly, taken somewhere safe and interviewed very carefully.'

Bill Downey nodded. 'You're right. Secure, careful, discreet. Who are you going to send to pick him up? It'll have to be someone good. Someone who understands this politically, understands the delicacy of it.'

Haines looked through the notes on Jason. She pointed to a name. 'That's the man for the job.'

Major Ward tried to put out of his mind the image of Stef Maguire in his bed. The way her hands curled up against the wall, her breathing mixing with the sound of traffic.

Is this wrong, what I'm doing?

He rubbed his eyes.

OK. He opened his computer, began following up his thought of the previous night.

As an RMP officer, he had limited access to the civilian police databases. He used it to take a look at Tom and Cathleen Fletcher. What interested him was their travel arrangements.

Tom Fletcher hadn't been out of the country for some years. His wife, though – Ward flipped down through the log of where she'd been. Three visits to Thailand, one to India in the past four years. Before that, a journey to Crete in the Mediterranean. All short trips – a week or ten days. Economy class. No excess baggage.

He looked at the details of who else had been on those flights.

He cracked his knuckles, thinking about it. Considered requesting further access to the civilian databases, going through to the civilian police.

The phone rang. Team Defence, direct from Whitehall. And after a few seconds, he made Cathleen Fletcher a much lower priority.

Stef Maguire worked a normal day. She interviewed two soldiers found scrapping behind the other ranks' mess hall. One of them curled his lip at her and she put him in a cell. Not a bad kid, she thought. Don't want to stop him shipping out with his mates. She went into a meeting with civilian police regarding the following day, Saturday. The troops would be bussed out progressively during the day, and more anti-war demonstrators were gathering outside the gates. There was a concern that they would cut the perimeter wire.

'Quakers, they're the worst,' said a civilian cop.

Back in the RMP post, glanced through Ward's door. He was on the phone, one hand cupped over his eyes, speaking. She walked back past twenty minutes later, saw he was off the phone. She slipped in and closed the door behind her. He looked up and smiled.

'How's your normal day, Stef?'

'I'm a bit sore.'

'Angry?'

'No, sore. I like it.'

He smiled, sunlight in his eyes. 'I've never met anyone like you.'

'This paranoid?'

'This passionate.'

'Steady, boy.' Silence. 'What's the matter?'

'Stef, something significant is going on.

I've been talking to Team Defence on the phone for half an hour.'

'This is about my ideas on Dan Simmons?'

'Not exactly.'

'You are working on that?'

'I said I'd take it on, and I am.' He looked at the phone and frowned. 'Are you OK for tonight? Because I could have a lot to tell you.'

Fletcher pulled up in the almost empty car park of the Sung food depot, the business with the half per cent pilferage rate. Its oriental canopy gleamed red and gold in the morning light, but it cast a shadow as he walked in through the doors. The woman at the desk saw him and reached for the phone.

A minute later, he was back in the concrete room with the shrink-wrapped chickens and the compactor and the two recipe women with their knives. And Kim Sung too – wearing a silky blue suit, white shirt, black tie. Kim Sung polishing his sunglasses, his dental work glinting.

'I told you not to come back here.'

'Don't waste another chicken. People in the world are hungry.'

'People are stupid, too.'

'I need to know something and I think you can tell me.' Silence. 'I said, I need to know something.'

'About oriental food?'

'Not exactly.'

'Then what?'

'A small detail. You seem to be a man who pays great attention to detail. I think you probably research your competitors thoroughly.'

Kim Sung looked at him a long time before replying. 'It's a good practice. The economic environment is far from ideal, and the wholesale sector is highly competitive.'

'Sure. And I need to find Gary Neale.'

Kim Sung went on polishing his sunglasses.

'Who?'

'Gary Neale. I need to know where he is.'

'Neale? I don't know anyone by that name.'

'Gary Neale knows about you. He thinks you're biting into his market. He's worried.'

Sung popped his glasses on, adjusted his cuffs. 'Has he got a food business?'

'I doubt it.'

'Strange. And why do *you* want to find this person?'

Fletcher said, 'I want to stop him.'

Sung looked at him over his glasses, a puzzled frown, thinking something over. Then he said, 'I know nothing about this person. I can't help you.'

'Yes, you can.'

The buzzing of the crusher echoed around the room. Kim Sung nodded at the two food demonstrators, who took a step closer, licking their lips. Fletcher said, 'When I find Gary Neale, it'll be the worst day of his life. He may never recover.' Kim Sung stilled the two assistants with a hand. 'This is your chance to get to Gary. And then you'll never hear from me again.'

The buzz of the machine. One of the women rubbing a thumb on her blade.

A flash of Kim Sung's metalwork. 'You're very tense,' he said. 'Tense, on edge. That's bad for you. You should take a trip to the coast.'

'The coast?'

'It might relax you. I know of a place on the east coast called Tundean. Heard of it?'

Fletcher had. A small town in Suffolk – originally a fishing village, now a holiday home place. The beach huts – he'd read somewhere – were selling for thirty grand each a few years back.

'Tundean?'

'Very smart place, quality people, nice restaurants. Just outside, there's a prestige housing development. Oh, and just next to that, there's a marina. You like marinas? All those classy boats. The biggest boat there is a huge motor yacht. Enormous thing.' He grimaced. 'A bit vulgar, frankly.'

'Is that what I'm looking for? A boat?'

'The name of the boat is *Contigo*, but you'll know the one when you see it. That boat is big enough to live on. I suppose some people just prefer to live on the water.' He went to the door, turned. 'Yes, a trip to the coast is the thing for you. And if you come back in one piece, and you want some work, let me know.'

'Thanks, but I'm a farmer.'

The recipe women winked at each other.

Gary Neale leaned on the rail, listening to Zibby, his man in the white trousers and black jacket, talking about what happened in the Pro Gym. Zibby was saying, 'They'll have to dry that gym out. Or turn it into a swimming pool. For people who like swimming in piss. The gym boys all saw it.' Gary's expression didn't change. 'Eh, Gary?'

'Yes, that's good, Zibby. So that particular message gets around.'

'That's it,' Zibby confirmed. 'Nobody says any names.'

Gary loosened his shirt. He looked round – one of the girls was sprawled out beside them on the foredeck, in a neat red bikini, her thighs spread to the English channel, her hands behind her head. Her face was tilted to this side, and her eyes were closed. Completely out of it. She was nineteen, the way Gary liked them, from some crap town in Latvia. They wouldn't believe it back

245

there, if they saw her on a boat like this.

He'd slapped her in the morning, and there was a leak of blood from her cute nose, over her lip, down her chin.

Gary said, 'This Honey Man, Fletcher, where is he now?'

'I don't know, Gary. But the boys from the gym burned his beehives last night. He must have got the message. He's probably pissed off somewhere to hide.'

Gary Neale watched the girl, her nose-bleed getting worse. 'I've made a few calls about him. Did you know he's ex-police?'

'Him?'

'He's ex-copper. I spoke to someone in Cambridge. He fell out with them. They say he's unstable. He keeps it under control, but he's on a fuse. There's a story he killed someone, way back.'

'A story. You're not saying he'd come here? To us? He wouldn't have the bollocks.'

Gary laughed and got Zibby by the neck, swung him around, threw him back on the railings so he had to hang on, laughing too. Gary said, 'Organic people, remember? Don't trust them. Everybody be ready in case.'

'You want extra people?'

'Get Tony and Steve, they're good. Just for a couple of days. If he comes out here, that's perfect. The sea's a big place. He'll just disappear.'

When Zibby left, Gary went and crouched on the decking, next to the sleeping girl, so deeply gone she couldn't feel the blood trickling from her nose to her chin, onto her throat now, into the swell between her breasts. If he left her here like this, she'd be covered in blood in half an hour. He reached out and brushed her hair with his fingers, thinking. Her nipples stood up and he rubbed them with his thumb, turning things over in his mind.

He couldn't lose, either way. If Tom Fletcher turned up at the boat, Zibby and friends would cut him to pieces. Even if he got away somehow, there was someone in the army who would take care of the problem.

If the army couldn't kill people, who could?

The girl was completely unconscious, the blood making spider patterns in her cleavage. Gary couldn't take his eyes off the blood.

The Odeon again. Coming back more and more. The way her hands scrabbled, then went still. All because she laughed at him.

Gary Neale stood and spat in the sea. He went downstairs. The two other girls were on the divan, playing cards for matchsticks. He whistled to one of them and pointed at the bedroom. She checked her last card, raised an eyebrow at the other girl, then walked over, unhooking her top.

Up on the deck, the girl in the red bikini opened her eyes.

Gary Neale closed the cabin door. He stood the girl against the wall. Half close your eyes, it could be the alley again, the closed-in space, the same thin girl right in front of you. He slapped her hard, and she hung her head, hand on her mouth. He slammed her back against the wall, put his hands around her throat. Her eyes were big and green, watching the sea through the window. He slid his hands off her, ran his palms down her shoulders, slid down on his knees in front of her.

He said, 'I'm sorry.'

She stroked his cropped hair, still watching the sea, trying not to yawn.

Jason woke with sunlight streaming under the window blind. Plane noise, vibration, stale air. He had a hard-on that really hurt. The girl soldier's tunic was hanging next to his, but the girl herself wasn't around. He checked his watch: five hours into a ten-hour flight. He lifted the blind slightly. He saw a small grey aircraft, flying parallel – looked like a fighter. An escort? Below that, down on the surface, a coastal city clear enough to see oil tankers in the docks.

The plane was lower than it should be.

What's going on?

He walked past the rows of sleeping troops, making for the rear toilets. In the galley, the girl was chatting to one of her mates. They both shut up and looked round at him as he passed.

What was that about?

He joined the queue for the cubicles. She came and stood next to him.

'What's the story, morning glory?'

'Hi.'

'You were well asleep there, Sergeant.'

'Knackered.'

'You were well asleep.' She took a swig from a water bottle. 'Do you know you talk in your sleep? You kept me awake, Sergeant, telling me all about yourself.' She winked.

He slammed the cubicle door shut, looked at himself in the mirror. He thought, *She's bullshitting. I didn't say anything. I did not say a thing.*

The plane lurched, changing direction.

About what, anyway? Auntie? Or my Lacon box? That'll be nice and chilled right now, no worries there.

Then the tannoy thumped and crackled. An officer's voice, the same whining he'd been hearing for fifteen years. 'A problem with the engines on this old crate–' he really said that. *Crate.* Talking about an un-scheduled stop for maintenance. In Turkey. Engines off, no aircon.

'Going to be a hot wait, I'm afraid. Get back to you soon, guys.'

Jason punched the mirror.

Friday Afternoon

Fletcher waited until the twins woke up, because he wanted to see them before he left. He played with them for a while in the back garden, he and Evie chasing Sally and Cathleen.

He kissed Cathleen. She moved her head away, her arms folded on her chest. Then she held him back and kissed his face.

Driving away, he paused and looked back. Nobody at the windows, of course.

He took the Land Rover out onto the road from Cambridge heading east to the Suffolk coast. After the outskirts of the city, he passed whitewashed cottages bright in the sun, roadside trees, pylons in wheat fields. In a while, the farmland changed to wooded hills, some capped with old windmills. He didn't take in much of that – just the long straight tarmac, the wheel in his hands. Towards midday, the horizon flattened and took on the empty, lit-up feel of the coast. There was a sign to a sealife centre, then another sign to the old nuclear power station at Harkness further up the coast. Ten past twelve, he picked up the sign for Tundean.

He pulled up on a headland just before the

town, got out and looked around. The sea was a slick green in the hazy sunshine. Tundean itself began a few hundred metres away: a pebble beach with those thirty-grand beach huts, then the town itself. It had a promenade lined with restaurants, a high street packed with shops that would have mystified the fishermen who had lived there in the past. None of those inhabitants were left, he was sure. There was a line of council accommodation visible further inland, between scrappy fields. He guessed that was where the last of them were gathered, making a living by cleaning the homes and retail spaces of the people who had bought them out.

Tundean. Of all the places for Gary Neale to hide himself. But he could picture Gary Neale here: a seat at the oyster bar whenever he wanted, browsing the galleries, convincing himself he belonged with these people.

Fletcher drove down, and along the promenade. He passed seafood restaurants and delicatessens, their windows stacked with champagne. A glimpse of the high street: a rising alley of antique shops and galleries. At the end of the prom, a car park with rows of German-built cars, a Museum of Tundean, and a flagpole running the cross of Saint George. After that, the housing development that Kim Sung had described, on the hillside. Then he rounded the corner and saw the marina further on. He stopped.

The marina. Impressive, he had to admit.

It was built into a natural bay: a wide semicircle of rocks under tall cliffs, a waterfall spilling a line down between them. It had a radial system of timber quays arranged like the spokes of a half-wheel, about ten berths on each pier. It looked well-subscribed – most of the berths were taken. There were modern yachts, restored wooden sloops, a few big power cruisers.

The spoke of the wheel furthest away from him was different. It had only one boat, right at the end of the quay, as if the owner wanted space between his craft and everyone else. It was a massive cruiser – by far the biggest in the marina – its white hull towering over the timber platform, facing out to sea.

Fletcher took a look with the binoculars.

A prow straight off a jet fighter, the raked hull studded with blacked-out cabin windows. A sun deck forward, with a woman in a bikini leaning on the rail, smoking. He watched her. She took a last long drag, threw the end over the side, stood holding the rail with her head bowed. Bruises on her arms. He focused on the hull just below her.

Contigo.

Gary Neale's home from home.

He kept looking. There was a control room with a swept-back roof, a massive radar array, then an even bigger deck at the stern. Another young woman – this one in a towelling gown, playing cards at a table. Then at the stern, more blacked-out windows, a dinghy on a winch, a steel ladder leading down to the quay where a man with white trousers and a black jacket was sitting in a canvas chair, hands behind his head. Not asleep, though. Eyes open.

Where the pier met the wharf of the marina, there were two other men in leather jackets, despite the heat, hands in pockets.

He doubted if any of those men was Gary Neale – they looked like hired help.

But there were three of them.

He drove down and parked near the wharf, in the shadow of the massive cliffs. The waterfall was splashing onto the rocks, making little rainbows. He walked out into the sunshine of the marina itself. There was an office building which looked closed. He knocked softly, made a show of checking his watch. He stood in its shadow, noting the two guards on the far wharf, the white flanks of the *Contigo* behind them. The only path to it led straight along the wharf, a hundred metres of clear space before reaching them. That gave them plenty of time to notice him and react. And then the next guard – the white-trouser black-jacket man on the chair. Plus whoever was on the boat itself in addition to the girls in bikinis.

An impossible approach. But he had to get onto that boat.

He walked along to the nearest quay, where a few people on an old timber-hulled sloop were washing the decks and polishing brass.

He considered.

Warm breeze, smell of the sea, the splatter of the waterfall. Above all that, the sound of the boats: a repeated chime and clang of rigging in the wind. He knew if he got this wrong, that sound would be his death bell.

He walked away.

Back on the main road, just past the curve of the cliff, there was a clump of hawthorn growing against the hillside. He drove the Land Rover into it, breaking off branches, forcing the car into cover. Not very well hidden, but the best he could do – and at least this side of the cliff was in shadow from the Tundean hill.

He zipped his keys and phone into a rucksack and jogged across the road. He clambered over the rocks, down to the pebble beach. A sign said, *Danger! Do not swim.* He pulled his boots off and stashed them between two rocks. He rolled up his combat trousers, and the sleeves of his work shirt. Then he slung the rucksack on his back and waded into the water. It was almost transparent at first, but after a few steps, it darkened, and he felt the pebbles give way to flat, slimy plates that made him slip and fall into colder water. He struck out forward, righted himself, felt nothing below him. His head just out of the water, he could see a current ruffling the surface near the edge of the cliffs, just where he had to go to get around and back into the marina.

He swam out there, keeping as close to the rocks as he could. Looking up, he saw the cliffs rising over him, some gulls circling at the top. In a few seconds, he was at the apex of the rocks where they jutted into the sea. He could see the marina and the white shapes of the boats. Then a swell took him, lifted him slightly off course. He felt the current take his legs, then his torso. *Danger! Do not swim* was correct. He glimpsed the *Contigo* in the distance, right out on the edge of the marina, then lost it as the current began rolling him over, twisting him towards the open sea. He got a mouthful of brine before he could strike out with his arms, the weeks of swinging the axe coming through in the power he could bring to the stroke, putting all his back into swimming until he got closer to the rocks and held on to the nearest one, getting his breath, while he looked at the marina from this new angle.

The obvious approach now was across the water, a straight line across the semicircular bay. But the surface was lit up with afternoon sun, and anything moving across there would be noticed by the *Contigo*'s guards.

The only sure way was into the marina and under the radial system of quays.

He swam slowly around the last of the rocks, his head just above water, the cliffs blotting out the sky. In a minute he came to the edge of the main wharf and held on to one of the big wooden posts supporting the first pier overhead. The post was set in a concrete sleeve, the water around it rainbowed with oil. He was cold now, with an ache in his back and jaw, but he kept going, swimming quietly from one post to the next, aiming for the central point of the wheel and then beyond that, the final pier where the *Contigo* was moored.

Sunlight came down through gaps in the timber, but otherwise he was moving in shadow. When he came to the first moored boat, he could hear someone singing on deck. He kept going, holding each post for a second before moving on. That way, he got past the line of boats – the final one a massive gin palace, huge propellers visible below the surface. He just hoped they didn't start up. That boat was small, though, compared to the *Contigo*.

After that, he hit the central area of the wharf: a group of concrete columns with the quays fanning out around it. He swam between the columns, crabs waving claws close to his face. Sunlight came down in patches, the chime of rigging overhead. Then he was through the centre, facing the other side of the half-wheel, the quays lined with more boats.

All except that last, empty one. Running out into the bay at about twenty degrees from the wharf, the long pairs of posts were lit by late sunshine off the water. Empty, until the white shape of the *Contigo*'s stern.

The water slapped around him, cold and green. Seaweed trapped in the pier slats dripped onto his face. He realised it was late in the day now – the sun fading – going behind the headland, he thought. Out on the sea, a ferry had its lights burning.

Fletcher waited, looking up through the slats. The two guards were up there, the soles of their trainers visible – one man tapping his foot. A burst of laughter, a cigarette end spinning between the slats down into the water.

Would they see him?

Fletcher filled his lungs and slipped underwater, the concrete sleeves of the posts looming grey then fading past. He came up when his lungs were hurting, lifted his head as slowly as he could, breathed in. The guards were behind him, the white bulk of the *Contigo* maybe fifty metres away.

He swam on, seeing the stern get bigger beside the last of the posts. Twenty metres away, then ten.

Then the engines started.

There was a shudder that he felt through the water, settling down to a low rumble, and a cloud of vapour floated out from the stern. He swam through it, moving quickly up to the boat. He looked up through the quay slats – no sign of the seated guard. He moved quietly out on the seaward side of the boat, looking up at it. Lights were on in some of the slit windows, a navigation light blinking on the radar array. He could see someone up on deck, too: not one of the guards, but that slim girl in the white bikini, looking out to sea, then disappearing into the stateroom. The engines revved again, burning fuel off through the stern vents as they warmed up.

The *Contigo* was getting ready to travel.

He swam closer to the boat. The smooth hull was rising slightly in the evening swell, the grey light glinting off the chrome railings along the superstructure. If the thing began moving now, chances were the propellers would catch him. Even if he avoided them – he would lose this chance to get to Gary Neale. The only way up onto the boat was a steel ladder running from just above the water up to the rear deck – but if he went clambering up there, he'd be seen by people on the boat. He looked up at the ladder. About halfway up, one of the windows was part open, a reddish light coming from inside. He would never get through there, he knew.

The engines revved again, the water pummelling his legs.

Try it anyway.

He climbed onto the ladder, his arms shaking with cold. Eight rungs up to the window – music coming from inside, over the engine noise. Without stopping, he ducked his head into the window, pushed it as far open as it would go, got his shoulders in. Pushing off the ladder, he got his chest through, overbalanced and fell right in, his rucksack catching on the window handle and tearing. He hit the floor, rolled over and got his breath. He lifted the rucksack clear.

He crouched on his haunches, water everywhere, and looked around.

A bedroom. Not luxurious, but something like a crew room, at the noisy end over the engines. There was a single bed with a crumpled duvet, a dresser and a wardrobe. A closed door – to the main boat, he guessed, and another door which was half open, light coming through. Sound of running water from in there, and a shadow moving.

He was spreading water all over the floor, his clothes sloshing even as he stood up. His eyes stung and his arms ached. But before he could get to the main door, the bathroom opened and a woman appeared in the doorway.

They stood looking at each other. She was barely twenty, he thought, with stringy blonde hair and hoop earrings. Wearing a towelling robe that was hanging open. Under that, she was naked – slim breasts, dark nipples, a tattoo of a fish on her navel, her bush clippered into a thin line. She had a joint in one hand, its sour smoke filling the cabin. She took a drag and held it in, staring at the water on the floor. He had no idea what to do if she started yelling. But she just breathed out, dilated eyes looking him up and down.

She gave a big, pretty grin. She said, 'It's a dolphin.'

'I'm not–'

'Not you. My tattoo. It's a dolphin. You were looking.' No attempt to close her gown.

'I mean, I'm not going to hurt you.'

'I know. You're the Honey Man. Gary was afraid of you coming here. That's why I left the window open.'

He said, 'And who are you?'

'Elsa.'

'Is Gary on the boat now, Elsa?'

'I think he's on the front deck.'

'Who else is here?'

'Zibby, the guard.'

'White trousers, black jacket?'

She nodded. 'And three of us, the girls.'

'You work here?'

She nodded slowly. He noticed bruises on her ribcage. She closed her robe suddenly.

'We don't fuck Gary, if that's what you think. He slaps us and begs for forgiveness.'

'I see.'

'So what are you going to do to him?'

'It depends what he says to me.' He went to the door, his clothes creaking with water. He listened. He could hear male voices talking from somewhere, the engine noise changing in rhythm, becoming faster. Then a metallic clang – a ramp being moved aside? 'Elsa, what about the other two guards?'

'They stay on the marina. This is the perfect time.'

He was starting to appreciate Elsa. He could hear the engines rising in pitch, the floor vibrating. Another shout from outside, then the engines really opened up and the boat began moving. The girl gripped the bed as the boat tilted sideways, angling out to sea, the cliffs slipping past the window, then a view of the whole marina as the boat righted and picked up speed.

He said, 'Where's it going?'

'Gary likes a trip at sunset. We go up the coast to the power station.'

'The nuclear power station? What the hell for?'

She shrugged. 'Gary likes seeing it.'

He put a hand on the door handle.

She said, 'Take your clothes off.'

'I have to find Gary.'

'Zibby will see the water on the floor. And it makes a noise, they'll hear you. Wait.'

She brushed past him, through the door. He glimpsed a stairway outside, evening light coming down from the deck, clouds and gulls overhead.

Did he trust her?

She reappeared, holding a bunch of clothes in dry-cleaner wrapping, threw them all on the bed.

'Gary's clothes. I'll keep Zibby busy.' She turned to go, then turned back. She took a big puff on the joint. Then she grabbed him by his wet collar and pushed her mouth against his.

Her lips were hard and wet, and he got a lungful of smoke that raced behind his eyes. He pulled away and she smiled, wiping her mouth. Then she left.

Something about that girl.

He threw his wet clothes out of the window and rubbed down with a towel from the dresser. The plastic wrapping contained a pinstriped suit and various shirts. Putting the trousers on, he found Gary was as tall as him, but wider. A black polo shirt bunched up on his arms. No shoes. In bare feet, he opened the door slowly. The stairway and the sky. His head still buzzing from Elsa's smoky kiss, wearing the fresh clothes of a psychopath, he climbed up the lurching stairs.

At the top, he raised his head out of the hatch, got a lungful of clean air and a good view of the rear deck. Glossy floorboards, railings against the evening sky, the huge radar dish above the pilot's cabin. Black jacket/white trouser man – Zibby – was in there at the controls, Elsa and two other girls grouped around him, taking an interest in the dials. It looked like a posed photo for a swimwear ad – except for the cuts and bruises. Beyond them, there were open doors to the main cabin, a kind of stateroom, warm lights inside. That was the way through to Gary Neale, if he really was on the forward deck.

Fletcher saw one of the girls put her arm around Zibby. Elsa leaned close to him too, her robe falling open. Fletcher walked straight up onto the deck.

The wind and light hit him. He walked quickly, feet silent on the boards. It was sunset, with layers of red cloud massing over the shoreline and the slate-colour sea tipped with mauve. Overhead, vapour trails breaking up pink and orange. Five paces.

He saw Zibby start to turn his head.

One more pace, and he was through the doors and inside the stateroom.

He felt the floor lift as the boat ploughed through waves, spray flashing past the slit windows. He kept going, across the room –

rubber flooring, heavy rugs – and into a second cabin lined with blank plasma screens. Beyond that, steps led down to a triangular space right in the bow, which had a divan bed. So where was the forward deck? He stepped into the room and looked up. The ceiling was open in a massive sun-roof, reached by a ladder, showing an oblong of turquoise sky.

Fletcher took a long breath, put a hand on the ladder. Then he climbed up – the rungs sharp on his bare feet.

At first, he thought the deck was empty. Then he stepped out onto it.

The deck was shielded from the rest of the boat by the cabin wall. It was triangular, a wooden floor fitted with spotlights that threw columns of light up into the spray coming off the prow. There was a chrome railing with a walkie-talkie dangling on a strap. Leaning on the rail, facing the shore with his back to Fletcher, a big middle-aged man, wearing linen trousers, polo shirt, boating shoes. Cropped grey hair, roll of fat on the neck. Just standing there, watching the coast, bracing himself as the boat ploughed up and down. Beyond him, the sun had set over the cliffs, the beach a purple band under maroon clouds.

Fletcher stood watching him.

So he'd found him – the man who'd sent Tonks with a gun, driven his family into hiding, burned his beehives. He thought how easy it would be to throw him over the side – drop the whole problem into the sea, then go back and deal with Zibby, dock the boat, go home.

But Fletcher stood watching Gary Neale.

The man suddenly noticed something further along the coast, craned his neck to see it better.

Fletcher knew what he really wanted here. He wanted to know why.

What's worth this much pain?

He took a few steps, grabbed the little radio and threw it over the side. The man spun round, then recoiled back and hunched his shoulders, turned his face up with a snarl. Still holding the rail in one hand, the slip-stream flattening his short hair, spray whirling past him in the floorlights. His face wide and flat, a big nose and thin lips. Dark eyes.

He was two steps away.

Fletcher said, 'I'm the Honey Man.'

'Yeah? You're wearing my fucking trousers.'

On the shoreline behind him, the Harkness power station appeared on the headland: a perfect white dome like a hole punched in the sky. Zibby must have seen it too, because the engines slackened and the boat settled in the water, cruising more slowly.

Fletcher said, 'You're Guru.'

'I'm not saying a word to you, son.'

'Why are you doing this?'

Gary Neale looked at him. His snarl turned into a grin, then a laugh.

'Is that why you're here? To ask why?'

'Tell me.'

'Or what – throw me in the sea? You're no bigger than me, son. And Zibby will get me out. He's a champion swimmer, did you know that?'

'It'll be dark soon. He won't even see you.'

'Clever boy. You think you've won?' Gary spat over the side. 'You have no idea. You think you're in the shit now – wait and see what they hit you with.'

'Who?' No answer. 'Tell me, Neale. Or I'll throw you in there now.'

'Who? Who do you think? I'm the top man, but compared to them, I'm a fucking amateur. They're the professionals.'

Fletcher felt the hairs on his neck rising, nothing to do with the sea spray on his skin or the cold wind coming off the water. They were approaching the power station, a vein of lights blinking on the reactor dome.

'Who are you talking about?'

'The army. The British army, you stupid copper. Ex-copper.'

Gary turned and leaned on the rails, watching the reactor. The white disc formed its own eclipse against the sunset, gulls circling around it. 'See the dome there? That's a special kind of concrete, it'll survive earthquakes.'

'You are involved with the army?'

'You want to argue with them? Do you? Then you're a brave boy, Honey Man, because I wouldn't. I've done a lot of things, but I would not fuck about with them. You're finished. Hey–' Neale pointed to the reactor '–they're pumping out from the core. You can see the steam coming off the sea. What a sight.'

Fletcher glanced at the vapour coiling over the beach, back at Gary Neale.

'Someone in the army? Why?'

'Why?' Neale shouted. 'What does it matter why? You're a fucking nobody anyway.' He shrugged. 'The sun's gone. Back to the marina now. That's part of the fun, get back before it's really dark.'

The engines powered up again and the boat pushed forward, smacking a big gout of spray over the deck. Then it angled right, turning around in a wide sweep to head back along the coast to Tundean. Fletcher saw the reactor slip away behind Neale, replaced by the sea, grey sky above black, a tanker on the horizon with green lights.

He said, 'Afghanistan. That's it.'

'Piss off. You're annoying me now.'

'That's why you burned my beehives.'

'Then buy some more. When I put diesel in this boat, know how much it costs? To fill it up? Twenty grand. How much is a beehive? It's nothing.'

The *Contigo* finished its turn and swayed into a course parallel with the shore, returning south. The power station was receding behind Neale's other shoulder, still circled by gulls riding on the thermals of its floodlights. The boat accelerated, ploughing through the swell.

Fletcher said, 'That's why my family's in hiding.'

'Family? This is business.'

'My twins.'

'Oh, learn a lesson, son. What's that? That there?' Neale pointed at the land. 'It's England, it's Britain, you stupid farm boy.' Shouting over the wind and the spray. 'You get it? This is what it looks like. It's a piece of vacant land in the fucking North Atlantic. Only question is, who owns it. *We* own it, me and my friends. You're a big boy and a big failure, Honey Man. You come up here wearing my clothes. You've failed.'

The boat was fighting the swell, bouncing and smacking on the water. Fletcher leaned back against the wall. Gary Neale put one foot up on the railing to steady himself, holding on with both hands. Then his right hand dropped to his ankle. Fletcher saw a smooth, hairless calf, socks. The hand came up with a blade, flicking it out, swinging it up.

Fletcher stepped back, but the knife caught him near the waist – a hollow feeling, but the real pain came in his neck as the linked-up nerves responded. Gary Neale raised his arm again.

Fletcher punched him in the face. A web of blood formed across Neale's cheek and then vanished, washed away in the slipstream. Neale looked surprised, but not shocked – as if the price of diesel had just gone up. Fletcher pulled himself upright, feeling the pain in his side. Then he brought his fist down on the top of Gary Neale's head. Neale crumpled and hissed. The knife flipped over the side like a fish thrown back.

Fletcher picked Neale up and rammed his head against the railing, then raised him again and slammed him down on the deck.

Neale lay there, not moving.

Fletcher crouched down, holding his own side. He could feel warm blood spreading down over his thigh. Neale's blood was pouring out of his mouth and nose, steaming on the floorlights. Their blood mixing, maybe.

Neale said something.

'What?'

Neale retched and shivered, hands trying to grab the rail for support.

'What?'

'Someone from the army is coming. He'll be here soon. He'll cut you to pieces. Then he'll find your crappy family.'

The boat was still racing at close to maxi-

270

mum speed, the shore becoming less empty, starting to flicker with light as they got closer to Tundean. One last cloud was left of the sunset. There was a star over the headland.

Fletcher carefully lifted Gary Neale's head. He said, 'Gary, tell me about the army man. Who is he?'

'He's a madman. He'll kill you all. You failure.'

'Who is he?'

Gary laughed.

Fletcher guessed he had five minutes before the *Contigo* reached the marina. Maybe less. He closed his eyes for a moment.

I can't do this.

Spray hit him in the face.

But I have to.

He broke Gary Neale's nose, then his left arm. Gary shook his head, didn't want to say anything. Fletcher was shaking, nauseous. He swallowed hard. He raised his bare foot and broke Gary's right leg below the knee – stamped straight through it and connected with the deck. Then he raised Gary's head in one hand.

'Tell me about the army. From the start.' Gary was dribbling vomit, veins bursting in his face. 'Come on.'

Gary said, 'They came to me last year. Off the record, but it was them. They wanted to know about the business. Import, distribution. Volumes I could shift.'

'And you told them?'

'They had stuff on me.'

'Why did they want to know?'

'It's an exercise.'

The boat slowed down a notch. 'An exercise?'

Gary was fading out. He was going into shock, his systems closing down. 'They said they were worried about soldiers smuggling gear back from abroad. They wanted to find out how they would do it, find ways to stop it.'

'What's this got to do with me?'

'Dan Simmons, the TV guy, he found out. He told you.'

'He told me nothing about any exercise.'

'It's not an exercise any more. It's out of control.'

Gary began curling into a ball, raising his hands to his chin. A linen-clad fetus soaked in blood and salt water, lit by halogen lights.

'Gary, who is it? Who's out of control?'

But Gary couldn't speak.

Fletcher straightened up. He was shaking. He was cold, true – the sea wind chilling the damp in his stolen clothes. He had a knife wound close to his kidney, he thought, was losing a certain amount of blood. And he'd just broken the bones of another man. But he knew that wasn't why he was shaking.

He thought he could come here and solve

the problem.

But an army exercise – that wasn't an exercise any more?

The problem wasn't solved, the danger wasn't past. Someone else was coming – someone from the army, worse than Gary, out of control.

Worse than Gary?

He tipped Gary Neale down the ladder. The big body crashed onto the floor and lay still. Fletcher rolled the sunroof shut. His main thought now was getting off the boat.

Friday Night

Fletcher stepped onto the walkway running alongside the hull. In the twilight, maybe Zibby would mistake him for Gary. He tried to see into the pilot's cabin at the rear, but it was dark in there. He made his way along the side, gripping the railing, bare feet smacking the wet surface. Through the side windows, he could see the blinds were pulled down in the two main rooms. He came level with the control cabin, looked around the corner.

No Zibby.

Just Elsa again, steering the boat level with the coast, her hair flecked with spray smacking up off the sea. Wearing a long leather jacket now. Jeans, trainers. She glanced over at him and smiled, then looked back at the sea ahead.

Fletcher shouted, 'Where's Zibby?'

She pointed over the side.

'What if he swims ashore?'

'He can't swim.'

'He's a champion swimmer.'

'Not now. We broke his arms.' She laughed, as if they'd broken his sunglasses. 'And Gary?'

'He's very sick.'

'Good.'

Fletcher was thinking through the next few hours: he had to get back to Tundean, retrieve his car, get back home – and then what?

Find someone in the army he could trust. Stef Maguire and Major Ward?

He said, 'I have to get back to the marina.'

'Wait a bit, Honey Man. Not such a rush.'

She pointed into the stateroom. He went over and stood in the doorway.

The floor rug was pulled aside, and the two other girls – dressed in jeans and jumpers now, and looking like off-duty models – were crouched over something on the floor. The redhead was twisting a dial set into a metal door. A safe. The stringy blonde reached over and gave it a final turn. She opened the safe smoothly.

Fletcher said, 'Why didn't you do this before?'

The redhead looked up. 'We're just silly girls, yeah?'

'How do you know the combination?'

'Zibby told us.' She winked and wiped her nose with her sleeve. She pulled out the safe's contents: two Glock handguns; five shrink-wrapped packets the size of bricks. She held them up: cash – smart red fifties. Half a million? Or a million? Also a wad of passports in an elastic band. She opened one, held up Gary's photo. The girls laughed and took the cash.

Out on deck, Elsa had slowed the boat right down. The shape of the headland was faint in the dusk. The boat itself would be virtually invisible from land by now.

He said, 'Thanks, Elsa.'

'It's OK. I like you.'

'Now take the boat southwest, you'll reach France or Spain.'

Elsa pointed at the English coast, said, 'Land of opportunity.'

He could see what she meant. Three women like this, all that cash, an economy in need of short-term liquidity.

He said, 'Just leave me at the marina.'

'Nuh-huh.'

The engines went down to a low rumble, just enough power to keep the boat straight. Elsa flipped off the navigation lights. The wind off the sea whistled over the railings.

He was aware of the three girls turning to look at him, their hair blowing out. There was a long pause. Then the redhead said, 'We needed someone like you.' She flexed her long fingers. 'You've been very useful.'

'We've, er, helped each other.'

'Yes. But you know what happens now.'

Nobody spoke. He could smell sweat, sun cream and cannabis. He could see their eyes in the glow of the instruments. He saw Elsa lick salt spray off her lips. He could see the redhead's nipples were hard. The blonde scratched her crotch thoughtfully. Then she turned to the wall beside the controls and unbuckled a fire axe that was mounted there and slid its cover off. She held the axe in both hands, running a thumb along the blade.

His heart thumped.

She said, 'Now you sink this stupid boat.'

She handed him the axe.

He breathed out.

The lower cabin had carpet over a fibreglass floor. In the centre there was a hatch. He lifted it and looked in. Striplights showed a space barely a metre and a half high: the inside of the hull itself. He lowered himself down, taking the fire axe with him.

So how do you sink a boat?

He crawled to the end of the space, found a wall with the stencilled warning *Air chamber. Do not pierce.* He smashed into it with the axe. The wound in his side stabbed in pain with the movement. But the other end of the crawl space had another air chamber, which he gave the same treatment. Then, under the hatch door, he swung the axe sideways, piercing the hull. Cold water spurted around him, but he kept hacking away at the fibreglass. When the water reached his knees, he dropped the axe and lifted himself back up to the cabin, the movement aggravating the knife wound again. He glanced down – water was flooding into the hold, over the air chambers. He went up the stairs, into the stateroom. The entire hull was starting to groan. The engines stopped, and an alarm sounded. He could hear the water behind him, rushing up into the cabin.

He found his rucksack in Elsa's room, and went up to the deck. The deck was empty, the crane for the dinghy gaping against the night sky. The boat was lower than he'd expected, the sea already over the engine vents, spuming vapour. Under the mist, the girls were braced in the dinghy, holding it off from the *Contigo* with oars.

The hull cracked and shrieked.

He made his way down the side ladder – the one he'd climbed up barely an hour ago – and made it into the dinghy. The pain from his wound became so bad, he lay down and just held on. He heard the outboard start. He shivered. From where he was lying, he could see the stern of the *Contigo* – what had been a massive white wall, now a thin band just above the water.

How deep was the sea here? A hundred metres? Deep enough to hide the *Contigo* and its contents for ever, he hoped.

He said, 'When we get to the beach, we all split up. We don't talk to each other again.'

He saw them exchange glances. He realised: *They think I'm slightly stupid.*

The engine opened up. The dinghy bounced a few times on the swell, then flattened down and made progress. Minutes passed with the whine of the propeller, the outline of the girls above him. Then waves began, and there were curses and shouted instructions. Another wave broke around them, and the dinghy lifted, almost capsized, then stabilised. Fletcher looked over the bow.

They were racing into the shallows. The motor cut, and they moved in on the last waves, crunching the shingle. He saw legs jumping out, felt the boat being dragged up the beach.

They left it up on the dunes. He heard their steps running away, the clink of the stones, then silence except for the sea on the shingle – like his own heartbeat. And a ferry klaxon.

He thought, *They think I'm slightly stupid, and they're right. Someone in the army was routing Afghan heroin through to Gary Neale, the Guru. Now he's coming to kill me and my family. And I might bleed to death here, tonight.*

He tried to raise himself, found the dinghy floor was slippery with blood. He looked up at the sky, the stars, an aircraft blinking.

He heard feet on the stones.

Footsteps passing, stopping. An outline against the stars.

Then someone got into the boat.

A smell of shampoo and cigarettes.

'Elsa?'

'I said I like you.'

She rummaged around in the dinghy, muttering, then kneeled beside him. She'd found the emergency kit. She balanced a torch, lifted his shirt, cleaned the wound and packed a wadding over it, wrapped a bandage around his trunk. Then she got in behind him, limbs wrapped around him, her mouth on the top of his head. She rolled the storm cover of the dinghy up over them both, and they lay there, shivering, until body heat calmed them.

She whispered, 'You want some of the money?'

'No, you have it.'

'What *do* you want?'

'I want to look after my kids.'

'That's a bit soppy.'

'I know. But it's what I want.'

She rolled on her back. 'You're a good man. I'm a good woman. I'm going to buy a place, you know? Somewhere I can live really peaceful.'

'Good luck.'

He tried to move, but couldn't. He closed his eyes. Sometime later, a klaxon sounded over the sea. He woke cold and his spine felt like wire. Elsa turned him over and put his face against her breasts, smoothing his hair. He heard her singing, in a low voice. He gave in, gratefully, and slept. He woke later, in the dark, saw her sitting on the edge of the dinghy, smoking, her joint sparking against the stars. She turned her face to him, then looked back at the sky.

When he woke again, before dawn, she was gone.

Cathleen stood on the decking at the back of Annabel's house, watching the trees buck in the wind coming off the farmland. She tried Fletcher's mobile again. It went to his voicemail – a few terse words in the voice she loved. She left another message, ended the call. A day of waiting, alone in this house, just the twins around her. She looked up at the bedroom window. They were in there now, asleep in their beds.

She thought of Fletcher the way she'd known him when they'd first met. He'd been a tall, slow-moving kid whose mother had just walked out on him, his father a morose drunk. All he wanted back then – and all he wanted now, she knew – was a real family around him, and a place to live that was their own.

She thought about phoning the police, telling them everything. How good that would feel, just to tell someone – apart from Annabel.

Her fingers moved over the phone pad, its screen lighting up.

She tried to find the opening words, a way

to explain what was going on.

She turned it off, went inside and bolted the door.

Major Ward lay on his side, looking at Stef Maguire. The bedroom door was open, and headlights from the main road crossed and recrossed her body, showing the pucker of her nipples, the panels of her torso. He watched her settling back, her hands behind her head, rubbing her face against her own arm muscles for a second, humming to herself. Then she looked at him.

'I didn't mean that to happen.'

He said, 'You sure?'

'I mean, before we talk about everything else going on.'

'Kind of hard to stop it, Stef.' He reached out and cupped her neck. The hollow of her throat was glinting like an opened-up quartz stone. He said, 'If I ever get that hotel in France, will you come and stay?'

'Yes, for sure. You'll need a security consultant.'

'Good point,' he said, 'France is a dangerous place.'

'Lethal. You might need a whole series of visits.'

He said, 'I would truly love that.'

'You mean it?'

'Yes I do, Stef.'

She got up suddenly and climbed over

him, her legs for a second straddling his face, thigh tendons sliding with lights. He put a hand out and she slapped him. He breathed in pollen, her body, watched her walking out into the main room. He guessed the Victorian horse soldier on the wall out there had never seen anything like it – this tall woman swinging her ribcage past the horse, her breasts pointing at the open window, leaning to pluck a flower from the vase, turning back.

She slid onto the sheets beside him, gave him the flower. It smelled of dust and the main road. He took a book from the case near the bed and put the flower in between its covers, pressed it, placed it on the bedside table. He rolled on his back and put his arm around Stef, touching her collarbone under its tendons, kissing her face. He thought, *Someone needs to take care of this woman.* He lifted a loop of hair off her ear, curled it and tucked it back down.

She said, 'Come on then, what happened today with the Dan Simmons situation?'

He took a long breath. 'You're going to hate this. Or possibly love it. I don't know how I feel about it myself.'

'Try me out.'

'OK. I was looking at civilian databases, Tom Fletcher and his wife. Something's not right there. But I didn't get a chance to check it fully. Because this other thing blew up.'

'Team Defence on the phone?'

'It was Haines, that politician in uniform. Trying to pull my strings again, saying she needs someone who understands the politics. But she's got a real problem, it could affect all of us. Bad timing too.'

'To do with Dan Simmons?'

'God knows, I hope not. Put it this way, we've got a situation going on. I've been asked to help solve it in an effective but highly discreet way.'

She rolled off him, their skin sliding apart, and kneeled up on the bed.

'Eh?'

He poured a glass of wine from the chilled bottle on the floor, handed it to her.

'James, what is going on?' She was staring at him.

He said, 'Tomorrow, I need a detachment of good people for an assignment. Problem is, my current team. There's something I can't put my finger on. I can't rely on them.'

'You can rely on me.'

'I can't involve you.'

'So I'm stable enough to screw, but not to do army work? Send me.'

He thought about it. 'Well, there are two men from other units I can bring in, guys I trust from the past. Three of you should be enough.'

'To do what exactly?'

'To go to Brize Norton to pick someone

up, bring him straight here to me. He's on a TriStar from Afghanistan, but it's held up in Turkey right now.'

'Who is he?'

'Well, he's an RMP sergeant who worked for me on Operation Alloy, the gun smuggling op. At the time I thought he was very professional. There were some aspects to his behaviour which I probably should have picked up on, but that's hindsight. You see, after Op Alloy, I was asked to run one more operation, anti-smuggling again, but a different kind of smuggling. We called it Operation Cut Out. I had him in my team again, he performed well. But Team Defence gave me information today that's changed my mind about him. I think he might have gone off the rails.' He spoke slowly, running it through his own mind as much as speaking to her. 'Yes, I think he's out of control, but I'm not sure in what way. I just hope it's not connected to your theory about Dan Simmons. We've got to be so very careful how we handle this.'

She opened her mouth to speak. He put his finger to her lips, but she brushed it away. He liked the little snarl on her mouth.

She said, 'Give me those two men you can trust, and I'll bring him straight here.'

'OK. I'll tell the men to rendezvous with you en route. You all need to be armed.'

'Why – what's this sergeant supposed to

have done? And what the hell was Operation Cut Out?'

'Listen, Stef. I'll explain.'

The stop in Turkey went on for ever. It was a shared military-civilian base, holiday jets lumbering in and out, black-painted helicopters parked in a secure compound to the west. The TriStar made it to an engineering hangar and just stopped in the heat. Without air conditioning, the cabin heated up in a few minutes. The flight officer came on, told them not to use mobiles, but everybody did – rows of thumbs whipping over the keys, texting the delay.

Jason tried to call Guru, to see what was the latest with the Tom Fletcher situation.

No answer.

Problems?

They sat baking on the plane. The girl beside him looked asleep – but pretending, he thought. With the blind up, Jason could see the shadows of engineers working on the tail engines, and a few ground crew standing around, looking puzzled. He bet they'd never seen anything this old before.

After an hour, the crew opened the access doors to let food and water on board. Some cooler air blew in, then died away. Jason tried to estimate the temperature. Around forty? But the baggage hold would be far cooler. At least, he thought so. Not hot

286

enough to break down the PEC-PAK. Or was it?

Down on the runway, Jason noticed two black-uniformed police. Berets and dark glasses, Turkish cop cool, just standing there looking up at the plane. A van pulled up. Another black uniform climbed out. With a dog on a leash.

Jason leaned forward – his shirt sticking to the seat. He raised the blind a little. The dog down there wasn't a guard Alsatian or Doberman. It was a little beagle, ears cocked, tongue wagging.

A sniffer dog.

He wiped his face with his sleeve. Crap luck. The engine, this airport, Turk cops with nothing to do except walk their stinking dog. He said, 'Fuck it.'

The girl reached past him and gently lowered the blind. 'You see the doggy? You like doggy?' She checked the seats behind – the occupants were near the open doors, trying to cool down. She whispered in his ear. 'Relax, Sergeant. I reckon it's a bomb dog. Just for sniffing explosives. You think they'll let it on here with us lot? Its brain will go bang.'

He thought maybe she was right.

'Thing is, Sergeant, why are you so nervous?'

'I don't like delays.'

'Nothing to do with your Lacon box.' She

leaned back and winked at him. 'Told you, you talk in your sleep. It's a sign of stress. By the way, who's Guru?'

'You don't know what you're–'

'Shh.' She touched his lips. 'We don't want people looking. Here's the deal for you. You've got five thousand dollars in your tunic.'

'You–'

'Hush, love. Give me the dollars, I say nothing. We get off this plane and wave goodbye.'

He thought about it, watching the cops playing with their dog, waggling its ears. The big thing now was just to get off the plane at Brize, find the Honey Man, fix him. This girl didn't matter. He said, 'OK. But not now. After baggage collection at Brize. There's a latrine in the corridor near the staff office. It's by a row of fire extinguishers. Meet me in there.'

She smiled and settled back, closed her eyes.

He watched her.

Women: proof again. Proof you can't trust them, no matter how pretty, how sweet. They all lie and thieve. The younger, the prettier, the worse they are. Of course, that's how it works.

There was only one in the world he could trust. And he was going to buy her the villa with the garden. Cool, green grass for her.

He felt his fifteen years' anger, the officers,

the humiliation at their hands, the way women treated him, his bad luck, everything starting to boil. Ready to spill out and burn.

Nothing, nobody, was going to stop him.

Saturday Morning

When there was enough light to show the tide was fully in, Fletcher started pulling the *Contigo*'s dinghy down to the water.

The pain made him lose balance, kept him on his knees for a minute. In the end, he got the dinghy there, ripped a hole in the side, floated it out, started the engine and pointed it towards Holland. The thing went out for fifty metres before it tipped over and went down tail first – not sunk, but waterlogged, just the nose breaking the surface. With luck, the tide would drag it out across the channel. Maybe, in the autumn storms, it would wash up on the beach again. Maybe not. But the *Contigo* and its contents would stay down there for ever.

He thought of Elsa, with enough money to live in peace now.

Something about that girl.

He turned away.

Red sun on the grey horizon. Gulls swooping over crab shells. Fletcher with a dull pain in his side that sharpened whenever he moved. But Elsa's bandage dressing stayed in place, and the shirt and trousers of a dead British gangster kept him warm as he walked along the coast road, onto the marina wharf, past the *Contigo*'s empty berth. He felt light-headed, his hearing acute. The sound of gulls, the chiming of the rigging. He realised that one sound was missing: the waterfall had stopped. As he rounded the corner under the cliffs, he heard it spluttering into action. It was man-made, he realised, running on a timer.

He picked up his boots from the rocks. In the Land Rover, he had a few seconds' silence, sliding them back on. He phoned the number of the Waterton RMP post. It rang out. He phoned Cathleen. She hadn't slept or been to bed.

'Tom, are we safe now?'

'Soon.'

Then he rammed the car out of the hawthorn thicket, slamming it back onto the road.

Tundean was deserted. The restaurants, the beach huts bright as pharmacy lozenges – Fletcher left them all behind, taking the long straight road back to Cambridgeshire.

He tried the RMP post a second and third time. In the end, Major Ward answered. Fletcher identified himself, asked, 'Where's Captain Maguire?'

'She's out on an assignment.'

'Then I'll talk to *you*. Someone in the army wants to kill me.'

A long pause. 'Who? And why?'

Fletcher took the Land Rover over a round-about, wheels screaming, other cars sliding away from him. 'Ever heard of someone called Gary Neale?'

'Oh Jesus.'

'He's got a friend in the army.'

'Gary Neale has a friend in the army?' Ward speaking slowly, a man thinking. 'I'm just putting – I mean, things are starting to come together in my mind. There is a person – God, this is horrific.'

'It is if you're me.'

'Fletcher, listen. The person I'm thinking of isn't even in the country yet. I've already sent a detachment to detain him when he arrives. There's no threat to you.'

'Really?'

'Yes. I think we'd better compare on this. It's a huge issue, I need your cooperation. I'll meet you. Are you at your house?'

'I'll be there in an hour.'

Fletcher drove at the highest speed the old Land Rover could make. He wanted to hear what Ward had to say, to be assured that whoever in the army had been working with Gary Neale was now out of circulation. He wanted to see Cathleen again, pick the twins up and spin them around in his arms.

Then – when everything was safe – he wanted a doctor to look at his wound.

He passed Cambridge in the distance – the block tower of the university library

292

glinting dull black in the sun – came onto the road heading out into the farmland. Sweat on his hands, sticking to the wheel. Sweat in his eyes, one lid trembling. Getting closer to home.

On the final road, just before the turning to his house, a raven swooped low over the road ahead, something hanging in its beak. Fletcher saw it was a baby rabbit. The little rabbit dropped free, and the raven soared away. No way to avoid it. There was a faint thump as the wheels crushed the animal. Fletcher glanced in the mirror. The rabbit was pulverised on the tarmac. And the crow had already settled on the red mess, pecking at the meat.

He powered on, and pulled up at the house in a spray of gravel. He expected Ward to be there, but the place was deserted. He checked the doors and windows. Before going inside, he walked around to the orchard and through the burned wreckage of his beehives. He went down to the cress pool. He breathed in the smell of cut wood, picked up some slivers and rubbed them between his fingers. He kneeled and ran his hands through the clean water.

Maybe the knife wound was making him ill, affecting his thinking. But he kept seeing the crow and the rabbit. Was it an accident? Or had the crow deliberately dropped its prey in front of the car – because it knew that was the best way to open up a victim?

Are crows that clever?

He shook his head clear. He scooped up some water and ran it over his face, and walked back to the house to wait for Ward.

Stef Maguire took an unmarked saloon past the peaceniks on the gate and drove west with the sun behind her. When she hit the M1 motorway, she stopped at the service station, where the two RMP men that Ward had called in would join her for the pick-up at Brize.

She waited in the car. She got a coffee and stretched her legs. The agreed time came and went, then another twenty minutes. She got out and stretched her legs again. Another ten minutes – and there was a danger now that crazy Sergeant Jason would be getting off the plane with nobody to detain him.

She phoned Ward – voicemail. She left a message – *Your reliable men didn't show – I'm going anyway*.

And she was looking forward to it. She had a baton under her seat and a 9 mm pistol in the door tray. She knew she could handle someone like Jason just fine.

Jason watched Europe below him, all those motorways and forests, then the Channel stacked up with container ships. And finally those pure white cliffs that always make your tired heart go *Fuck*.

Then RAF Brize Norton. Another seventies' leftover, peeling and faded. The first thing that greets you – the smell of the drains. Welcome home and thanks for risking your arse.

He lost the girl soldier at baggage reclaim, her gang of mates milling around her. He saw his Lacon box come through, let it go around the conveyor twice, to see if anyone took an interest. But everyone was focusing on their own kit, glad to be off that shitty plane. He stacked the box on a trolley with his kitbag and wheeled it out of the hall. He took the corridor to the staff area, past the fire extinguishers, into the little latrine half-way along.

The latrine smelled of piss, had a cubicle and a basin with rusty taps.

She was already there. Plus one of her mates, a spotty teenage squaddy. Jason had the feeling they'd just been snogging. He closed the door behind him and slid the bolt.

They all stood looking at each other. Jason pointed at the boy.

'You her boyfriend?'

'Yeah, Sergeant. And the price has gone up. Now it's ten thousand.'

So Jason broke the kid's jaw – at least he thought he must have, the crack it made. The kid crashed back through the cubicle, fell right in there, curled up on the floor with his legs sticking out. The girl put her knuckles in her mouth, staring at the boots.

Jason said, 'You're a nice girl.'

'Don't do anything.'

'It's OK.' He rubbed his hand for a while, looking at her. The kid in the cubicle gasped and twitched. 'You and me, we'll just forget it, eh?'

The girl smiled and nodded. She looked at the door.

He said, 'Wait.' Cupped his hand behind her head, got a good grip on the back of her neck. Soft, hot skin. She got the idea. She put her mouth up to his, lips open, a string of saliva. He smiled. She used her tongue. Her boyfriend groaned on the floor. She put her hand on Jason's crotch.

He nodded.

She levered his fly.

He got a grip on her hair and slammed her face down on the tap. He felt her cheekbone break. He lifted her up by the hair. Her eyes were rolled up blind, her mouth making silent words, like a gypsy woman he'd seen once at a fairground. He dropped her and she folded up, gagging.

He opened the door and backed out with his trolley. The last he saw of her, she was wedged under the basin.

He let the door slam.

He corrected his tunic. He adjusted his headgear and his bootlaces. Straightened his shoulders. Slewed the trolley around in a big arc and headed for the exit.

Outside, the light made him blink. Scores of people milling around, being met by others in uniform or by families. He waited, thinking, *They must have sent someone. They must have.* He called Guru again. Still no answer.

What's happened to the guy?

The crowd thinned out. A few metres away, he saw a female RMP captain in battle dress. She was built like the kind of woman who causes trouble in the armed forces. They looked at each other. He was aware of the box beside him. He saluted.

She acknowledged it. 'Sergeant Michael Jason?'

'Yes, Captain.'

'Any problems, Sergeant?'

'No, Captain. Someone's picking me up.'

'That's me. I have orders to take you home.'

The house was hot and silent, dust swirling in the light as Fletcher unpeeled the bandage over his stab wound. The cut was small, but it felt deep and the edges of the skin were grey. He put an adhesive bandage on it, wondering for a second where Elsa was by now. Safe and well, he hoped. Safe and rich.

He ate some bread and honey, drank a litre

of orange juice. Then he found a change of clothes: old work trousers and a denim shirt, baseball boots. He balled up Gary Neale's clothes and took them outside to the beehives, dropped them on the pile of charred wood. He threw on some petrol and watched them burn. As the fire died down, he felt nauseous. After Ward, go to hospital. Definitely. See a good Health Service doctor – maybe an Aussie, or one of the Russian kids they have now.

He closed his eyes for a second in the sunlight. He looked up and saw Ward.

The major was standing in the orchard, wearing a jogging suit, trainers, massaging his side. He was looking with interest at something Fletcher had almost forgotten was there: the little camera still taped to the apple tree. Ward looked at Fletcher and stopped massaging, raised a hand in greeting, walked over. Stared at Fletcher's appearance, the way he was standing.

'What the hell happened to you?'

'I'm OK. Tell me what's going on.'

Ward looked round at the apple tree. 'Why is there a camera back there?'

'This place is full of cameras. I take security seriously. So what's going on?'

Ward squinted in the glare, brushing a midge from his eyes. 'Look, I'm going to be completely open with you, because I'm asking for your discretion. We all need to handle this sensitively, given everything that's going on.'

'Don't stop there.'

Ward examined a piece of charred honeycomb, turned it over with his foot. 'OK. What you have to understand, Fletcher, is the level of threat that we face. Our people are overstretched, often exhausted. Some – a small minority – are completely pissed off with everything. They feel poorly equipped and underpaid, you've seen that in the news a hundred times. And they're out there in a country where the ability to make serious money is just a hand's reach away.'

'Heroin.'

'It's like putting hungry people in your orchard here, when the apples are ripe. Saying, *Don't touch the fruit.* You can't expect them not to touch the fruit. It's just inevitable. Some of our people at some point in time may start trying to source heroin direct from the Afghans, back to this country. We can't let that happen.'

'Tell me about a certain exercise. Is it out of control?'

Ward shook his head. 'I can't comment in detail. But exercises have taken place. We've done research that says, if a handful of our people took it into their heads to do this – how would they do it? Who would they need to link up with to distribute it? Now, I have to say that a certain member of my team, at the time a very effective soldier, was part of that.'

'Part of talking to Gary Neale? Who is this soldier?'

Ward seemed about to answer, then shook his head. 'I can't comment on individuals. But you've been in the police, you know how some individuals of that type – Neale's type – can be persuasive, seductive. Have you met Gary Neale, talked to him about this?'

'I'm not commenting on individuals. You're saying Neale persuaded him to do it for real?'

'As I stand here, I don't know. God knows what passed between them. Our man is rather–' he paused '–well, he's none too stable. Ultimately, I think Dan Simmons stumbled across this connection and the discussions they had.'

'And what happened to Dan Simmons exactly?'

'That's the next stage for me. To be sure what really did happen. The MOD will hate me for this. But look, the man I'm talking about couldn't have killed Dan Simmons. He's been out of the country.'

'Where exactly?'

'Afghanistan.'

'That says it all. Now he's coming back to try to kill me and my family.'

'No danger of that.' Ward kicked a piece of

300

wood. 'Look, I sent a team of people to detain him, straight off the plane, bring him here under guard, where I can find out exactly what's going on. And I'll take the investigation on from there.'

Fletcher listened to the tall grass. 'Bring him *here*? To the barracks?'

'Yes. He'll be in custody until we understand more. He'll be locked up, I can assure you of that. I'll personally keep you in touch with developments. Because, as you can imagine, I'm asking for your discretion here. This is an important time for us, a sensitive time. I don't want journalists sniffing around. And frankly, at the moment, I don't want the civilian police either. Can I count on your understanding?'

Fletcher had a sudden image of Gary Neale's body curled on the floodlit deck, the *Contigo*'s hull slipping under the water.

'OK.'

'Thank you.' Ward was looking at him closely. 'Are you sure you're OK?'

Fletcher said, 'I need a drink of water.'

In the kitchen, he gulped a glass of cold water, looking out of the window. Ward seated at the table beside him. Fletcher said, 'When exactly will this man be in custody?' No answer. He drained the glass. 'When, Major?'

He turned. Ward was looking at a photo

on the wall. Mounted in a silver frame. It showed Fletcher starting work on the house two years ago, grinning, holding a sledge-hammer. His arm around Cathleen, who was smiling, her face up to the camera.

Ward sipped his water. 'Who's that?'

'My wife, Cathleen.'

'A great looking couple you make. This must have been terrible for her.'

'Her and the children.'

'Yes, of course. You're a family man, aren't you?' He flexed his shoulders and stood up. 'Well, I'll call you soon, let you know what's happening. I've got my best people assigned to this.'

Fletcher closed the front door, listened to Ward's car driving away. He went out to the back and sat on the kitchen step, against the kitchen door. The warmth of the wood calmed him. He watched butterflies flicker along the orchard.

Was the situation over?

Gary Neale had spoken about a madman. Now Fletcher knew it was some renegade soldier coming back from a war zone. Straight into custody.

Fletcher rested his head back against the door.

If this really was over, they could come back. Cathleen, Evie, Sally. He could start work again. Restore the hives, finish the cress pool. Dig out that last big tree stump, the old oak with the lightning damage. He smiled. Build a little playground here for the twins. Swings and a slide, they'd love that. Should have done that before now. He closed his eyes with the sun on his face. Smell of the burned wood. He heard a bee drone past, ravens calling, the movement of the elephant grass. All the sounds of home.

Major Ward drove out of Fletcher's gate, through the field of elephant grass, then pulled over. He put his hands over his head for a minute, his eyes closed, thinking back.

No, there was no mistake. He was right about what he'd just seen, what he'd just confirmed. He was absolutely right.

He slammed the wheel. Civilians. You cannot trust them. You cannot trust them.

He checked his phone. A text from Stef, estimating her arrival time back at Waterton. Two hours now.

He had two hours to sort this mess out.

He called into the RMP post. Told his staff to get a mobile phone number for him from the civilian police database. He dialled it.

The woman who answered sounded exhausted and defensive.

'This is Major Ward of the Military Police.'

'What – what do you want?'

'I need to come and see you urgently.' A

303

terse response. He said, 'No, don't hang up. And don't phone your husband either. This is something you might prefer your husband not to know about.' A long pause, audible breathing. 'Does that make sense now?'

Haines used the gym in the MOD building in Whitehall, did thirty hard minutes and then warmed down, showered, went into her office. She was expecting something from Major Ward to say that Sergeant Jason was securely in custody, but there was no message. She flexed her neck, feeling tension there.

Then she relaxed. Ward was smart, and he was on board with this. Everything would be under control.

Stef Maguire leaned back in her seat against the car door and looked at Sergeant Jason next to her. He was calm, flexing his shoulders like a man who's just been on a TriStar for twenty-four hours and now has a two-hour drive back to barracks. He had a sharp face, lines around the eyes, sweat across his shaved head, now he'd removed his headgear. His kitbag and Lacon box were in the boot. She was interested in why a sergeant needed a box like that. As a precaution, she made him switch his phone off and stow it in the glove box – he grunted and rolled his eyes at that. But he was doing everything she told him to.

She said, 'Who were you expecting to meet you?'

'One of the boys, Captain. With all the delay, I didn't know who.'

'Well now I'm taking you to Waterton Barracks. Major Ward has a lot to ask you.'

'About what, Captain?'

'You realise you're famous, Jason? You've caused a lot of unwelcome publicity with your stay at the Palace Hotel.' He nodded slowly, looking out of the window. 'But the army wants this done quietly. So that's the way we'll do it. OK?'

'OK.' He wound the seat back and closed his eyes.

She watched him for a minute. He wasn't really sleeping, she thought. But she'd already texted Ward to confirm she had Jason, with an estimate of their arrival time at Waterton.

She drove out through security, onto the main road. There was a small group of demonstrators, waving placards with messages against *Poppy Crush*. She left them behind, settling the car on the road. She could smell Jason's body. Glancing over, she saw his profile. He opened his eyes.

He said, 'You're in Ward's team?'

'Yes.'

'How is he these days?'

'He's just fine.' She thought of his hands

305

on her thighs, put that out of her mind. 'And I hear you've done some work for him too.'

'Yeah, Operation Alloy, you've heard of that? Assessing ways of smuggling weapons.'

'Any good stories?'

He laughed. 'They thought they could hide stuff inside Warriors and Land Rovers. We found handguns, grenades. There was one guy, we opened up his Warrior, looked in the engine bay, there was a complete fucking mortar plus rounds. He was going to sell it in Birmingham.'

'Best place for it.'

'Yeah.'

'And then another operation, last year, correct?' He didn't answer, sliding his window down as the traffic bunched up into a long crawl. 'I said, isn't that correct?'

'Yeah, correct. Operation Cut Out. The same approach, looking at drugs. You can see why they wanted to test that out. You been in the Stan yourself?' She nodded, and he turned his head fully to look at her. 'Then you know. There's opium product everywhere. Half the time you're tripping over it, it's growing on trees.' He laughed. 'So the temptation's there for some of the boys. If they can get it through the system.'

The queue came to a halt, smell of car fumes over Jason's body smell.

'And what's the answer?'

'What answer?' He'd stopped calling her *Captain*, but she let it go. She wanted him to relax, keep this journey low-key.

'How does someone in the army get it through the system? Stuffed inside a vehicle? In the engine bay or what?'

He shrugged. 'We looked at it a few ways, did some simulations. Ward will tell you all about it. Basically, it can't be done. I mean, you could try, but the vehicle searches we put in after Alloy, you'd be caught. Put it in your kit, there's the sniffers. The dogs and the new sensor wands, you get stopped by a random check, nothing gets through that. We tried all the ways we could think of. A few times it got through, but not often.'

'You actually simulated it? With real heroin?'

'Same as the weapons simulation. If you don't simulate it, you don't know how they do it, you can't stop it. We'll probably simulate smuggling something else next. Magic carpets or something.' He yawned.

She said, 'Bad flight, eh?'

'Nightmare.'

'Where did you get the heroin from?'

'Little villages in the Stan. They've all got factories.'

'What happened to the stuff when it actually arrived back here?'

'We incinerated it.'

'Incinerated it? Where?'

'At Waterton Barracks. There's a secure incinerator. Woof, up in smoke. It's what the civilian police do with what they catch.'

'Did it always get incinerated? None got mislaid?'

'You're joking.' He drummed the dashboard, peering past the long line of cars.

'Is that *no*?'

'It's no, come on. Hey, we're moving now.' The queue thinned out and they picked up speed. 'Can I ask you something, Captain? Where are the others?'

'Other what?' she said.

'Other MPs. I mean, it's just you? Nobody else? To pick up the monster of the Palace Hotel?'

'You're not under arrest, Jason. We're having a cool drive to Waterton. I just hand you and your kit to Ward. Then you explain what happened in the Palace Hotel.'

'OK.'

He drummed his fingers on the dash, miming the cymbals, making the sounds. She noticed the way his mood could swing around rapidly. Ward was right, there was something out of control about him. She was glad she had that baton stashed under her seat and the 9 mm pistol under a cloth in her door pocket. Jason hit a final note, stilled the drums, turned to her. 'Something else I want to ask you. You heard of someone called Honey Man?'

308

She let the implications of that settle in her mind. She said, 'That's an interesting question, Jason. Why do you ask that?'

'Just a name I've heard.'

'It's new to me.'

She let her hand fall to the pistol in the door tray. She wanted this man out of the car, into an interview room at Waterton. She could manage this situation, though.

They crossed over the M1 motorway and she picked up speed, heading east. Waterton should be an hour now.

Jason said, 'Reason I ask is I just thought you might know who Honey Man is, where to find him. I'd like to meet him personally. Really I would.'

Fletcher opened his eyes. He blinked. There was a grey haze over the sun and the step was cooler. He'd been asleep for a few moments. He looked around. The grass was hissing in a new breeze, the apple trees bowing. He wiped his eyes.

He'd just been dreaming of that crow with the rabbit in its beak. Settling on the crushed remains, pecking.

Are crows really that clever?

Have they learned, by watching cars and rabbits, the best way to get what they want?

He pulled himself to his feet. He went into the kitchen, rifled through the cupboards for a box of painkillers. Took a handful with water and stuffed the rest in his pocket.

He was thinking of Major Ward examining the camera in the orchard. Massaging his side. He'd seen someone do that before, somewhere.

He dialled Cathleen's number. No answer.

He went out to the Land Rover, and started the engine. The morning was clouding over.

Saturday Midday

Sergeant Jason looked asleep again, but Stef Maguire believed that was another of his mood changes. They were making good speed, fields flashing past. She phoned ahead to Waterton, made sure the RMP post was expecting them. Suddenly, Jason said, 'I can explain.' Still with his eyes closed.

'What?'

'Everything I've done. I can explain.'

She said, 'Not now. Wait for Ward to interview you.'

'No, no.' He punched the dash suddenly. 'I can explain, about me. I want *you* to know.' He looked around. 'We're here now.'

'We're about half an hour from the barracks. Next turning.'

'No, we're *here*. Where it matters. I'll show you what matters.'

'What do you want to show me?'

'Where it all started. Don't you want to see that, Captain? Stay on this road.'

She thought about it. He was volatile, but he wanted to tell her something. She slowed for the exit to the Waterton road, then changed her mind and passed it.

He said, 'Thanks. Second on the left now.

It's narrow.'

She said, 'Jason, I'm armed. Try something on, I'll shoot your knees off.'

He nodded. 'That's what I expect from an officer.'

The road led into a dip, beet fields on either side, scrappy verges of marsh grass. At the end, there was a scrawled sign saying, *marows + spuds for sale.*

Behind that, a mud road leading to a house standing alone in a lettuce field. An irrigation spray near the road was laying mist across it, but she could make out a sagging roofline and a fenced garden with chicken coops.

She said, 'What's this?'

'My aunt's house. She's still here.' His eyes were clear and bright.

'Why are you showing me this?'

He craned forward to see past the spray. He whispered, 'Everything I've done is for her. I'm going to take her away from here.' He looked at her, his face changing, becoming defensive, like a bullied kid. 'I've done nothing wrong. I just wanted you to see why I've been working so hard. Pushing myself so hard. It's for her.' The only sound was the water spray, clicking as it turned. 'Come and meet her.'

'We need to get on, Jason.'

'Come and meet her.' He opened the door and slid out, circled around the front of the car and crouched down, feeling the lettuce leaves.

She thought, *Shit.*

She got out, leaving the door open. He was walking towards the house. No other human being within sight. Just the empty farm road, high clouds, the water spray.

She took the pistol and followed him.

She noticed the chicken coops looked empty.

At the house, she saw him open a gate and walk around to the back. She was a few seconds behind, walking around the side of the house past windows cloudy with grime and piles of rotten marrows. At the back, there was a garden of overgrown grass. Jason was kneeling in the centre, by a patch of dug-over earth.

She stood behind him, holding the pistol.

He said, 'She's never been to Spain. I just want to take her somewhere warm. Somewhere she can rest.'

Stef looked at the patch of earth.

'You're saying she's in there? She's dead?'

He stood up suddenly and turned. His fingers were black with earth and there were veins across his cropped head. He took a step towards her. She lifted the pistol and slid the hammer back with her thumb.

He said, 'No need for that. I just wanted to show you.'

She said, 'You've shown me. Now drive.'

Cathleen left her children at their nursery, saying she might not be back until late afternoon. She didn't know how long this was going to take, or what direction it would follow. She drove back to Annabel's house and went to the drinks cabinet under the massive TV screen, poured herself a vodka, drank it looking through the slatted blinds. The sky was full of moving clouds – shadow, then sun.

She had another vodka.

A red car pulled up at the kerb. She recognised the man who climbed out. Major Ward: his big, tanned face. He was in uniform, unhurried, taking time to straighten his tunic, put his cap under his arm. He looked tense, though: a big crease between his eyes as he walked to the front door.

She saw net curtains moving in the house opposite.

He rang the bell. He shook her hand, wiped his boots on the mat.

They sat in opposite chairs, Ward touching his fingers together. She was glad of those vodkas, the way it put a pane of glass between them. She thought she probably looked rough – but he didn't look great, his face sweating. He said, 'Look, Mrs Fletcher, you know your husband's been facing some difficulties–'

'You could say that–'

314

'Which started with the death of Dan Simmons at Waterton Barracks.'

She looked away, at the reflection of the two of them in the plasma screen – Ward just a big outline.

She said, 'What do you want?'

'Dan Simmons was an interesting man, wasn't he?'

'He was a nice enough guy.'

'He was interesting. He wanted to make a controversial film about heroin distribution.'

'If you say so.'

'Correct.' She watched him tap his fingertips together. Big tanned knuckles. 'He had some files on his laptop.'

'Why have you come here?'

'Before he died, Dan Simmons referred to your husband. Why?'

'I should never have let you in here.'

'But you did, because otherwise I'd have gone to ask your husband about this.' That silenced her. 'That's better. Now I realise there's been a disastrous misunderstanding. The real secret is yours, Mrs Fletcher, isn't it?'

She put her knuckle to her mouth and bit the skin. 'This is nothing to do with you.'

'It is now.' His voice was soft, but he was watching her closely, his eyes hard. 'You see, Mrs Fletcher, I took a good look at Dan Simmons' files. I thought something in there wasn't right. I also looked at your travel arrangements over the past few years, where you went and who with. That was certainly interesting. But it was only today, something clicked in my mind. Regarding Dan Simmons, and what he was talking about.'

'You bastard. Don't use this against me. Don't tell Tom.'

His outline in the screen was blurred by the edges of tears in her eyes.

He said, 'I think you'd better come with me.'

'You can't make me.'

'Of course I can't make you.'

'You have no jurisdiction. You're not the police.'

He shrugged. 'Obviously not. You can stay here if you wish. But you've got a lot of explaining to do. And you probably want to do that *before* your husband finds out. Am I right?'

Cathleen put her face in her hands. She didn't want him to see her cry. She'd come this far, done what she had. She saw herself in the past – like a figure in the plasma screen – making the decisions she had made. She looked up, wiped her eyes. He was watching her, expressionless.

She said, 'I love my husband. Don't tell him.'

Fletcher found the driveway of Annabel's

house empty, the new age garden filmed with dust. Inside, a note from Cathleen saying the twins were at the nursery, but nothing else. He tried her phone, but it was switched off.

At the nursery, he scooped the twins up and held them close to his chest for a long time, until they wriggled free and went back to playing in the sandpit.

He arranged with one of the staff to baby-sit the girls if he wasn't back when the nursery closed. In the Land Rover, he took another couple of painkillers, trying to think where Cathleen could be. Sand from the children's pit on his hands, grit between his teeth.

At Waterton, Stef Maguire took Jason straight from the car into the RMP post. She put him in an interview room and locked the door on him. She watched him through the glass: standing, hands behind his back, looking up at the window grille.

The task of digging up his garden – that was one for the civilian police. She went to find Ward.

She stopped and walked back two paces. Through the glass panel in the door of the next interview room, she could see a woman in civilian clothes.

Stef watched her for a few seconds. Jeans and a jersey. Long, coppery hair tied back. Hard to see her face, because she was seated, facing away from the door. Not just civilian clothes, Maguire thought, looking at her posture. *This woman is a civilian.*

The woman turned suddenly, looked Stef in the face. Shadows under her eyes, neck muscles rigid. The eyes unblinking, uncommunicating, then flicking away.

Stef walked back into the main area, saw Ward's office had the blinds drawn. She knocked and heard him shout, 'Yeah.'

She went in.

He looked up at her. 'Stef.'

'Don't sound so pleased.'

'I am pleased. I've just heard from my two reliable men. They crashed their car en route – fractures and concussion. I can't believe you handled Jason alone.'

'He's in room three.' She threw him the key – he caught it and smiled.

'Good going. I'll get started on him, then.'

From outside, the noise of trucks being loaded, moving equipment in readiness for Poppy Crush. Ward made for the door.

She asked, 'Who's the woman in room two?'

He stopped. 'Don't you recognise her?'

'No.'

'Think back to Dan Simmons' files. The girls.'

'The interview with the heroin addicts?'

'No, come on,' he said. 'The photos. The nude photos.'

'You're kidding.'

'No. I went to see Fletcher just now, to re-assure him. I saw a photo of his wife on the wall. It's been clicking away in my mind, because I'd seen her very briefly when we went there, remember? She's the naked one in the swimming pool. Wearing the hat and nothing else. It's Cathleen Fletcher. She doesn't deny it, by the way.'

She tried to remember the woman's face, under the hat. Maybe that *was* the woman in the interview room. 'But what's going on?'

'I think I've just resolved this whole situation. But we'll get round to her soon enough. First, our Sergeant Jason.'

'But what's she *doing* in here? She's a civilian.'

'I'll explain. After Sergeant Jason.'

'Whoa, hold on–' He was moving past her. She said, 'I'd like to be present at the interview with Jason.'

'No need.'

He was already out of the door.

Ward sat opposite Sergeant Jason, and studied him. The man looked tired, sweaty, on edge. Nothing wrong with that. His kitbag and a Lacon box were stacked in a corner.

Ward said, 'Well, Jason. I haven't seen you for a while.'

'What's up, sir?'

A pause. 'I hear you cooperated with

Captain Maguire.'

'She had a gun, sir.'

'You didn't expect that?'

'No.'

Ward switched on the old recording machine on the table, confirmed his identity and Jason's.

'Tell me about the Palace Hotel, the Belgian girl.'

He saw Jason's eyes widen, getting the story straight. 'I was en route back from the reconnaissance for Poppy Crush, sir. Still in civilian clothes. There was a girl in the hotel, we got talking. She was really pissed up. Later, I heard she fell out of a window.'

'She started talking in hospital. Said your name.'

'Like I said, I met her.'

'She said you threw her out of a window.'

'Don't know about that, sir.'

'Did you or did you not throw her out of a window?'

'No, sir.'

Ward saw him glance away for a moment. *He did it, the little shit. Violent, devious rat.* He said, 'That incident has caused unwelcome attention at a very sensitive time. And there are rumours about *further* revelations.' Jason didn't blink. 'Any idea what that means?'

'No idea, sir.'

'No idea at all?'

'No, sir.'

'And now there's something at Brize, too. A double assault in a latrine, two private soldiers who were on your flight.'

'Oh, that. I heard there was a fight in a latrine, sir. A boy-girl thing. Nothing to do with me. I might have been nearby.'

'Nothing's ever to do with you, is it? You're always just nearby.'

'Sir.'

Ward put his fingers together. 'So what's in your kit?'

Silence.

'Come on, Jason. We've worked well together in the past. Now I'm asking myself questions about you. About what you're really up to, who you're associating with. If there's anything in there, tell me now.'

He could see Jason thinking again. The lips almost moving, not quite. Looking at the voice recorder.

'Nothing in there, sir.'

'What if I examine your kit myself?'

Jason looked up at him, his eyes appealing. Like a dog, Ward suddenly thought. The farm boy with his perverted aunt.

'I think you need help, Sergeant. Counselling. You're a violent and reckless individual. Open your kit.'

The bag contained personal oddments, stinking clothes. The box had maps, photos, all legitimate. Ward looked at Jason, who glanced at the recorder again. Ward pulled open the foam lining. There was a package of some kind, sealed in thick plastic. He held Jason's eyes, gave him a look that said he knew exactly what it was. He said, 'You fucking idiot.'

Jason swallowed.

Ward went over to the microphone and said slowly, 'You idiot, your kit's a mess. But there's nothing in here that shouldn't be.'

Then he turned the recorder off.

Jason leaned back against the wall, closed his eyes. 'Thank you, sir. You're the only good officer I've had, sir. That really understands me.'

'Bullshit. We don't want this blowing up just as Poppy Crush starts. They'll crucify the whole army for that. And you were in my team, it'll rub off on me as well. Everyone wants this to go away. To be precise, they want *you* to go away. You are going away, aren't you?'

'Yes, sir. I'm going for Voluntary Release. I'm moving to Spain.'

'With your auntie?'

Jason's lip curled. 'Sir.'

'Don't do that with your mouth, you look like an animal. Now listen, we're going to incinerate this.'

Jason tried to smile. 'Yes, sir. You've been good to me, sir. You're the only one who has.'

Stef Maguire saw Ward walk past her office door. Sergeant Jason was behind him, his face blank, holding something in a bin liner. She went out and called, 'Sir.' Ward turned, an eyebrow raised.

She said, 'What about Cathleen Fletcher?'

'What about her?'

'She's a civilian. Under what process are we holding her?'

'We're not holding her. She's free to leave at any time. But she's ready to help us.'

'Help us with what?'

Jason just looked at the ceiling. Ward took a long breath, frustrated. 'I'm going to interview her.'

'About what? Having an affair with Dan Simmons?'

'Oh, come on. Do a simple sum. About the death of Dan Simmons.'

'The death of—'

'Isn't it obvious? We both knew the Team Defence line was too simple. You said yourself the death was suspicious. Cathleen Fletcher lives nearby, she has a secret to hide.'

She couldn't think what to say, except, 'This is crazy.'

'What did you say, Captain Maguire?'

Sounds of the trucks outside, shouts of men loading. Dust in the air. Ward's eyes that had seen her body spread for him, full of authority now.

'Sir, this is just crazy. She can't possibly have–'

'Dismiss.'

'And we need to bring in the civilian police–'

'Dismiss, Maguire.' A smug look on Jason's face. Ward lowered his voice. 'If you can't play an active part in this team, make yourself useful. Go and help load the trucks. If you don't mind getting your hands dirty.'

Ward and Jason walked out together.

She'd seen that a hundred times, of course. Two men siding with each other against her. The crude instinct coming through. She watched them walk away together along the tarmac, past the RMP buildings, Jason swinging that bin liner with something in it.

Yes, she'd been through that before.

But she'd never heard anything as wild as the idea that Cathleen Fletcher had got onto an army base and shot Dan Simmons because he had photos of her naked.

That made her think of last night again.

She closed her eyes.

When she opened them, the world looked different, with harder edges.

In the old incinerator building, Ward flicked the lamp switch. The overhead light cages made shadows across the brickwork. He slid the door bolt shut. Jason standing there with his bin liner.

'Go on, then, Jason. You know the drill.'

'Sir.'

He watched Jason go over to the furnace – a big steel carcass with a round door – and fire up the controls for the gas burners. The man was like a dog, he thought again. Servile, obedient – but resentful underneath that, always waiting for a chance to bite. The furnace clanked and groaned as it warmed up, Jason wiping his face as the heat spread through the room. He was twisting the bin liner in his hands, wringing it like a chicken's neck. Then he checked the furnace temperature on the gauge and put his hand near the iron door to feel the heat.

'I think it's ready, sir.'

'Do it, then.'

'Sir.'

Jason opened the door. The inside was lined with iron ribs, pulsing blue and red, blasting out heat. He threw the bin liner in there, and it puffed out for a moment. Then it vaporised. The block of heroin inside it was already burning, turning molten black, the flames going right through it. Total incineration.

Jason closed the furnace door. He looked close to tears.

Fletcher tried everywhere he could think of. Friends' houses, even the doctor's surgery. He tried her mobile for the tenth time. In the end, mid afternoon, he drove through the field of elephant grass back to their house.

He came and stood looking at it in the dusty sunlight. The blinds were down, and that made him think of Monday, when she'd been up at the window, smiling down at him, her hip against the frame.

He walked around to the back, into the orchard. He felt his head spin again, cramps shooting through his stomach. He held onto the nearest apple tree for a moment. It was the one with the camera he'd attached, the one that Major Ward had taken an interest in.

His mind went back to Ward in his track-suit, standing near the camera, flexing on his feet after a run. Massaging his side for a second. His right hand under his left arm, as if he'd pulled a muscle there.

The hand under the arm. Flexing, working the strained muscle.

Fletcher walked over to the wrecked bee-hives, looked back at the camera tree. He had to wipe sweat out of his eyes. He re-played the image in his mind. Ward's right hand, reaching under the left arm. He'd seen that before somewhere. A man reaching under his arm like that.

Ward looking round. *'Why is there a camera back there?'*

It had been Little Tonks, Fletcher realised.

Little Tonks in the car that night, reaching under his arm to slide away a gun in a holster.

In the stillness, Fletcher heard the grass rise and fall. He felt the hairs on his hands bristle.

Stef Maguire went up to a soldier who was using a sledgehammer to bang a signpost into the ground. The sign had arrows in opposite directions:

Hunstanton beach 60 miles. Afghanistan 3660 miles.

She told the man to have a break, then she threw his sledgehammer in the back of her car and drove out of the barracks, through a knot of peaceniks waving placards against Poppy Crush and chanting slogans. She left the noise behind, drove the mile to Major Ward's house. Took the hammer up the communal stairs.

The door gave out on the third blow, crashing onto the hallway floor. She trod over it, entered the flat and kicked open the bedroom door.

She stopped.

In the early morning, when she'd left on the assignment to Brize Norton, the room had been grey with light and smelled of their lovemaking. Now it smelled of Ward's deodorant, and the sunlight showed the dust stirred up by the door falling in. It was tidy, except for a pair of trainers on the floor. The bed was neatly made, pillows aligned, the duvet uncreased. On top of it, a grey jogging suit had been thrown there, the jacket on top of the trousers. She stood looking at it.

Yes, she'd left in the early morning, a last kiss in the hallway. Ward must have gone out somewhere, wearing this gear. He'd gone to reassure Tom Fletcher, he'd just told her that.

Then Ward had come back and changed in a hurry, and gone where? To bring in Cathleen Fletcher? Stef reached out and lifted the zipped edge of the jacket.

Inside was a leather shoulder holster, empty. Its straps tangled in the sleeves of the running suit. She picked it up and smelled it. Just leather, and Ward's sweat.

She threw it down. That could be explained. An RMP major from a barracks shipping out to Afghanistan. He goes jogging, carries a weapon for defence against terrorists.

Yes, that could be explained.

She looked under the bed, in the bedside cabinet.

She knocked over the litter bin, then kicked it against the wall. Its contents flew out – scraps of tissues, a condom box. The flower she'd given Ward the night before, her fingers still damp with sweat. Now ripped up, dumped in with the rubbish. She spread the pieces with her boot.

Why did you tear that up, Ward? Why did you put it in the trash?

She slammed open the wardrobe. A spare uniform, sweaters, trousers. A few storage boxes which she tipped out on the floor. Socks, boxers, ties and cufflinks. A filing cabinet with a simple lock. She went back to the hallway. An elderly neighbour was peering in, gawping at her uniform and the sledgehammer.

She said, 'Army business.'

She used the hammer on the filing cabinet. The lock flew off across the room and the top drawer slid open.

Lots of divorce stuff. Whole wads of solicitors' letters. Statements of liabilities, demands for settlement. Some other material about the purchase of a hotel in the Loire. She spread that out on the floor. Invoices from a French property broker. Commercial mortgages on the land and building – skimming through, she saw four hundred thousand, six hundred thousand Euros, another one for three hundred thousand.

So he'd already bought the place, it wasn't just a dream. It looked as if Ward was getting ready to retire young.

There was a photo gallery of the hotel attached to a letter. Grounds with a fishpond and an apple orchard. A garage with a collec-

tion of vintage cars, invoiced separately –
another two hundred thousand Euros. The
hotel itself a beautiful old mansion, a cob-
bled courtyard, *Hotel Etoile* above the door.
Geraniums. Turreted attic windows.

*Is that where I would have slept, Major? In a
cosy little attic, with you bending me over the
bed?*

The next letter had a demand for overdue
instalments on the mortgage. A three-page
letter from a French lawyer.

She heaped the documents together,
dumped them back in the cabinet and
slammed it shut, breathing hard, looking at
it. The hammer blow had moved the whole
cabinet sideways. Behind it, there was an
area of the wall cut out and sealed over. A
removable panel.

She punched it and got her fingers under
it. It came away to reveal a small cashbox.
Dust swirling around her, she broke that
open with the sledgehammer.

Nothing in it at all. Except a small cardboard box, the end taped over. She shook it.
Heavy clunking. She shook it out on the
carpet, stood looking down at it.

Bullets, 9 mm. Not the British army brass,
but a cheap silver alloy. Probably Croatian.

Last time she'd seen these, a spent one was
lying on the wet grass next to Dan Simmons.

In fact no, she corrected herself. Last time
she'd seen these, a box like this one was

tucked away in Dan Simmons' locker.

Guru. Who's Guru?

She put her hands on her thighs and retched, her stomach dry. Then she stood for a minute, sweat running down her face.

Thinking, *Paranoid?*

I should have been more paranoid, not less.

She turned and saw the ripped flower on the carpet. It hit her then. She knew why he'd thrown it away. The same reason he'd seemed surprised to see her when she walked into his office just now at the RMP post.

Because Ward wasn't expecting to see her again.

Two reliable men to go with her to Brize Norton – they didn't exist, did they? Ward had sent her to Jason alone. He'd been expecting Jason to take care of her. Would she have ended up in the garden, next to the aunt?

She picked the flower up and put it in her pocket. Put the Croatian bullets in the other pocket. Straightened her uniform. Picked up the sledgehammer and went to the door.

She stopped and turned around. She stood there looking at the duvet. Then she pulled it off the bed. She put her hands on the sheet, twisted it in her fingers, wrenched it up off the mattress. She put it to her face and inhaled it.

Fuck.

She could smell herself, her hair, her perfume, her own arousal, Ward's sweat and his semen too.

She dropped the sheet.

She kicked the vase of flowers off the dining table.

She trod over the shattered front door, expecting it to open downwards into hell.

The kind of hell that waits for screwed-up female captains if they're not very, very careful on this earth.

Jason waited half a minute, watching Ward standing over by the door. Sweat pouring off Ward's face, drumming his fingers on the wall. He looked stressed. Not surprising.

Jason went to the controls and turned off the gas. The furnace hushed, then made a single clang as the iron carcass cooled down.

Jason said, 'That was my property.'

Ward said, 'We have to destroy everything, you understand? Any possible evidence. Anything that connects to us.'

Jason said, 'What a fucking mess, Guru.'

'Don't call me that.'

'You called yourself that–'

'And don't get lippy with me,' Ward shouted, then calmed down. 'I've just saved your arse.'

'You saved your own arse.'

'Do not get above yourself, Jason. Do not get above yourself.'

The officer's voice: whining, nagging. Jason said, 'You took care of Simmons. Why didn't you just shoot Tom Fletcher?'

'I left him a sign, remember? I warned him to shut up. The next day, I met him, but Maguire was there. You think I should have shot her too?'

'You should have found some way to shut him up before now. I've spoken to you on the phone every day since Tuesday.'

Ward was looking fucking terrified now. He said, 'And every time, I got on to Gary Neale – that animal. Tried to get him to sort it out. His people made a mess of it, useless civilians. Then you told me *you* were going to do it.'

'I've been on a frigging TriStar. Why didn't *you* do it?'

'I went to see Fletcher just now, he had a hidden camera pointed at me. I only just noticed in time. You think I should have shot him on camera?'

'Well, I'm here now. Where is Fletcher?'

Ward just laughed, shaking his head.

Jason said, 'What's the matter with you?'

'He didn't know.'

'Bollocks.'

'Address me with some courtesy.'

'Bollocks, sir.'

'He didn't know about us. Simmons was talking about Fletcher's wife. Simmons had a relationship with her.'

'So what's the problem?'

'He didn't know about us, but he knows now. He knows about the army talking to Gary Neale.' Another big clang from the furnace. 'I tried to get through to Neale this morning. No answer. And I checked with the marina, his yacht is missing. The coast-guard are out looking for it.'

Jason wiped the sweat out of his eyes. 'Where's he gone? Abroad?'

'I don't know. But Fletcher's been some-where overnight. He's been in some kind of combat.'

'You think he *found* Gary Neale?'

'Possibly. And Maguire's a problem too. She's been sniffing.'

'You've been sniffing her, Major, am I right? That was clever.'

'It slowed her down for a day. Then I thought you'd take care of her on the way from Brize.'

'Is that what you thought? You can't get rid of her, but I will?'

'I told her about Cut Out, but she's suspi-cious, I know she is. And Fletcher could be phoning the civilian police now, or the media. We have to stop them both, we have to—'

'Stop your whining. Your *whining*.' Jason slapped his own head. 'I've had all your whining voices half my life, telling me what to do.'

'Yes, I'm telling you what to do.' Sweat

dripping off Ward's chin. 'You destroy everything now. All the relevant material, anything remaining. That means any remaining
supplies of this stuff. And destroy Tom
Fletcher–'

'And Maguire?'

'Yes, Sergeant. And Maguire.' No hesita-
tion at all.

'Just get them all together in one place –
invite them round? Where?'

'We have our safe place, don't we? Quiet
and secure. Anything could happen there.'

Jason said, 'Get Fletcher and Maguire to
the safe place? How?'

He looked into Ward's eyes. He saw the
panic passing, the old officer's look coming
back until Jason knew he wasn't on the
same level any more. He was the dog again,
the one who fetched things obediently.

Ward said, 'You take Maguire to the safe
place now. I'll make sure Fletcher arrives
there as well. Then you earn your keep. You
destroy everything.'

'Maguire I can do. I can do Maguire. But
Fletcher – how will you get him there?'

Ward reached for the door bolt.

'We have an asset, Jason.'

'Yeah?'

'Yeah, Sergeant. Think.'

'What?'

'What's still sitting in the interview room?
Fletcher's wife.'

Saturday Afternoon

Stef Maguire parked outside the MP post, noting that Ward's car had gone. She took the sledgehammer and dropped it next to the funny signpost. Then she picked it up again and finished hammering the thing into the turf. She hammered it a metre deep.

A few soldiers stopped to watch her, and there was some applause as she threw the hammer away and jumped up the steps into the post. Ward's office was empty, so were the interview rooms. No sign of him or Cathleen Fletcher.

She sat at her desk and composed a two-hundred-word email detailing what she knew. She addressed it to the Provost Marshall – the commander of the Royal Military Police – and Team Defence, and her own solicitor as a back-up.

She read it through. Then she sent it off like a missile.

Walking back out, she saw Sergeant Jason standing on the steps, bareheaded, his hands behind his back. He'd been watching and waiting for her, she could see that.

She came and stood next to him. He saluted. They stayed there watching the activity along the roadway in front of them: troops assembling along the path, their kitbags beside them, coaches arriving to pick them up. Some of the soldiers lounging, closing their eyes in the sun. Jason said, 'Hope they all come back safe, Captain.'

'Where's Ward?'

'He's gone off base.'

'Where's Cathleen Fletcher?'

'She's gone with him.'

'Where?'

'I'm sorry, Captain. He didn't say.'

She turned her head to see his profile. She could see veins on the side of his temple, bulging. His hair stubble damp with sweat. 'Are you stressed, Jason?'

'No, Captain.'

'Look at me, you piece of shit.'

Jason turned his face to her. 'No need for that.'

'I know what you and Ward are doing. I can restrain you right now if I want. You ever seen a man kicked in the balls really hard? I mean, really hard? It takes a week to walk again.'

'Thing to remember, Captain, is the major and me, we got a lot of friends on this base. People who understand us.'

A team of soldiers rose to their feet as another coach pulled in. A few looked over at the two MPs standing under the shade of the porch over the steps. A few raised hands to Jason, gave thumbs up. She saw Jason raise his right hand, holding it there a few seconds like a blessing as the troops began clambering aboard. She thought, *Jesus. What is going on in this place? I can't trust any of them.*

She breathed in. She eased the Browning pistol out of the back of her waistband. She nudged it against Jason's spine. He froze. She said, 'I think you're smuggling Afghan heroin into this barracks.'

'No way.'

'Ward's used you. You're just a mule.'

'Don't call me that.'

'What's he paid you? A few per cent?' She pressed the muzzle into his kidney. 'An hour, maybe two hours, this will all be out in the open. Just in time for Poppy Crush – fantastic. And you know what happens to you and Ward then? A public lynching. You will both be torn to bits.' He was silent, sweat glinting in his hair. 'But he's murdered someone, you haven't. If you behave now, I'll say you cooperated. I'll stand up and say you saw sense at the last moment. That sounds good in a court martial. Ward will come off a lot worse than you. About twenty years worse, Jason.' Sweat was pouring down his skull – and then she made a connection that explained a lot about Ward. 'And they'll shut him in prison with the same men he put away after Op Alloy. That's a death sentence.

He knows they'll kill him in there, and the army won't care, won't protect him. Think about that. How long do you really want to spend in there beside him, watching your back?'

Jason stood still for half a minute, his lips moving silently. Then he said, 'You will say I helped you?'

'Yes.'

'OK. It's true, he used me. He said it was a simulation, Operation Cut Out, and it was at first. Then he told me to bring in more and more. I can give you all the ways I did it, and the dates. And not just me, there were others too. We said it was a test, but we never incinerated the stuff. He kept it. He gave us cash. We called him Guru in conversation, never used his real name.'

'How much did you bring in?'

'A lot.'

'Where did it go?'

'There's a civilian called Gary Neale. His people picked it up from us, sold it through on to the streets.'

'You're saying you brought it on to the barracks? And these Neale people picked it up? I can't believe it.'

'Not the barracks, no. We drop it off at a safe place. A storage place we use. Then Neale's lot collect it from there. So we never see each other.'

'Where's Ward now?'

'He's there, in the safe place. Everything's there – that Cathleen Fletcher woman is there, and Tom Fletcher will be there, and Ward. Plus evidence of what he's done, maybe some of the Afghan product still around. You want all that? That's where everything is. I can give you the map reference. Then lock me in a cell.'

'Nice idea, but no. You're driving again.'

Fletcher was flagged down by a civilian policeman about a hundred metres before the main gate to Waterton Barracks. The policeman was the new kind of copper: trousers tucked into boots, unshaven, leather gloves. Behind him, the road was closed off with yellow tape, a line of cops in Day-Glo jackets holding back a rabble of demonstrators. Fletcher got out of the Land Rover. A chant hit him:

Poppy Crush
Not for us

Placards against the blue sky, jostling the police line. In the middle of the road, two elderly men kneeled with their hands clasped, signs around their necks:

Quakers for peace

Fletcher said to the unshaven cop, 'I need to get into the barracks.'

'That's not going to happen, is it?'

'I'm not involved in all this.'

'So go home.'

340

The crowd began baying suddenly – animal sounds, hissing and screeching. A coach was coming out of the barracks, the windows blacked out. As it came past, the demonstrators surged, the police staggering, then linking arms, holding them back. From somewhere a bottle hit the road, close to the Quakers. One of them reeled back, blood spurting down his face. A cameraman ran in close to get that: the blood pouring onto his white shirt.

The cop said, '*That's* the front page.'

Fletcher said, 'I've got to get in there.'

'Go home.'

'You have to understand–'

The cop swivelled on him.

'I order you to disperse and I have the power to detain you–' the voice was rushed, like a rosary '–for a period allowed by the Terrorism Act and thereafter by application to a court, you want the rest?'

'I'm just saying–'

'You want to be arrested?'

Another coach appeared. The police were ready this time, the protesters howling as they were held in line.

Fletcher turned away, walking back to his Land Rover. He heard a car behind him, screeching out of the gate area. Another surge from the crowd. He heard tyres slick on the road, an impact. He turned.

A black saloon car was steering around the

peaceniks, a few demo people slapping on its windows. The car snaked left and right, knocking one protester over. There was a moment of chaos – bottles flying, a placard slamming off the bonnet, then the car straightened and blasted away from the barracks, along the straight road and off into the fens.

Tinted windows, hard to see anything. The driver was a man, he could just see that. Combat uniform, thin face, scowling. Not Ward. But the woman beside him looked like Stef Maguire.

He tried to run back to his Land Rover, but the police put a line of men across the road, linked arms holding everyone away while another coach rolled out. He tried to push through, was pushed back. By the time the police line folded away, the road held just TV vans, police vehicles, one last coach. And his Land Rover.

He leaned on the hot metal of the bonnet, holding his side, getting his breath back. Feeling tears film in his eyes.

Haines cleared the last of her paperwork and tidied her desk. Summers came to the door.

'Want to get a drink?'

'Have you heard from Major Ward?'

'No, but he'll have it buttoned down. Come on, it's Saturday. Let's get a drink.'

She went to shut down her computer. There was one last email, from a captain at a Waterton address. She opened it.

Summers said, 'I'll drink on my own, then. What's the matter? You've gone white.'

She said slowly, 'We need to put a team of people together.'

'To do what?'

She turned the screen to him.

He reached for the phone.

She put her hand on his.

She said, 'Let's just think. Before we make the calls.'

Those vodkas back in the house were hurting Cathleen's eyes now. She was driving a red Alfa, Ward sitting beside her, flipping through the numbers on her mobile. His camouflage tunic was unbuttoned and he was sweating.

She followed his directions onto a narrow road, between cabbage fields with workers tending the plants.

Ward looked up and noticed the field workers. He said, 'I saw people working like that, once. I was watching with binoculars. We hit them with a cluster bomb. We had to use a bulldozer to clear the mess away.'

She didn't know what was worse – being trapped here with him, or going back to face her husband.

She said, 'Where are we going?' No answer.

'OK, fuck you. I'll get out.' No answer. She looked across at him. 'I said, I'm getting out.'

'I'm taking you somewhere safe for interview.'

'Interview about what?'

'Dan Simmons.'

He took her phone again and dialled. 'Fletcher?'

She could hear Tom's voice, shouting.

Ward said, 'Calm it down, Fletcher. I might have to phone Gary Neale. Except he's gone missing. Any idea where?' She heard Tom's voice quieten. 'That's better. Look, I have your charming wife here with me. Yes, she's fine. A little bit stressed, but we all are. Want to speak to her?' He held out the phone long enough for her to say *Tom* – then took it away. He said, 'Don't worry, Fletcher, I'm taking her to our safe place. The safest place possible. I suggest you come and meet us there. I'm sure you want to see Cathleen again. And I'm sure she's got a lot to tell you.' He looked across at her and winked. 'Haven't you, Cathleen?'

He pointed ahead for her to keep going along the road. No other buildings, cars or people around – just the open fields, scrubby hedges, clouds and pylons. Old wartime bunkers beside the road. There was a rail crossing in the distance, the barriers raised. She slowed the car a little, but Ward flipped the phone into his other hand and reached inside his open tunic. He came out with a pistol, held it pointing loosely at her. She felt her heart thump and her bladder constrict. She speeded up again, the car racing along the narrow tarmac towards the crossing barrier. Beyond that, the fields were planted with green wheat, rolling into a shallow valley. He said into the phone, 'Let me give you the map reference, OK? And when you get here, I think Cathleen will want to talk to you. She'll have something–'

No. She'd tried to find the words, thought about it, couldn't face it. No.

'–something to tell you about Dan Simmons–'

She punched her foot down on the brake, putting all her strength into it. The car twisted and she saw Ward lurch forward, dropping the phone, the gun in his hand pointing at the windscreen. The momentum lifted her up in her seat and by then the car was sliding across the road towards the rail crossing, the wheel spinning in her hands, tyres howling. The car twitched and spun, the back sliding around in a full circle, clouds racing across the windscreen until they hit the barrier, the car flexed over sideways and slammed back down.

There was a noise close to her, a sharp crack that made her ears go dull. The window beside her exploded, showering glass.

It went quiet. She could hear her own

pulse, her own throat swallowing. Warm air blew in. She smelled the tyres burning, and another kind of smoke over that, like fireworks. She tasted blood, thick and hot, and realised her mouth was filling up with it. Something had happened in her neck.

She tried to speak. It came out as *Sally and Evie*.

Fletcher replayed the words and sounds in his mind.

I'm taking her to our safe place.
The safest place possible.
The map reference.
Cathleen will want to talk to you–
No map reference, no more words.
Road noise, tyres. Silence.
So where was she?
No answer from Cathleen's mobile now. He sat at the side of the road, watching a sparrowhawk high above the tarmac, wings flickering against the sky, looking for its target.

Our safe place.
The safest place possible.
He thought back to a photo: the print that Stef Maguire showed him here in his Land Rover, after she'd thumped the bloated gym rat Little Tonks out in the field, that afternoon of the fen Blow.

That photo had a caption. He was trying to remember it.

Safe place? The safe place? Their safe place?

He moved in his seat. He felt in his shirt pocket, found the strip of painkillers and punched some out into his mouth. *Their safe place.* A picture of trees. Great. Trees and weeds, a derelict house. And the gates, of course. Big timber gates, creosoted, the slats in a distinctive diamond pattern. Creepy kind of gates.

Who in this world could help him find where they were?

Fletcher started the engine.

After the fucked-up demo zone around the barracks, Jason relaxed a bit and drove with fingertips on the wheel. Maguire in the passenger seat had her left hand in her lap, holding the Browning pistol she'd already stuck in his face on the journey from Brize. She wasn't left-handed, though, he knew that.

Leaving Waterton behind, he took a narrow road between fields separated by ditches. It went on for miles, out into wheat fields with old wartime bunkers near the road, clouds on the horizon.

She said, 'Why Guru?'

'Huh?'

'Why did Ward choose the name Guru?'

'Made him sound like an expert.' He laughed. 'Hey, you know why he sent you to pick me up from Brize? He was hoping I'd figure you out, maybe sort you out.'

'I'll sort him out.'

'Good, because you and me, we're getting on OK, aren't we? I've got no problem with you at all.'

He looked at her and smiled. They went over a junction, onto an old tarmac road heading into a plain, towards a rail crossing.

She said, 'There might be another reason he sent me.'

'Yeah?'

'Yeah. Maybe he thought I'd sort *you* out. You're as big a risk to him as I am. Maybe he thought we'd argue, only one of us would come back. One less problem for him. Think about that.'

They drove in silence for a minute, the Maguire woman flexing her hands. Jason thinking, *Would Ward do that? Throw us in together, see who came out alive?*

He laughed.

At the rail crossing, there were tyre marks across the road and window glass glinting in the light.

He said, 'Careful with that gun, girl,' and they went over the rails and thumping down again. The road angled around and followed the edge of a field, the railway line on a raised bed beside it.

She said, 'This is the middle of nowhere.'

'Too right.' They came to another rail crossing, this time the warning lights flashing in

348

the late sunlight. Jason slowed and stopped, though he could have dodged over the rails. A bell clanged and the automated barriers swung down. He said, 'We'll have to wait a bit. Then we're almost there. Ward will be there, I know that.' The train approached: a transport pulling noisy cargo skips. Jason shouted, 'It's just beyond here.'

The last wagon rolled away and the barrier lifted. Jason drove over the crossing, onto a narrow road that led alongside the train line, the rails parallel to the tarmac for a long way ahead, a series of signal lights on gantries casting shadows in the late sun. At the end of that, they diverged: a curve in the road, the railway angling the other way. Jason pulled up at that point. 'This is it. Our safe place in the country.'

She kept the gun on him, but she peered ahead through the windscreen. He looked down there too.

The safe place.

At the end of a ploughed field, there were two clumps of trees. Between them was a large and half derelict building. Two storeys, with all the windows boarded over, holes in the roof. Set behind old timber gates built with a weird diamond pattern, surrounded by a chainlink fence growing with weeds. She said, 'I've seen that place before. Dan Simmons had a photo of that building.' She looked at him, raised the gun. 'He came here and saw what was happening. Is that when Ward decided to kill him?'

Jason shrugged. Behind them, the alarm bell of the rail crossing began to sound again. In the mirror, he saw the barriers sliding down.

She said, 'What's in this building?'

'It was an old mental hospital, back in the sixties. It's kind of grown wild. It's weird inside. Really weird.' Behind him, he saw the yellow nose of the locomotive approaching from the distance, leaking fumes into the evening sky.

'What's in there now?'

'I told you, that's where Ward's taken Fletcher's wife. They'll both be in there by now.'

She craned her neck around, trying to get a fix on her location. The pistol still pointing at him from her other hand. The train sounded its klaxon behind them. He smiled.

She said, 'What's funny?'

'Not funny. Just thinking you're pretty.'

From her left pocket, she took a pair of handcuffs. She snapped them open, clipped one cuff around the wheel, tried to snap the other one on his left hand. He pulled it away. She raised the gun at him.

He said, 'You won't shoot me. I'm just the junior, you know that. You might shoot Ward, not me.'

He opened the door and slid out. Cool

evening air on his face. The railway tracks clicking with the approaching train. He watched it get closer, the clunk of the wheels echoing across the fields.

Maguire got out of the car too, stood leaning on the door with the gun out of sight. He looked at the train: the driver's vision was just a curve of clean glass in the grimy window. Down here, they would look like two squaddies out for a stroll. She said, 'Get back in, Jason.'

He smiled at her. She *was* pretty, he had to admit that. Healthy, fit and strong. But he knew about the pretty ones – they were the worst.

The train was right on top of them now – the engine rolling past a few metres away, smelling hot. Then he saw Maguire jump. The train was squealing and groaning, but the wheels were clunking more slowly, coming to a halt. He looked along the line. A red signal down there on the curve, the engine already rolling around the angle – hiding them from the driver completely.

He saw that this train was different from the last one: not the cargo hoppers, just steel box wagons with ventilation slits. Then the train halted, but the squealing noise carried on. He realised the squealing wasn't the wheels, it was inside the wagons.

He shouted, 'Jesus. Just look at this.'

It was a cattle train.

The trucks were crammed full of animals: slaughter cows, he guessed, their eyes, lips and nostrils cramming against the slits, exhaling in bursts, long pink tongues licking desperately and some starting to tear, spattering blood into the air. There were scores of these jabbing tongues, as far as he could see – the front of the train around the curve, the rear of it extending back towards the crossing.

The animal sounds carried out across the field, louder than the idling engine up ahead.

He thought, *That's luck for once.*

And he started moving.

Stef Maguire had the handcuffs in one hand, the pistol in the other. When Jason began walking around the car towards her, she let him come around so they could see each other. Then she threw the handcuffs to him. They landed at his feet and he stopped.

The train suddenly moved forward, then halted with a shriek. The livestock began kicking the steel walls, jamming their snouts into the ventilation slits, their tongues steaming. The whole train stank of piss.

Jason picked up the cuffs and clinked them in his hand, looking at her. A jolt went through the train wagons again, and she saw froth spattering out around him. He wiped his face.

She said, 'Get in the back of the car and cuff yourself to the headrest. Sit there and do nothing.'

She saw him shrug and clip one cuff onto his left wrist. A train klaxon sounded in the distance and the cattle in the wagons began kicking the walls. Jason walked over to the rear door of the car, reached for the handle. He fumbled it, kept pulling it, but it didn't open. She thought, damn, the child locks are on or something. She went around to take a look, still with the gun on him. Then he wrenched the door open, brought it straight onto her hand. She dropped the gun and it fired through the window, blowing a cloud of glass up against the wagon – bits smacking Jason across his cheek and one eye. The pistol clattered away under the car. Jason kept moving: his hands fastened on her neck – one wrist trailing the cuffs. She tried to knee him, then kick him, but he lifted her up off the tarmac and brought his forehead down on her face. She heard her nose break, felt seconds of concussion. She said, 'You animal.' Blood pouring down her chin.

Jason knew that was how they saw him, these women. To them he was just a beast, like the cattle here. To the officers too, just a dog for fetching what they wanted. He knew what he was doing, though. He had vision in one eye – the other felt cold, the lid closing on bits of glass.

He turned Maguire around and rammed her head against the wagon, pushed her face against the nearest slit. He felt her trying to wrench away as cow teeth chewed the metal edge right in front of her, then a bleeding tongue spattered her with red froth. He had his hand around the back of her neck in a way that would break her spine if she struggled, and she knew that, face half turned to him, eyes shut against the animal tongues. Because he felt like it, he ran his free hand inside her tunic, felt her nipples, then down into her trouser front and felt her bush. Then the train really started moving. There was a big jolt as it started up, the wheels squeaking, brakes releasing with a gasp. The wagon wall began to slide away from him, her face scraping across the metal, onto another air vent where a cow blew a whole mouthful over her, over him and his hands too, as the train shuddered and swayed away from him, coming to the end of the wagon now, a big steel door banging with hoof blows. Her hands grabbed at the door, her fingers clawing under it, the animals inside there banging and howling.

She shouted, 'No.'

She was strong, but he pulled her away, held her by the neck.

'No. No.'

She stamped on his foot, her boot heel

breaking the top bones. He grunted against the pain. He punched her head against the wagon again until she stopped struggling. Then the wagon finished and there was a gap: a sudden view of the field beyond, with level blue sky, plus the greasy couplings moving over the rail sleepers and gravel.

He threw her in there.

She went down past the coupling hooks, her body hitting the track itself. She tried to get her balance, but she fell sideways. He staggered back and watched.

The first wheel of the next wagon took her leg away – blood spattering out – then as she twisted, the next set of wheels cut her head clean off, just sliced it off and left it between the rails as the other wagons rumbled past. Left her body headless with her tough arms stretched between the sleepers, hands reaching out, fingers scrabbling for just a second.

He lowered himself down, sat watching the spaces between the moving wagons: each gap flashing that field and sky. In the end, it all went quiet.

He calmed his breathing down.

Maguire's blood was pooling between the rails, spilling out down the embankment. Her head lay facing away from him, hair strewn out across the sleepers. He thought, *That's what happens. When they treat you like that, it's what happens.*

He dragged himself over to her and felt in

her pockets for keys. He unlocked the cuff, rubbed his wrist, watching the train rolling away to the west.

He laughed. He reached out and stroked Maguire's head. It was warm and matted up with blood, grease from the train and gravel dust. He lifted it by the hair and threw it out into the field. Then he rolled her body off the rails, watched it turn over, its own arms around itself, hugging itself, going down into the long grass, and disappearing.

Big strong arms.

Not strong enough, girl.

The boys are going to win this.

Jason assessed his situation. Blood in his eye, but he could still see. He could just move his left leg, could try walking. Could probably just drive, let the car roll down the hill, roll into the old hospital to meet up with Ward and Cathleen Fletcher.

And Honey Man. He'd be there, walking into it.

He made it over to the car, and reached underneath for the gun.

Fletcher pulled up in a small Fenland town, on a road of cinders. At one end, the Pro Gym stood silent against the sky. That was of no interest to him now – he didn't even give Little Tonks a second thought. At the other end of the street, he pushed open the door of the lumber yard he remembered from that night. A big Nissen hut with a corrugated roof, *We Make Anything* over the doorway.

Inside, a sales counter, smell of sawdust and the whine of a machine from the back. A young guy wheeling a trolley of planks stared at Fletcher.

Fletcher said, 'How long has this place been going?'

'Years, I suppose. You better sit down before you fall down, mate.'

'You make gates, for houses?'

'Gates, anything in wood. You OK?'

'Is there someone who's worked here from the start? From years ago?'

Fletcher went to the address the boy gave him, was told the person he wanted had moved out, got rough directions to his forwarding address. In the end, he found him in a house off the high street. An archway led into a concrete square, with four doors leading off. The man opened his, folding up a newspaper. Behind him, a sofa, TV showing racing, a can of beer. He was approaching seventy, probably. Scarred hands – woodworker's hands, Fletcher hoped. One hand cupping his ear to listen, then pocketing the fifty quid Fletcher gave him.

'I don't know how you found me. Years ago, that was. And yes, I remember those gates. Big gates with a diamond pattern.'

Red eyes going distant, thinking back. 'It was a while ago. But there's no scrap value, boy. No metal in them. They're just timber.'

'That's fine. Where's the house?'

'Not a house. We made them for a hospital. A special kind of hospital. They closed it down twenty-five, thirty years ago.'

'Where is it?'

'But there's nothing of value there.'

'There is to me.'

Summers put his phone down for the last time and looked over at Haines. They'd been making calls for so long, the sun had gone and the office was full of grey light.

He said, 'You were right. It's a good team. It's low-key.'

Silence, both of them watching the lights come on in the buildings outside.

She said, 'You want a drink now? Because if this doesn't work—'

'Let's get a drink. Two or three hours, we'll know.'

Saturday Night

Fletcher stopped his Land Rover on the road near the rail line. He felt hot, but there was cold sweat on his back. It was after sunset, the sky to the west jumbled with red clouds, grey-blue overhead. He could see the old hospital down there in the fields, half hidden by the trees.

He reached into the car and lifted out his axe. The blade glinted in the dusk.

He walked down across the ploughed field towards the two clumps of woodland. Night animals were moving: he saw a bat circling and moths lifting from bushes. He was limping and unable to walk fast, but he kept a straight line along the furrows, holding his axe in one hand. His boots were raising red dust from the soil, blurring the air around him.

He remembered – back at the marina, facing the *Contigo* – the way he planned things, being logical. But now he just felt the rise and fall of his feet, the weight of the axe, a momentum he couldn't and then didn't want to stop.

He came onto a rough track that led between the trees, potholes with water that caught the red horizon as he splashed through them. He noticed tyre marks – truck-sized. Midges swirling under the trees. Then he looked up.

Up ahead, he saw the old gates, warped timber with that diamond design. Just like the photo.

He headed for them, limping steadily, trailing the axe. A plane flew high over the gates, leaving a vapour trail. He began to run, jogging unevenly, the pain from his side jolting into his spine. He ducked under tree branches, swerved between others fallen across the track. He came to the gates.

Rusty hinges set into concrete pillars. They were part open, their diamond shapes slicing up the mauve and red sky. Beyond them, he saw old gardens with tall weeds, a fountain leaning at an angle. A parked car: a black saloon gleaming in the dusk, one window shattered. Then a building. He pushed through the gates, stopped and looked around.

There was nobody visible.

Beyond the fountain, the big, two-storey hospital in pale stone. The upper windows were boarded with plywood, those on the ground floor bricked up. There was an ornate entrance porch sealed with breeze blocks. He went up to it and felt across the blockwork: it was solid, hadn't been disturbed. Another bat came overhead, swerving around the gable wall. He followed it.

At the side of the building, two metal chimney stacks towered over him, jutting against the sky. An early star shone between them, and another vapour trail.

At the back, there was a courtyard with flagstones visible between weeds and bushes. The rear wall of the building had another row of bricked-up windows, and there was another doorway here. Not sealed with breeze blocks. It was smooth and pale in the twilight.

He felt it. A big steel plate, recently fitted. Secured with steel hinges and a padlock.

He listened. The noise of a vehicle on the distant main road, and midges buzzing close. In the undergrowth, an animal rustling.

He put his ear against the cold steel door.

From inside, a faint rushing sound.

He listened again.

A low hissing, like water gushing out of a pipe.

He felt the padlock. It was tempered steel, a vandal-proof casing, fixed to some kind of bolt inside.

Who or what was really in there? Cathleen – and Ward, army people, Military Police?

He went to the nearest bricked-up window, lifted his axe and swung the back of the head against the bricks. They gave way in a spurt of dust against the darkening air, and

Fletcher expected to see the interior beyond that, but he could just make out a layer of metal plate.

There was no quiet way into this building.

He went back to the steel door and looked at the lock. The thing was indestructible, but it was held on by a welded hasp. He twisted his axe around in his hands, took a breath. He swung the axe high and brought the blunt edge down on the metal ring. The sound hurt his ears, went out across the field and then echoed from whatever was inside. It took another three blows before the welding broke and the lock dropped away. Fletcher hooked the edge of the axe behind the door and pulled at it.

The hinges turned and it swung out.

From inside there was a smell of decay, and that hissing sound again, and a faint red light that spread along the axe handle.

He stepped inside.

The light and the hissing were coming from a tall heater unit – a patio heater fuelled by a gas canister – just standing there in the middle of a big open hall. In its red glow, Fletcher looked around.

He realised the place was alive.

Not with army personnel, but with dry fungus.

The hallway floor had once been paved in tiles, now most of them broken or missing, and big mushrooms were sprouting up through the gaps. Fletcher trod on one, and its contents puffed out across the floor. The walls on three sides were part in shadow, partly lined with ceramic tiles that refracted the gleam of the heater. At the back, there was a carved wooden staircase up to the first floor. To either side of it, a series of arched doorways leading into darkness.

Where in this place was Cathleen?

He stood listening, heard only the hiss of the gas heater. He took out his pocket torch, went to the first of the doors on the ground level, and looked through.

In the torchlight, he could see a corridor lined with cupboards, their doors hanging open. Massive fungal formations grew out of them, spooling across the floor. He looked in the next doorway: rows of skeletal beds, twined with sheets heaped with rodent droppings.

The last doorway led to a set of stone steps going below ground, the ceiling growing with stalactites. In the torchlight, he could see that many of the growths had been snapped off, and the steps themselves had footprints in the dust.

He went slowly down there.

At the base, a wooden door with a stencilled sign, *Danger Poison Do Not Enter.*

He opened it and shone the torch in.

An old cellar. In the centre, a wooden pallet. Stacked up on it, a number of small plastic bags. He shone his torch on one of them. Inside the plastic, a whitish powder.

He stepped back.

Heroin. How much was here – twenty, thirty kilos?

He turned and went back up the steps into the hallway.

He shouted, 'Cathleen.'

The word echoed around the ceramic walls. The gas burner guttered and flared again. He went over to the staircase. It stood out into the centre of the hall, an old carpet piled at its foot. Ornate banisters on either side made big shadows against the walls. He put his foot on the first step: the carpet was crumbly and dry. He put his weight on it, and found it was solid stone. No creaking. He trod on the first step, then the second. He had his axe in his right hand, holding it just under the blade, the torch in his left hand putting a disc of light onto the stairs. His own shadow from the burner moving ahead of him. His eyes coming level with the top step.

In the torchlight, he saw that the first floor had a large landing, growing with mould. There was the framework of what had once been dividing walls of separate rooms, their floors littered with debris, a few bedsteads bare of everything except coil springs making shadows against the plywood sealing the windows.

He called Cathleen's name again. No answer.

He shone the torch around. The ceiling itself was partly open to the sky, elsewhere a mass of mushroom growth: domes crowding over each other, bulging down almost to head height. Beyond these destroyed rooms there was another dark corridor leading left and right to the rest of the upper floor.

Someone shot at him.

The noise was loud, but the amount of growth on the ceiling deadened it, because there was one echo, then silence. Fletcher crouched down, head below the top step, and turned his torch off. He couldn't feel any injury, but he could smell the gun smoke, and he thought he'd seen a flash from the far corner, behind one of the smashed wall timbers.

He felt his heart thumping, the pain in his side multiplied by his sudden movement. Was that Ward? Where was Cathleen?

A male voice called, 'Honey Man.'

Not Ward's voice, he was sure of that.

'I know what's going on, Honey Man.'

He flattened himself against the cold stone steps. His torch was off, but the gas heater down there was still on, outlining him. He could just see the heater from here, glowing orange. He heard a movement on the upper floor. If the man got closer, he wouldn't miss a second time. Fletcher pocketed the torch and slid down the steps, hitting the last one with an electric pain in his waist.

The whole space was still lit by that gas burner.

He pulled himself over to it, grabbed the dial and slammed it off.

Nothing happened.

That movement overhead again, someone moving slowly across the floor. Dragging one foot, maybe. Tread and drag. The man would be at the stairs in a few seconds, in the shadows up there, seeing Fletcher lit up in this circle of light.

Then the burner hissed and spluttered, using the last of the gas, and went out.

The noise upstairs halted.

Fletcher felt blind, the dark after the orange glow leaving him with just angles and shapes. Then the building began to reappear around him: moonlight through the roof coming down through the stairwell, showing the ceiling up there and the stairs themselves. Fletcher heard the man moving again, closer to the stairs. No torchlight, just that dull tread.

Fletcher jumped over to the side of the stairs, pressed himself against the staircase itself, under the gothic banisters. He didn't think he could be seen by the man on the top step. Anyone up there would have a view of the stairs and the shadowy hallway.

The voice called down, 'I know about you,

Honey Man.'

He stayed quiet, against the splintered panelling, the axe against his side, its head down. Over his shoulder, he could only see the banisters in the moonlight and the bulbous growth on the ceiling beyond that. What did the man mean, *I know about you?* Fletcher thought, *I should be saying that. I know about you, about your heroin.*

He waited, resting the axe head against his boot. He could raise it, take a swing at the stairs. But where exactly was the man?

The man said, 'You're there by the stairs, yeah? Which side?' There was another shot, the flash showing the whole of the lobby, staying on his retina. Some tiles smashed out from the wall and clattered across the floor. 'You and Cathleen and Dan Simmons. Not us. Not what we're doing. Dan Simmons knew about us, but he was talking about you.'

Fletcher heard more movement on the landing, then silence. Why? Because the man was off the landing, on the top stair now, the solid step not creaking or moving. He looked up, but the flash on his retina plus the moonlight made it hard to see. All the man had to do was reach over, point the gun down here, loose off some shots. He didn't have to see, he could just keep firing – one side, then the other. How long before he did that – a second more?

Fletcher stepped away from the stairs. He

angled back and swung the axe down, the pain shooting through his side. He turned that pain into an upward swing, a curve that took in as much of the stairway as he could reach, the axe head catching the moonlight as it smashed through the banisters. After the wood, he hit something solid. The impact jarred his hands, threw a big spark over his head into the dark. Then he realised that was a shot, the man had fired again. Fletcher was exposed now, reeling backwards with the axe in his hands. He looked up. Against the moonlight, he saw a man with hands spread wide, one of them holding a short pistol, his face staring down. Looking right at him.

The first howl was stifled, like a child crying under its breath. The next one was louder. The man slumped down in the middle of the stairs, his legs giving way. One hand had the pistol up against the banisters, the other was reaching down to his shins, moving, pale in the moonlight. He cried out again, a breathy noise through clenched teeth, ending in a grunt. Fletcher imagined taking another swing, the blunted axe going right into his torso. The man started weeping, trying to hide it, but crying under his breath, plus little yelps that rang around the stairwell. Fletcher reached out and put his hand on the pistol. Took it away from him and put it in his back pocket.

The man didn't resist. It left him with

another hand free, which he clamped on his lower legs again.

Fletcher put down the axe and shone the torch on him.

The man was as pale as the hospital fungus, his mouth clenched, teeth bared. One eye closed under dry blood. Camouflage uniform coated in dust and spores. Fletcher shone the torch lower. The man must have been crouching on the steps, because the axe had hit both his legs: one just above the ankle, almost severing it, the other mid shin, right into the bone. He was losing blood, lots of it, pouring down over the stairs. The man was panting, half-sobbing now. He looked up at Fletcher.

'So you're Honey Man. Pleased with yourself?'

'Where's Cathleen?'

The man grunted, clutching his legs. 'You've cut my feet off. I'll lose my feet.'

'Where is my wife?'

'Help me.' The voice was slurred, and the torch disc showed veins rigid in his face. He stank of sweat and the canvas smell of his uniform.

'I'll help you. Tell me where Cathleen is.'

'I don't know.'

'You do. Where is she?'

'Ward's taken her somewhere. He said he was bringing her here, but they're not here, you can see that.'

The man twitched, his head drooping.

Fletcher took his own belt off and put it around the worst leg, the ankle wound, and tightened it. The man bucked and twisted his head, breath bubbling in his throat. Fletcher couldn't see if that was stopping the blood, but it was on tight.

The man said, 'Give me a hit. Inject me with heroin. I'm dying.'

'You've got a tourniquet on. You'll live for hours.'

'I've shot myself.'

It sounded like a child saying, I've wet myself.

Fletcher shone the torch over him again. The jacket was stained black around the waist – a shot through the stomach maybe, the hand close to the body when the axe hit his legs.

The man said, 'In the basement–'

'I've seen it. Your stockpile.'

'There are syringes in there too. Give me a hit. I've seen stomach wounds. When the shock wears off, it's agony. And I'm not doing prison. They'll kill me in there.'

'Ward's taken Cathleen somewhere else? Where?'

'I don't know. Somewhere safe.'

Fletcher went and lit the gas burner again. In the red glow, he went down under the stalactites to the cellar. Beside the pallet of heroin was a bag of syringes and bottled water. He opened a syringe, sucked it full of water, ripped open a heroin packet, took some grains with his dusty fingers and dropped it right in. Put the plunger back and shook it. This wasn't how Tonks' girl had done it while breastfeeding her baby back at the gym, but the stuff dissolved anyway, and the needle was dripping. He took it back up to the lobby.

The man already had his sleeve rolled up, a strip of cloth wound below the biceps. Fletcher shone his torch on the forearm.

'What did you mean, you know about me and Cathleen?'

'Give me the hit. I'm dying.'

'What did you mean?'

'I don't know. Ward said, say that, destabilise you.'

'Destabilise me?'

'Give me the hit. I can feel my legs now. Please.'

'Destabilise me how?'

'Ask Ward.'

Fletcher looked down at him. Then dropped the syringe into his outstretched hand and stood back. The man said nothing, grunted, exhaled, found a vein and slid the needle in. Like a bee sting: the barb in the skin, but slower, quieter. The man leaned back, the syringe still hanging from his arm. Fletcher turned to go.

'I'm as good as you, Honey Man.'

371

Fletcher walked over to the door, trailing his axe behind him on the floor.

The voice called, 'I just wanted a place to be myself, you know? With someone I love.'

Fletcher opened the door. He stopped. His hand on the steel plate. His hands all over the building, his axe in the man's legs. His sweat and hairs, probably, on the banisters, the stair panels. Gary Neale's yacht was bad enough, but this place was a DNA lab.

Fletcher went back to the gas burner, turned the dial to max until it roared. Over on the steps, the man's head was angled back, mouth open. No sign of breathing. He looked like a body on a funeral pyre, the wood piled up around him. Fletcher pushed the burner over. It clanged on the floor, rolling over a few times across the debris. From the doorway, he saw it all catching, the outside breeze sending spores of blue flame across the entrance hall, up the cool staircase thermal. He left the doorway open.

Looking back from the edge of the copse, he saw the roof take light. From the field, he saw it collapse, the red glow dimming for a second and then jumping up brighter than before, sparks flying up against the moon.

On the main road, he pulled over by a drainage channel. No traffic either way. No red glow in the sky – the fire already dying down. The moon reflected in the water.

Everyone just wanted a safe, peaceful

place. This renegade soldier, Fletcher himself, even that young woman Elsa on the *Contigo*. Some people find it, some people don't.

The soldier had said, *Destabilise you.*

Destabilise me how?

Ask Ward.

Where would Ward have taken Cathleen?

If not the safe place – then where?

He opened the door and threw the pistol out into the drainage channel. He didn't hear it hit the water, but he saw the moon fly apart.

He stopped the Land Rover in the field of elephant grass, a few hundred metres from his house. He pulled the blunted axe out after him and stood looking at the house beyond the trees.

Could Cathleen be there?

In the moonlight, he could see the white gable wall. No lights in the windows, and the floodlights off.

The grass rustling.

His vision was blurred, making two moons over the house.

He shook his head.

He walked towards the gate, taking the longest strides he could, the pain jolting his legs and torso each time. He trailed the axe head down behind him for a while, but it clunked on stones in the road, and he hoisted it up on his shoulder.

The gate was open. The padlock not smashed, but unlocked.

Fletcher had a key. Only Cathleen had the other one.

In the courtyard – not Cathleen's car, but an old red Alfa. Ward's car. The lights smashed, one window blown out, glass fragments strewn across the seats.

What did that mean?

He stood with his axe over his shoulder, looking up at his house. He saw the four big windows and a door, like a child's drawing. He pushed the front door and it opened. The inner door was half open too. No sign of forcing that he could see. Someone had unlocked this. He pushed the airlock door open.

The entrance hall. Moonlight from the staircase. In the kitchen, pans glinting on the shelves.

He sniffed the air. The familiar house smell, warm and dry. And something else, which he'd scented not so long ago.

Sweat. The canvas smell that came from an army uniform. Someone in uniform had been standing in the room, very recently. Maybe a minute ago. And standing for a while, sweating.

On the centre table, there was a coffee cup and a few letters stacked together – the way he'd left them in the morning. Something else. A dark circle. He reached out and picked it up.

Cathleen's bracelet.

He held it in the light, felt it, put it back. Did she leave it there, or someone else?

He listened. Who exactly was in the house right now?

He went to the staircase, looked up. The moon was shining through the landing window. He went slowly up the stairs, holding the axe by its head. He stopped on the landing. Black and grey light. No sound at all, except a creak in the roof that sometimes happened after a hot day. He looked into Evie's room. The bedclothes were folded on the beds, the toy box and wardrobe closed. He opened the wardrobe. Hangers and clothes, stacked toys, nothing else. The same in Sally's room. The bathroom was empty, smelled of bleach and soap. He stood outside the big bedroom, listening. That ceiling creak had stopped.

He pushed the door open.

The room was lit by moonlight through the window, still dusty with soot from the beehive fire. The bed seemed untouched. He looked in the wardrobe, under the bed. No other sign of Cathleen, nothing she'd left.

He went to the window. Through the soot, he could see the grass, the orchard, and the shapes of the hives.

He looked again. Near the orchard, the open channel in the elephant grass – where he'd stood waiting for Gary Tonks' accomplice a few nights ago. A man's shape. And something distinctive about it. He realised what it was – combat trousers tucked into boots. Through the dust on the glass, he was sure he saw that.

A soldier.

Downstairs, he stood in the kitchen doorway. The breeze from the garden smelled of grass and burned wood. He stepped out into it, bringing his axe behind him, the head trailing on the turf. The cool air made him dizzy for a second, sweat chilling between his shoulders.

He began walking over to the channel in the grass wall, where it rose as a dark block against the shifting stems.

Halfway, a man stepped out in front of him.

They stood looking at each other in the moonlight. The man was in camouflage uniform – trousers tucked into his boots – bareheaded, and held a Browning pistol in his right hand, pointed at Fletcher's chest. The man wasn't Ward. He was younger, in his twenties, thinner and lighter. He was studying Fletcher with his head tilted slightly back. Behind him, another man stepped out of the grass. Another soldier. He wasn't looking at Fletcher, but across the orchard to the hives.

Fletcher said, 'Where's my wife?' No reply. 'Where's Ward?'

No reply. From the other side of the orchard, another uniformed man appeared out of the grass, holding a pistol in two hands. Another came out beside him. Then from the hives, another one, making his way between the boxes. Fletcher realised the whole orchard was full of soldiers – seven or eight of them, some armed, some not, all dividing their attention between Fletcher and the hives. Was it the hives – or the slope going down to the cress beds?

The man in front of him kept the pistol steady.

'You are Tom Fletcher?'

'Yes.'

Taking a good grip on the axe by his side. The man's eyes flicked down over that, back up to him.

'Listen, Ward's here. He's down in the stream.'

'Where's my wife?'

'She's down there too.' The young face eyed Fletcher. 'She's down there with him.'

'Is Maguire here?'

The man looked at the man next to him, back at Fletcher.

'Maguire's missing.'

'Why haven't you arrested Ward?'

'You'll see.'

They parted to let him go through, pistols lowered.

He walked ahead. On either side, he saw other soldiers watching him from the grass, or standing between the apple trees.

He brushed past some of the saplings, blossom tumbling through the air. He began to run, using the last of his energy. In the beehives, he ran through the low buzz from the bees. He saw two last soldiers watching him. He crashed over the burned wreckage, smelled the wasted honey. Then beyond the hives, it was darker, and he hit the earth track leading down to the pool. He slipped and went sprawling, leaving the axe behind, a jolt of pain in his spine. He came to rest on his front, raised up on one arm, near the edge of the slope. He tried to get his breath. He could feel heat spreading down his side, and his hand came away sticky. The wound was bleeding. He could still hear the giant grass, shivering out in the dark.

He grunted and shook his head.

He pulled himself over to the bank of the pool. A warm breeze was coming up off the water and he could smell the cut wood.

He crouched and looked around.

There were stars over the trees beyond the pool. The moon behind him just showed the water ridged with current, ribbing around the branches, moths drifting across the surface. In the centre, that massive oak. He couldn't see anything else. Or anyone else.

He slid his legs over the bank and stepped into the water. The sediment gave way, and he felt the pebbles below. The water was cool, just over his knees.

He shouted, 'Cathleen.'

Something exploded out of the trees, a white face swooping over him, then going up across the slope. An owl. Its wings had shaken the branches – and moths were sparking out against the stars. They spiralled down, and the pool was quiet again.

A voice said, 'She's here.'

The words echoed. Ward, he was sure of that.

He said, 'Where are you?'

Silence, then the noise of a vehicle from back near the house. And when that stopped – just the faint sound of the elephant grass.

No.

Not the grass.

Human voices. Whispering, then cutting off.

He said, 'Cathleen?'

'I said, she's here.'

Fletcher stepped further into the pool. In the dark, with the outline of the trees, the stars, the faint moonlight, it was hard to locate the voice. He waded out, the water up to his thighs, ripples spreading around him.

'I'm here, Tom.'

Cathleen's voice.

The hawthorns moved in a sudden breeze. Fletcher realised he was losing blood, and sweat was pouring off his chest and hands. The water looked cool and clean, good enough to drink. He said, 'Where are you?'

No answer.

Only one place. One place for Ward to hide her, keeping her there.

He waded out to the oak. Close up, its jagged top sliced across the stars. He put a hand against the trunk. His fingers curled inside one of the axe cuts, the wood splintering in his fingers.

He heard that whispering again. Right here in front of him. On the other side of the oak.

He moved slowly around the trunk. He knew what he was going to find. Major Ward, holding Cathleen hostage. Maybe with that Browning pistol he'd brought to the house in the morning, tucked in his shoulder holster, putting his hand there to take it out, then changing the movement into a rub of the muscles once he saw the camera on the apple tree.

Fletcher kept his fingers on the bark as he moved around the tree, flexing his other hand.

The space behind the oak was in shadow from the moon, a wedge of dark water spreading back to the trees. The surface was full of stars and dead moths. In the middle,

Major Ward.

Fletcher came right round, into the shadow, and stood there looking.

He said, 'Jesus.'

Ward was there. He was kneeling, the water around his torso, his hands on his knees. He looked as if he'd been there some time. He was shivering, his face showing against the dark. His eyes were raised to the oak tree itself. Fletcher followed his line of sight.

Cathleen was sitting in the hacked-off ledge of the trunk, her feet out of the water, just her face and arms showing. He couldn't see her eyes, but he could see her hands. They were extended, gripping a Browning pistol pointed straight at Ward's face.

She looked at Fletcher, looked back at Ward. She said, 'Where are the children?'

Fletcher took another step, the water spooling around him. He reached out for the gun, but Cathleen kept it on the major. He reached again. Just for a second, and hard to see in the shadows, she pointed it at Fletcher.

He stepped back.

'The twins are OK. I've seen them.'

Another owl called from the fields.

Another vehicle pulled up on the gravel of the house.

Then she was pointing it at Ward again, keeping him down in the water.

There was silence. Ward shook himself, cupped some water and splashed it over his face.

He said, 'She crashed my car, grabbed my gun. Are you proud of her?'

From beyond the slope, the floodlights on the house came on, sending a pillar of light up against the moon. It increased the light a little – sharpening the print of Cathleen's hands across the water.

Cathleen said, 'I phoned the barracks. I said they could come here and take him away.'

Ward swayed, seemed to overbalance. He pushed one hand down into the water and came up with something. Cathleen pushed the gun into his face and he opened his fingers: a handful of black silt slipping back into the water.

He said, 'That's what I am now. That's what I am to them.'

Fletcher said, 'Cathleen, put the gun down.'

'No.'

He still couldn't see her face clearly. 'Cathleen, put it down. We don't care what happens to him. They can take him away.' Silence. 'Let them take him away. That's why they're here.'

She said, 'I don't think so, Tom. It's been an hour now. They know we're here, but they haven't come down. They're waiting for something.'

Moths spun past. Ward said, 'Clever man, aren't you? You found out what you wanted to know.'

'I've seen the heroin in the old hospital. And your friend said you know about Cathleen and me. What does that mean?'

Ward laughed. 'I could close my mouth now, do twenty years in prison. Maybe fifteen—'

'Shut up, then—'

'But I won't last fifteen days in there. They'll break my bones. And my name, my family name. A disgrace. So maybe I'll keep talking.' An owl called. A plane went overhead. 'Fletcher the clever man, the investigator. Is that why Dan Simmons mentioned you in his dying words? Honey Man?'

Fletcher felt his back running with sweat. 'Dan Simmons knew me when I was a private investigator. He uncovered your criminal activity, he was afraid, he wanted to pass the information—'

'Really? Is that what he wanted to tell you?'

'But I knew nothing. Because Dan Simmons was an idiot. He didn't—' Fletcher saw Cathleen's hands move, angling the gun down at Ward '—he didn't write the letter.'

It was perfectly still. He heard a few voices from up in the orchard. Cathleen's breathing. And the sound of water as Ward stood up.

Ward steadied himself, his hands spread beside him. His arms dripped water, twisting in the light from beyond the slope. Fletcher saw Cathleen raise the gun, point it at his mouth.

Ward said, 'You believe that? A man saves his last breath, his last words on earth. He uses them to pass on information about drugs?' He laughed, water dripping from his hair. 'What a fine country we would be, if all our citizens used their dying breaths to reduce the level of illegal importation.'

Cathleen's hands moved on the gun, tightening.

So still, this air. Fletcher could smell himself – two days' sweat, salt water, blood. He could feel his hands shaking on the tree. He heard the pulse of his own eardrums, the swallow in his throat. And Ward's laughter.

'You're a big man, Fletcher. But you're an idiot. Who called you Honey Man?'

'Dan Simmons.'

'Simmons and Cathleen. That was their name for you.'

The grass sighed. Moths flashed past. Fletcher had never felt air this still.

'They called you Honey Man. He had pictures of her on his laptop, did you know that? Taken somewhere hot, in a swimming pool. Was it Crete, where they went together that time? And I don't think your friend Dan saved his last words on this earth to report crimes, Honey Man. I think he was talking about his legacy in this world.'

Cathleen said, 'We had a life here. We weren't hurting anyone. We were happy–'

'Happy with your lie.'

'It wasn't a lie,' she said. 'We had what we wanted.'

'You wanted a lie, then.'

'You invaded our life. You threatened our children.'

'Yes, the children.' Ward nodded slowly. 'But Cathleen, when are you going to tell them who their father really was?'

Cathleen made a long, low cry. Then she shot Ward in the face.

Just above one eye, going down. His hands flew out and pulled at the air, as his head jerked back. Fletcher thought he saw the bullet, a spark flying off at an angle into the trees. There was a fraction of silence, then the spray of Ward's head hitting the water, and the flutter of all the moths in the bushes setting off, twisting up into the dark.

When the echo came, Ward was already on his back in the water, the lake feeling across his mouth. The echo sounded twice and stopped. Ward's face turned to the light from the house. Just the slight current moving the body. The water around him darkening.

Something flopped on his chest. Cathleen had thrown the gun on him. It bounced off his uniform and sank.

Cathleen jumped down from the tree, her feet making crowns in the water. She stretched out her hand. He took it and kissed it, pressed it to his face.

They went up into the neighbouring field where the cabbage was growing. There was an irrigation pump there, hissing in the dark. They sat against the wall of elephant grass, with their arms around each other, looking into the dark empty field.

Fletcher closed his eyes. He breathed in Cathleen's hair, her sweat, the grass smell. They talked for a few minutes, then she just pressed her face against his chest. The pumped water and the grass set up a kind of whispering.

He could hear the soldiers' voices from the orchard, the beehives, then down in the pool – calling to each other, shouting.

The breeze dropped and the ground felt warm. Fletcher twisted Cathleen's hair in his fingers, the way he always had done. He felt her move against his chest, her head thumping his ribs. She twined her fingers in his shirt, pulling him close. She was sobbing, making sounds like someone suffocating, rubbing her face against his chest.

He listened to that and the sound of the water spray.

A helicopter came from the east, circled once around the field, then switched its searchlight on. It lit up the field, the grass, the spray, then came lower. Fletcher held Cathleen to his chest, watching it. It was a civilian police model, settling jerkily. It descended just the other side of the water pump – the searchlight shining through the spray. The helicopter feathered its blades, churned the air around the pump.

For a second, there was a rainbow – oily-looking, full of hot fumes, rippling in the beat of the engine. Then the helicopter settled and cut its power, the blades slowing with a long octane sigh.

Someone got out and came walking towards Fletcher and Cathleen, outlined in the searchlight.

Someone crouched down in front of him. A smart suit flecked with mud.

'Cathleen Fletcher? Tom Fletcher? I'm Inspector Brzinski, Cambridge police.'

The water spray still pulsing.

Cathleen said, 'Ward abducted me. He was going to kill me. I grabbed the gun, it just went off.'

Fletcher said, 'The rainbow's gone.'

The man looked behind him. The helicopter was leaving a fuel haze against the spray. The man wiped droplets off his face. When he looked back again, Fletcher and Cathleen were standing up, covered in earth and blood, their hair strung with water, dripping in the light from their house across the fields.

One Month Later

Fletcher spent three days in hospital, in the care of a young doctor from Moscow. The first day, the police questioned him for two hours. They went outside – and he guessed they were phoning their colleagues who were interviewing Cathleen, comparing their accounts. They came back and did another hour. In the end, they left with blank faces.

After that, he lay listening to the nurses talking about their boyfriends. The wound in his side was cleaned and trimmed, and a drip fed him with antibiotics to counter the infection that Gary Neale's knife blade had introduced to his bloodstream.

Cathleen and the twins visited in the afternoons. The twins played hide-and-seek around the bed. Cathleen sat beside him, holding his hand. They didn't speak much.

When they left, he closed his eyes.

In the evening, he watched the TV screen over the bed. Fields full of poppies, whole valleys, lighting up with flame. Armoured vehicles ploughing through them, their tracks ripping the flowers into a red storm. Interviews with men of the Cambs regiment, snatched and blurry against a backdrop of fire.

When the Russian doctor discharged him, he went home and worked long hours on the smallholding. He replaced the burned hives, collected the honey from the others, sealed and labelled it in jars. The elephant grass was harvested too, baled and taken away, leaving the area pixellated with cut-off stalks. The house felt suddenly exposed, other buildings now visible in the distance, light slanting across the fields, and rain – as the weeks passed – tumbling from hot clouds.

He finished preparing the watercress beds, burned the roots he'd cleared out, chopped the last of the old oak tree into firewood. In late June, he built a dam of sandbags, diverted the stream and drained it for a morning. Put in the panniers to grow the cress, filled them with black compost, filled that with seed.

Around midday, his phone rang. He answered it, looking at the seeds settling into their earth.

He ended the call.

He thought, *How did they find me?*

He thought, *Not so difficult, really. Not for people like that.*

He knocked through the dam and let the stream flow back in. The water was clear, sparkling with sediment. He watched it flow out across the pool, washing against the panniers. Then it went still, just the print of the breeze, reflecting storm clouds, and his own face.

Thinking about that call, what to do about it.

He looked up. At the top of the slope, the twins were watching him. Green eyes under their lashes, freckles, summer tan on their cheeks. Their black hair coiling out like oil smoke against the sky.

He walked up the slope to meet them. He stood between them and put his hands out, felt their smooth fingers link with his. The three of them stood, looking across the field to the house. The poppies had come. The earth was covered in red dots, flickering around the white hives, studding the margins of the elephant grass field – a long swathe of stalks running out to the horizon, poppies already growing over them.

Sally and Evie's hands hot and powdery in his.

Between the poppies, Cathleen was coming towards them. Brushing through the red flowers, making the petals fly loose.

Fletcher gave her the twins. Feeling in his pocket for his car key. The sky going electric grey, the beehives pale in the gloom.

Early evening saw him in a delicatessen with a blue neon sign over the entrance. The door was open, cool air smelling of salt and static. Fletcher sitting at a counter, looking out at the seafront. A promenade strung with diamond bunting, parked cars of premium class. Holiday people, second-home people, yachting people. Stopping at the bars along the front, leaning on the railings outside, looking up at the clouds massing over the sea.

Fletcher stirred a coffee, checked his watch.

Seven p.m. The twins in their bath now, ready for a story.

Big electric flash off the sea, the promenaders flinching and raising their collars.

Someone slid in next to him. Pushed a newspaper across. He looked at it sideways:

The *Tundean Weekly News*. Headline: *Harkness reactor – leak denied.*

Foot of page: *Vanished yacht: wreckage found.*

The mystery of the Contigo *may be close to–*

He looked away, out over the sea.

Long fingers picked the paper up, folded it over. Long fingers with clear, neat nails.

A burst of thunder came through the door, rain spitting on the glass in front of him. The neon light on her nails on the paper.

He turned to look at her. She was watching the sea too, cradling a glass of champagne. Her hair was scraped back, glinting with raindrops, her earlobes with studless holes. He recognised her profile – the last time he'd seen her she'd been sitting on the *Contigo*'s dinghy, smoking a joint, outlined against the moon. Now Elsa looked relaxed, in a modest summer dress, bare shoulders, a cool tan on her throat as she turned her face, lifted her chin and studied him.

The neon sign flickering in the static.

She said, 'You think they'll find the boat?'

'No.'

'But they found things on the beach–'

'Stuff is going to come loose, Elsa. They'll never find the boat. Don't worry about it.' She didn't answer, sipping her drink. 'Is that what you wanted to talk about?' But she sat watching the rain fingering the window, and the black sky beyond it over the sea.

He took a long look at her. No jewellery, no watch. Fine hairs on the tanned skin along her arms, and her shoulder damp with rain.

What is it about her?

'You look great, Elsa. What are you doing these days?'

'I'm being careful. I'm careful with myself, with the money. I lock the doors and sleep ten hours a night, no dreams, no waking up.'

'You're lucky.'

She touched his face. 'To be honest, Honey Man, you look tired.'

'I've had a blood infection. I don't sleep

well. I work a lot, physically, but I can't sleep.'

'Does a blood infection do that?'

'It does to me.' He smiled. 'I had this Russian doctor – know what he said? *You're not such a young guy any more.* Doctors, eh?'

'Russians.' They were quiet for a while, watching the sea. Then Elsa said, 'How are your kids?'

'They're not my kids.' It was a release, finally saying it aloud. 'I thought they were, but they're not.'

He felt Elsa turn to look at him for half a minute, then back at the sea.

She said, 'Do you dream at all?'

'I dream about–'

The deli lights went off. People groaned, *Power cut.*

In the half dark, Elsa said, 'Go on.'

'There was a woman called Stef Maguire, a soldier. I only met her a few times, but I dream about her. She's dead now.'

'God bless that woman.' Elsa dipped her fingers in champagne and crossed herself. 'Why did you come here to meet me, Honey Man?'

'You phoned.'

'But why did you come here?'

'You said you wanted to talk about the boat, the *Contigo*. And we have, and more besides.'

The storm sent bursts of rain against the

window, Elsa's eyes following drops sliding down to sea level.

She said, 'I'm buying a farm.'

'A farm?'

'It's in Italy, up near the Swiss border. Hot summers, cold winters. There's an orchard and a vineyard. It has fields for keeping horses, and there's a stream with fish. It's God's own garden. And I'm thinking of putting in beehives too.' She finished her champagne and turned to him. 'So I need someone to come and help me with the bees.'

'But Elsa—'

She put a finger on his lips. 'Seriously. Just think a while. Then decide.'

Fletcher stood on the empty seafront. The gutters were running with storm water, but the air was hot enough to raise a sweat on his back. There was rain on his shaved head, in his eyes – and looping through his mind, something his wife Cathleen had said a while ago, when they were talking after making love. *The brain has a receptor for opiates. A piece of the mind with no other function. We're all born wired up for poppies.*

But there are other things in this life like poppies. There are things that you need to keep you alive, things you have to believe in, even if your conscious mind is telling you to give them up. You believe in these things and you keep using them although you know it's an addiction, you know it's a lie – because if you don't, what else is there left for you in this world?

When the sun burst through the black clouds over the sea, Fletcher made his decision.

Author's Note

I'm grateful to the people from the armed forces who gave their time to comment on this book. In particular, Flight Lieutenant Mike Gallagher gave insight into RAF logistics and arranged privileged access to a major airbase in Oxfordshire. Captain Emma Cannings patiently advised me on aspects of army life and the mission to Afghanistan.

Nick Sayers at Hodder tactfully suggested that I scale down the paganism, and I have to thank him for that and all his other advice, as well as Anne Clarke and Eleni Fostiropoulos for their dedicated work on all three books.

I'm also grateful to Camilla Bolton and Madeleine Buston for their marvellous support from London, Jan Michael and Susan Ridder in Holland, people who've helped to spread the word including the two JAGs in Reading, Uta Protz and Peter King in Cambridge, Jeff Pierce in the USA and Pam Lawrence in Canada.

And finally, of course, Ruth.

If you've enjoyed this book, take a look at my website, www.patrick-lennon.com, which has some bonus scenes from *Cut Out* and background on the whole Tom Fletcher series, a discussion forum, a log-on to my newsletter list, and the chance to win some limited edition gear.

The publishers hope that this book has given you enjoyable reading. Large Print Books are especially designed to be as easy to see and hold as possible. If you wish a complete list of our books please ask at your local library or write directly to:

Magna Large Print Books
Magna House, Long Preston,
Skipton, North Yorkshire.
BD23 4ND

This Large Print Book, for people
who cannot read normal print,
is published under the auspices of

THE ULVERSCROFT FOUNDATION